Invidia

part two in the

Chronicles of the Damned

series

a story by
R. N. Matos

Edited by

J. Matos

&

N. M. Matos

1

Copyright

For information, please contact:
thedamned@gothicgraphix.net
www.chroniclesofthedamed.com

Look for R.n. Matos on Facebook

ISBN: 9-78098-3069508

Printed in the United States of America

Contents

Being that this is my second book in the series, I want to express my gratitude to the people who have helped me make this possible. Especially, since never in a million years did I expect to write even one. It was, and continues to be, a long learning process which left me with a greater appreciation for the things that authors like Stephenie Meyer, Charlaine Harris, and Anne Rice were able to achieve. I may not like all their work, but I have a new found respect for their achievements. First, I want to thank my wife, who put up with all the late nights and grouchy mornings. I appreciate my daughter keeping me sane by keeping me on my toes on New Mumbasa and Reach; allowing me a little escape from all these words and deadlines. Then there's my Mom and Dad for the moral support, phone calls, encouragement, and loads of material for another novel I hope to write in the near future. Then of course, I thank my brother who surprised me with more help than I ever expected. I want to thank my growing army of fans that continue to send me messages of encouragement. Above all, I thank God for putting all these people in my life.

The world took the events at Giza in stride. Just like a great many other things that were once taboo are now acceptable, the confirmation of the existence of not just vampires, but werewolves and who knows what else was accepted without incident. Of course, there were the expected reactions from the ultra conservative sector that see evil in everything they don't understand, but they were few and far between- very few, much too few for Joe the Plumber to bother with. Politicians sat by wondering what all this would mean. Certainly there would be the rise of a new civil rights movement, but which side does one take in these matters? How does one impose the law on beings that could easily overpower you or simply disappear? There were even rumors of mind control, which really unsettled more than just a few in Washington. The Potentate wasn't going to wait around for politicians and radical organizations to make up their minds about how to handle the situation. The Praetorian Guard have their orders, the Protectorate is on alert, and the New Minority is revving up their propaganda machine. Humanity, will accept them or perish.

The Canis were not very keen on their unexpected celebrity status. The experiences of thousands of years among the humans have left them with a preference towards continued anonymity. Thousands of years of battling the Legion taught them cynicism of any and all Legion- good will. They let the Legion continue their flamboyant ways. It makes it easier to keep an eye on the parasites. Still, that doesn't mean they'll not act should the need arise. The rest of the world might think the vampires are looking to coexist and strive to just be accepted as just another being on God's green earth, but for the Canis, the war is far from over. The only thing that has changed is there are now more combatants in the struggle and whatever actions are taken must be executed with a heightened level of discretion. The Canis will organize, consolidate their efforts, and appoint a leader. With Mathias gone there is only one clear choice for the job, but will he accept the position? The future of the Canis and possibly mankind is held in the balance of this decision.

The world has proven to be a stranger place than anyone had imagined. It is even stranger now for Katrina Le' Giroux with the rumors that Vlad is still walking among the living. After more than 400 years as the lead assassin for the Potentate she's become calloused to all the death, but this new assignment is different. It challenges her loyalty, her sense of honor, and her resolve. She has left the life she built in search of the truth and will do anything to find it. In the back of her mind a voice haunts her saying, "In the end will it all be worth it?"

Vatican City Archives

Prologue II

Somewhere beneath St. Peter's Square, deep below the streets where the tourists and the pilgrims meet, a foreigner has infiltrated the hallowed catacombs where the sacred scrolls of ancient scripture are stored.

I wish I'd never been given that stupid assignment. Of course, it really wasn't the assignment. It was my damn persistent curiosity for the things that are never good for me that got me into this mess. Well, let's not get over-dramatic. It isn't that bad. I can do without the freaking flea bites after a full moon and why in God's name haven't the werewolves- oh excuse me 'Canis'- come up with some kind of stretchy material, uniform, or something like the X-Men? I'll never know. My new monthly scourge is putting a pretty dent in my wallet. Then again, there are the upsides. There is one in particular that makes it all worth it. I guess one could call it my new found animal magnetism. The once dreaded assignments to celebrity functions have become a playground where I frequently magnetize. Then again, the flip side to that is this bullshit. Bruno and his fucking obsession with Vlad and all his little Dragon Patrons or whatever they want to call themselves. I've been stuck in this hell hole somewhere in the bowels of the Vatican looking through all these manuscripts for a week.

The reporter's life has drastically changed since his encounter with Frank Talbot and the Canis. His once mundane existence has taken a decidedly more exciting turn.

This Katrina babe must really be important for Bruno to put so much emphasis on her. If he's fixated on her she must be a real dream of a character. Still, I fail to see why the big cheese among the Canis wants anything to do with an assassin like her. So far, I've discovered that Katrina's ancestors once worked with The Church. It seems it all starts with The Church. They were mystics of some sort that somehow intervened in all affairs of miraculous nature. There was a disagreement with the Church over the Joan of Arc incident and they severed their ties with the Holy Roman Empire. It looks like that happened a lot during that time. According to the Jesuit manuscripts, the House of Arcadia, as the mystics were called, popped up years later as council and advisers for the House of Bourbon with the Huguenots. I bet the Pope was just thrilled to death over that one. It took a lot of digging, but this stuff is priceless. Note to self: make sure to do more research on the House of Arcadia. I wonder what will happen when the priests around here realize I'm not actually an emissary from the French embassy researching royal blood. As best as I can tell, this all happened before the big split and, of course, Vlad was in the center of it all.

My head hurts. I can't keep all this shit straight. Damn it! I must have dozed off when I wrote this chicken scratch yesterday. Who the hell is going to read this? I can't read this. Fuck it!

He grabbed the manuscripts of interest and bundled them into some robes someone had left hanging on the wall. He threw a bundle to each of the escorts Bruno had sent with him.

"Bubba One, Bubba Two; take these things and meet me at the train station."

He threw the halogen lamp he had been reading by in the trash can. The contents burned slowly and smoke rose from the canister, it caught fire, and the alarms went off.

This place will be busier than a Thai hooker on port day. Now we can get the hell out of here. Those guys sure do look worried. There must be a lot of important shit in there. I hope they don't let the fire spread too far. Bruno might get pissed and cause me some real discomfort.

The infiltrators disappear into the crowd and make their way through the caverns running for the exit. Their advance is hampered by the monks and security rushing to put out the fire.

"Alto, Alto!" A voice called from behind.

Oh shit, it's the Swiss Guard! What the hell? How do they know? Forget it, they ain't catching me. Great, Bubba One and Bubba Two disappeared. I'm the only idiot getting chased.

The chase ensued through the corridor at breakneck speed. The catacombs twist and turn like a maze. In the panic of the chase the infiltrator forgot about the powers that come with being a werewolf.

Damn it, which way do I go? If I make it out of here those two morons are gonna hear it from me. They're gonna hear it from me good.

Deeper into the catacombs it goes.

This looks like a good escape route. Just a little further; I can see an exit.

His escape route was suddenly blocked by his pursuers. His surprise turned to horror as the scene unfolded.

Shit, where did those two Vatican goons come from? What in blazes? They're changing! They're Canis!

"Hey look fellas, how 'bout we just put the pig stickers down and we discuss this nice and calm like fellow lycanthropes."

The guards were not impressed by his retort and thrust with their lances, which he barely eluded by sidestepping and pressing against the wall.

"Wow those are sharp!" he said, infuriating the guards, eliciting snarls and growls.

"Don't get excited! I didn't mean to touch. I'm just scared shitless. Come on boys - turned, born, we're all God's furry creatures."

The guards had had enough. This time they charged to kill.

I guess stalling with wit isn't going to work.

Something happened that not only surprised the guards, but completely shocked their quarry.

Oh shit, the Bubbas!

"Where did you guys come from? I'm so glad you showed up when you did. I couldn't morph. Why is it I can't morph when I need it and right when the time is at its most inconvenient, bam I got fur? Explain that to me. By the way, that was beautiful the way you guys just popped up behind them and took their heads off with those funny, curvy, Gooky knives. Is that what you call them, Gooky knives?"

The Bubbas sneered at him as they wiped the blood off their blades onto their victim's uniforms.

"Ahh, I guess not. I don't know what you call them, but it was beautiful and right on time. No wonder Bruno sent you two."

This time the sneers were accompanied by growls.

"Okay I get it, shut up. I tend to talk when I get nervous. The more nervous the faster I talk."

The annoying little man finally irritated his escorts to the point where they made theirs at the end of a Gurkha.

"Okay, okay I'll shut up, I'll shut up, just don't stick me with that thing."

Man these guys are intense. I always wondered why those Vatican Guards wore those funny get ups with the poofy stretchy material. Canis in the Vatican, Bruno is going to be real interested in that. We should be able to blend in with the panicked crowd and get out of here. Yeah, no problem two ten foot tall monks and a priest with blood all over his tunic. Yes Sir, real inconspicuous.

A Day to Remember

Chapter One

Paris, 1567- Antoine Montague Le Giroux was glowing with excitement as he ran through the streets of Paris, following his equally excited messenger of the court. He tripped, slipped and tumbled over merchandise barely able to stay on his feet as they passed the market place. He made many promises and left many IOU's in the wake of his mad dash to the chalet. In the stupefying ecstasy of his excitement he left his horse at the gates of the palace with the stable-hand holding the reins. He rushed through the streets lost in the dream of the arrival. Antoine was oblivious to everything around him ignoring even his unique senses which were alerting him to imminent danger. He ran and ran; laughing like a mad man. As he neared the corner of Notre Dame an angry mob of Catholic villagers was forming. Their hatred and discontent fueled to frenzy by the words of the man standing at the steps of the cathedral calling them to action in the name of God.

"Brothers and Sisters, how long will we stand idly by as our holy fathers and sisters are murdered while in the service of our Lord and fellow man? We can't stand idly by while our leaders make concessions to these heretics compromising our beliefs for the sake of peace!" He said with distain as Antoine and his messenger turned the corner.

Antoine was a known adviser to the court of the Huguenot prince, Louis I de Bourbon. The conflict between the church and the Huguenot prince was brewing into an all out war once again. The first one ended in an unsatisfying truce between the factions known as the Edict of Amboise. The scars of the events that led to that bloody war still festered.

At this moment, Antoine didn't care. He needed to get home and no mob was going to stop him. His messenger ran straight towards the crowd attempting to plow open a path. He was swallowed by the crowd and beaten for his efforts. Antoine faired the same. As the mob fell upon its victims swarming over them like bees, they were suddenly dispersed by a palace guard on horseback.

The guard had Antoine's horse in tow. The horses kicked and bucked as they pushed everyone off of Antoine and his messenger. The guard reached down and pulled the messenger up by his collar. Antoine jumped on his horse and the three managed to ride out of the square to safety. They rode hard through the streets passing by the growing mob of angry Parisians. It would have been a long trip indeed on foot to the Chalet le Giroux in Orleans eighty miles away. The horses were frothing at the mouth when they passed through the gates of the chalet.

Antoine jumped off the horse and ran to the door. As he reached the top of the stairs he was greeted by a maid holding a baby wrapped in a bundle of fine linens. He took the baby in his arms and raced across the foyer, up the stairs and into the grand chamber to his wife's bedside. She had been washed and the linens had already been replaced. She lay back on her pillow, looked up at Antoine and smiled. He kneeled and brought the newborn's face up to its mother's and kissed them both.

"I wish to name her, Katrina," said his wife, Estella Arias Le Giroux.

"Katrina is a fine regal name," replied Antoine as he smiled with his face bloodied up from the beating he took at the steps of Notre Dame.

"And what happened to you?" asked Estella.

"Oh nothing to worry about my dear, I was so excited I fell off my horse," replied Antoine, hoping to make light of the situation.

"Antoine, do you forget who you are talking to? You cannot lie to me. First, I'm your wife, second you stink at it and then, of course, I'm an Arias. Did they hurt you?"

"My dear, on this day, the Devil could not harm me. My soul shines with the love of a father and nothing can break that shield."

"I guess the guard on horseback had nothing to do with it."

"Perhaps, I suppose he helped a little bit. Didn't you have enough on your mind at that moment than to fill it with my troubles, too?"

"If I had not, you may not be here. Did you really think that guard hopped on his horse and came to your rescue on his own accord? Your horse has more sense than that fool."

"Promise me you will keep those special feelings under

wraps. We have enough problems without everyone now suspecting us of witchcraft. Also, you must show me how to do that trick one day. It might come in handy in court."

"You know better than to call it a trick. You make it seem like we are some kind of dancing bears or circus clowns. Besides you can do it, you just need to trust your feelings and project your thoughts with a clear mind."

"Ah, is that all? Well then, I believe I'm burdened by an unclear mind and a general mistrust of feelings I don't understand. So, I guess I will have to remain the performing bear in the house of Le Giroux."

"For shame, Antoine! Well, as long as you don't try to dance," she replied saucily with laughter.

The maid walked in with the messenger and asked, "What is the child's name, Madam?"

"Mademoiselle Katrina Le' Giroux daughter of Antoine Montague Le' Giroux and Estella Arias Le' Giroux," replied Antoine.

The messenger wrote down the name on a parchment and turned to leave. Antoine looked back at his wife. She glanced at him and just nodded. He too could sense the danger that awaited them, but she could see it clearly.

"Wait, don't go yet. Stay here till morning it might not be safe," Antoine called out.

"We must get back. I need to get this parchment back to the registry," replied the messenger.

"As do I; I must return to the garrison and help repel any incursion into the palace," said the guard.

"Well then, at least drink with me to the birth of my daughter," Antoine suggested hoping to delay them for their safety.

"Oh please, you must. Our family won't be here till tomorrow and we must have a toast to our child's health. I would also hate for the salted pork our cook made to go to waste. I believe the poor soul expected the family today and made too much," exclaimed Estella.

Estella knew that it was difficult times and not only was food scarce, but good food was just about non-existent. Good wine and a salted pork meal would be too much to pass up. The two men looked at each other and gave in. Whether by their will or not, Antoine will never know.

The servants prepared a table right in the grand room by Estella's bed. The maid brought Estella a burgundy gown and helped her sit up in bed as the men turned their backs and averted their eyes for the sake of Estella's modesty. She blushed, flattered by the thoughts that crossed the guard's mind and chuckled under her breathe listening in on the young messenger's embarrassment.

Antoine poured the first goblet of wine and invited the men to join them at the table. He passed the bottle to the servants. When everyone's cup was full, Antoine raised his glass. They toasted to the birth of the mademoiselle, drank to the ancestors and then drank to the king. They then sat at the table and the cook brought in the pork still steaming from the heat of the brick oven.

She was followed by a handful of kitchen hands holding platters of vegetables and pastries. As they drank the wine the pork began to disappear. When the two bottles that Antoine had called for were done, the guests thanked their host, asked to be dismissed and got up to leave. Antoine once again looked back at his wife expecting a sign.

"Oh please give my best to the prince," she called out to the men as they left.

Antoine knew it was more of a signal to him than an actual farewell to the men. He walked with them to the gates and dismissed them.

"This will surely be a day to remember," said the messenger before they rode away.

Antoine returned to the house to be with his wife and newborn daughter. They went up the stairs and settled in for the night. The servants secured the gates and locked all the doors and windows making sure to turn off all the lanterns. The horses were locked away in the stables and the dogs released to secure the grounds.

That night two shadowy figures climbed over the wall. They were making their way slowly across the yard using the shrubs and topiary as cover. Their movement alerted the pack of dogs. The dogs approached slowly, stalking their prey, but when they reached the area where the intruders had alerted the pack there was no one there.

Estella woke up startled by her senses. She snatched up the baby, cradled her, and hid with her in a linen chamber. The dogs started barking; the noise alerting the residents of the house. Antoine woke up groggy from his deep sleep. The entire house was bustling with servants running around by the light of torches and lanterns. They all ran to the doors and stood guard waiting for something to happen. Antoine stood in the grand hall downstairs trying to get a sense of the situation. The dogs continued to bark crazily, growling and howling frustrated by the elusive trespassers. The tension grew as the moments past in anticipation of what was about to happen. The tension swelled smothering the sound out of the air. Even the dogs went silent. Then the crashing sound of glass broke the tense silence of the night. Everyone looked up in the direction of the grand room upstairs.

"Estella!" shouted Antoine as he darted to the stairs.

One of the intruders stood at the top of the stairs as if daring the gang of servants to approach. The other walked into the grand room, looked around, then walked directly to the linen closet where Estella was hiding and stood in front of the door. Estella was sitting holding her baby and completely sensing everything that was happening beyond that door. She knew the man outside her door was not a man at all; she knew he was picking up on her body heat and his intentions were anything but good. The thing outside that door had evil plans for her baby and even worse for her. She closed her eyes and held her baby tighter as she sensed the monster reaching for the door.

At that moment, one of the dogs crashed through the window knocking the intruder to the floor. He bit the monster on the neck; blood spurted from the wound, and sprayed the wall as he shook the life out of him. In a flash, the other fiend rushed into the chamber.

He drove a blade through the dog's heart and dropped him to the ground. He crashed through the door that hid Estella and her baby and snatched the baby up. Estella shouted and struggled to get her baby back but the brute just slapped her away knocking her back into the closet. The monster turned towards the window and found himself face to face with the snarling fang filled face of a Canis in full transformation.

The fiend realized he was surrounded and would not make it out of there alive. Out of desperation or frustration he threw the child out the window. The Canis closest to the window leapt after her and snatched her out of the air just before they both hit the ground. At the same time the remaining Canis attacked the remaining intruder. The unmistakable sounds of crackling bones breaking under flesh, the ripping of the meat and the tearing of ligaments filled the air and added to the horror Estella was experiencing through the senses of the packs victim. Antoine rushed past the gruesome scene to reach his wife and try to comfort her.

"Where's the baby?!" she yelled as he approached.

He ran back passed the ugliness in the center of the room, down the stairs, out the door and finally outside to the spot where his daughter had fallen. He arrived to find the baby cooing and cackling in laughter with the dog sitting right next to her. He stood there shaking his head as he looked at the dog and said, "Pardon the expression, but I think the cat's out of the bag."

The rest of the dogs appeared and they all swiftly ran towards the wall and jumped over it. Antoine picked up his baby and brought her in to her mother. All the servants were huddled in the hall whimpering and wailing from fear. There was nothing to say. He walked past them as quietly as possible, took Katrina up the stairs and placed her in her mother's arms.

Estella looked up at Antoine full of astonishment and said, "She feels them."

Estella was right. Katrina could feel them, but not the way a descendant of the House of Arcadia should have. She was too much like her father. She had a heightened sense of awareness, but lacked the sharp focus that made her mother, grandmother and previous Arias women so powerful.

One day, a few years later, as she walked the streets of Paris with her mother her ability shined.

Estella haggled with a merchant taking advantage of the end of day rush to clear the stands.

"Come now, be reasonable. The streets are quickly clearing and it would be such a shame to let these provisions spoil on your back as you carry them back home. I'll give you forty for the whole batch."

She could have easily won the negotiation with her influential talents, but Estella reveled in these challenges to her character. The thrill of the chase was usually more satisfying than the quarry.

Bored with the spectacle, Katrina wandered off. She wandered so far that Estella could no longer sense her. She was on her own for the first time since her birth. She walked the narrow corridors that wound through the different quarters of the city. She watched as dirty angry faces stared back at her with scheming eyes. They stared at her hair, they gawked at her shoes, and they glared at her dress, but no one dared to approach her. It was as if they could not believe what they were seeing was real. They might have thought it was a trick by the king to snare a thief and any minute some soldiers would jump out and imprison them. All seemed content to keep their distance.

All except for one; this one followed closely in the shadows of the setting sun. In the distance, the sounds of a panicked mother and the frantic search that followed danced like flames and echoed through the air bouncing off the cavernous walls of the corridors of Paris.

With every step she took into the darkness of the approaching dusk, Katrina invited the predators that lurked about her. Emboldened by the setting sun a couple of ill intended dregs approached. They stopped in front of her, towering over her like giant oaks smothering the little girl. One touched her shiny hair and grinned eerily. Those who watched what was happening scurried away in fear.

Katrina sensed the danger and let out a panicked shriek. The two men quickly grabbed the little girl and darted off into the darkness. From nearby an unseen figure stood and watched it all unfold, then followed slowly from a distance. The shriek alerted Estella and the search party, and they rushed to its source.

They scurried about like rats in a maze, frantically searching for the little amber haired girl with rosy cheeks and pearl filled smile. Estella struggled to focus her senses, but could not detect her daughter. It was as if there was some great barrier preventing her from reaching her precious little girl. The search became more frantic as the little girl's shrieks became more frequent and excited. The soldiers pulled their swords from their scabbards as they neared the sounds echoing through the streets. Estella was filled with fear as she read their thoughts and failed to sense her daughter's presence.

Finally, coming around a corner leading to a long dark alleyway they were shocked by the strangest scene they could have ever imagined. Shadows danced upon the walls of the dead-end street like pagans round a campfire. A light that broke the gloom illuminated the spectacle. A tall man loomed over the little girl as she danced and laughed hysterically with her awestricken playmates. The two thugs danced around with flowers in their teeth; dancing bears at a circus and Katrina was the ringmaster. As the soldiers approached with Estella walking slowly behind, they too joined the festivities, almost as if in a trance. The lurker turned his gaze to Estella, and then slowly walked past everyone without saying a word taking with him the light that filled the space.

"Katrina!" yelled Estella, realizing what had happened.

At that moment the men stopped dancing, as if coming out of a dream, looking around dazed and confused at their predicament. The soldiers quickly snapped to action and arrested the two naked street dwellers. Katrina cried as her play things were taken away. Estella quickly erased the scene from the memories of those around them then held Katrina deep in her arms.

"Don't ever do that again my dear. There are some that

would not understand," she whispered in her ear.

Katrina looked up and with an understanding far beyond her years nodded her compliance. Estella was still troubled by the man she saw looming over her daughter. Like any mother in her place the worst rushed through her mind. As she pondered different possibilities, Estella heard her daughter say, "It was an angel mommy. His name was once Enoch."

Redheaded Bastard & Green Eyed Devil

Chapter Two

For several years Katrina struggled with the talents that gave her premonitions, visions, nightmares and caused her to hear voices. She kept all this from her family for fear of reprisal against her family, especially in the terrible era of the Inquisition. Being a member of a family that supported the Huguenots was cause enough to keep such things to one self. The church had agents of the Inquisition everywhere and even the anti-establishment and protestant Huguenots did not tolerate anything that might even resemble witchcraft. She suffered much as a result. Children her age did not understand her, labeled her the Queer One and banished her from their everyday adventures.

Katrina abandoned human companionship and befriended the stray animals of the city and the wild ones from the forest that surrounded her estate. Estella and Antoine grew accustomed to her forays into the dark forest. They were accustomed but still fearful of the dangers that lurked in those woods; dangers both natural and supernatural. Katrina sensed them both and at times found herself drawn by some eerie feeling that invaded her soul. She would be filled with irresistibly strong feelings of attraction that on several occasions led her to dark figures in the woods. These dark figures shied away whenever she approached.

"Hello there," she would call trying to ingratiate herself to the strangers.

"I'm Katrina; I live just passed the meadow. I'm not here to hurt you. Won't you come out? Oh, don't worry I won't tell anyone." She would wait for a response, but none ever came.

"I don't have anyone to tell, even if I wanted to," she whispered as she turned away.

They were always puzzled by her presence. She never saw them, but she could feel their apprehension. She named them the Darklings. She envied them and found herself wishing she could be like them. Free from all the mundane trappings that encompassed her everyday life as a member of the Huguenot court.

Katrina never understood her role or her family's role in the House of Bourbon. She watched as the prince met with her father and mother behind closed doors. She saw how the rest of the court tried so hard to put on a pleasant face and a friendly smile. She would often imagine what they were actually thinking behind the façade of courtesy and it was never nice.

Then again, was it all her imagination? Even at court she

was an outcast. So Katrina made the forest her home away from home. At least there she was certain to never run into anyone from the Royal Court. Estella's fears waned to tolerance after the fifth time Katrina brought home a wolf or bear companion. She resigned herself to the fact that as long as her companions were around no one else would dare bother her. She still worried that others might contrive her fancy ways with animals as some sort of enchantment and misconstrue the situation into some perverse form of satanic behavior. No one outside of the family paid much attention to Katrina and in this case it was a welcomed blessing.

At the age of ten Katrina was summoned by the Huguenot court to the Royal Academy. Up until that time she was educated at home by her mother and grandmother. Estella was not happy. She knew what awaited her daughter and was not looking forward to watching her go through the experience. She pleaded with Antoine, but he felt that rejecting the invitation would call the wrong kind of attention to the family. They settled on a compromise; Grandmother Arias would go with her as her escort.

Katrina had mixed feelings about the adventure. She was excited about leaving the confines of her estate, and anxious to meet children of her age, but she too could feel the nervous dread caused by the specter of rejection. She wished it was not so, and hoped she could make new friends. That hope was crushed the first day she entered the gates of the Academy.

The carriage transporting Katrina and Grandmother Arias stopped at the gate to the palace. The gate guards challenged as expected and then saluted the carriage in. Katrina leaned out the window to see the topiary and statues that lined the avenue leading to the rotund in front of the chalet on the far west side of the palace. Grandmother Arias pulled Katrina back into the carriage just before stopping at the academy doors. "Act like a lady and remember your manners," Grandmother Arias scolded.

She was not at all happy about having to take time from her daily routine to chaperone a ten year old at such a snobby affair. Grandmother Aria's contempt for school mistresses was deep rooted going back to her days at the convent school and Sister Rozzelli. Still, she would not allow her granddaughter to embarrass her in front of the faculty of stuck up elitists.

Katrina stepped out of the carriage and even though she could barely contain her excitement and wanted to just burst into her class ready to make friends, she contained herself and waited for Grandmother Arias to escort her to the door and make the introductions. Katrina could hear her grandmother attempting to assure her as her enthusiasm waned the deeper they traveled into the corridors of this educational institution. Her curly red hair made her stand out among the other girls and instantly inspired envy among her peers, which was then followed by ridicule and harassment. Katrina tried to make the best of it. She noticed that no one smiled. She wondered how they could see where they were going; they had their noses turned up so high.

She scanned the courtyard in the hopes of finding a friendly sympathetic soul, but was disappointed by the constant hostility that surrounded her. She then caught the mischievous scheming of a sinister group of girls. A young girl near to Katrina's age had arrived with her entourage of chaperones. She looked very distinguished in her colorful robes though obviously a foreigner. She had a regal demeanor and a striking presence. The small procession walked along the path between the topiaries on the side of the carriage trail coming from the main gate. There was string that was stretched across the path; it led into the bushes, wound around a stock, traveled up into a tree and was tied to a wasp nest hanging over the path from a limb. Katrina broke into a dead sprint. Her grandmother yelled for her then caught the same scheme unfolding. Just as the two escorts were about to trigger the snare, Katrina ran past them, jumped across the path and pulled the young lady away from the nest that fell right on the spot the girl would have been. Angry wasps peppered the entourage with their stingers and chaos ensued, but the young lady escaped without a blemish. The girl looked at Katrina with a cold stare of indifference; her stare was then diverted by the sound of little girls giggling from the balcony. She looked at Katrina once more and continued down the path. Her escorts scurried to her side struggling to catch back up as the wasps continued to attack them.

"You're welcome," Katrina said under her breathe as she watched her highness walk towards the main doors of the Academy with her escorts in tow.

By the time Katrina reached her assigned seat in her classroom, her enthusiasm was completely drained. She sunk into her chair and barely looked up as the mistress rambled on about the virtues. She blocked out her schoolmates jabbing thoughts looked up and peered through the corners of her eye at the classmates around her. One face out of the twelve in the room looked back at her and smiled. Or so it seemed, Katrina shortly realized she was laughing at her. Through her increasing focus Katrina realized they were all laughing at her dress. Apparently it was somewhat out of fashion.

That didn't bother her as much as the comments that started rolling about her mother being a witch. Even at a low whisper the words sounded loud and clear in Katrina's ears. Katrina was used to the name calling; it had been a part of her life for as long as she could remember. Living isolated from the public tends to intrigue the baser forms of curiosity in people and left without explanations they arrive to the most sensational of conclusions.

Then of course, there is the obvious; her bright red hair. This genetic trait passed down from her great- grandmother made her a target of suspicion of being a hell spawn conceived in sin with the Devil himself. Everyone in this place was a Huguenot, but it made no difference when it came to rumors of supernatural or superstitious subjects. The Huguenots were just as feverish in their pursuit of witches and heretics as the Holy Roman Empire in those days. The atmosphere was charged with animosity of one sort or the other. If "Redheaded Bastard" was the best they could come up with it did little to annoy Katrina, a well hardened callous had formed over that one a long time ago.

And yet, nothing removed her confidence that in this room was a potential lifelong friend. She could feel it. She just had to identify her. The opportunity came sooner than she expected. The day wore on much as it started. The snickers, sneers, and whispers continued. In art class the mistress handed out paper, brush, and paint. She instructed everyone to just use the colors and paint at will anything their hearts desired. The ring leader of the Banshees, a name Katrina had already come up with for her tormentors though never uttered out loud, was one of the older girls; a spiteful thing named Alice. Alice walked up to the mistress and asked for some red paint. The mistress was reluctant to supply anymore paint, first because it was very expensive, and also because it seemed an excessive amount of one color for such a small paper.

"Well, here you go, but let me see what you are working on," she said as she passed the jar of red paint to Alice.

Alice took the paint and led the mistress in the direction of her easel. As she passed Katrina's work area, she stopped suddenly and unexpectedly causing the mistress to bump her on the back. Alice exaggeratingly stumbled, dropped the container on Katrina, and spilled red paint all over the dress she was wearing. Katrina was beside herself with anger, not so much at the act, but at the fact that she saw it coming, and did nothing to prevent it. She leapt from her bench, swung her pallet aiming to strike Alice across the face. Lucky for Alice the mistress jumped in front of Katrina's blow and saved her from the inevitable cut and paint on her face.

"Young lady, what has gotten in to you? Is this how you react to an obvious mistake; an accident? How quickly you are to judge," said the mistress.

"That was no mistake, she planned the whole thing," she replied plaintively, her voice lowered by injured pride. "There isn't even any art on her paper; how could she need more paint?" Katrina asked as accusatively and sarcastically as possible.

The mistress dragged them both by the arm over to Alice's easel and looked at the paper. It was completely bare. "That still does not make your reaction appropriate!" The mistress scolded Katrina. A stunned look came over the mistress's face, as she realized that there is no way Katrina could have known there was no paint on Alice's paper. Alice's easel was standing across and facing away from her in the art circle. She took a moment, closing her eyes and taking a low deep breath to calm her nerves with the justification that someone must have told her.

"Class, I hope I don't have to remind anyone that art time is for artistic forms of expression not involving conversation," said the mistress.

The mistress took Katrina by the hand and escorted her to a chamber where a robe was picked out and she was allowed to change her clothes. This dress was far worse and even less fashionable then the one she had on. It was basically a choir robe, and not even a primary singer's attire, but a low ranked backup choir smock. The room erupted with laughter when Katrina returned to class in her new clothes.

"Silence, continue your work!" ordered the mistress.

Katrina was completely humiliated and embarrassed. Still, she would not let this get her completely down. She did her best to continue drawing the serene landscape of a place she had never visited before, but had seen so many times in her dreams: the New World. Unbidden, dreams of this far away land came to her more and more and became a device to escape the torment of the little voices and the snide insufferable looks. The puzzle of these images was a siren's call to freedom from the incessant little indignities that wore on her daily. The drama of the day would have ended had it not been for Rebecca; the young lady from that morning's wasp incident.

Rebecca was another ostracized little girl whose parents hoped to gain favor among their peers by enrolling their daughter in the Academy and entering that social circle. Rebecca's "questionable background," olive skin, and green eyes made her the target of foul offenses and ridicule. Her father had been doing some trading in the Persian lands and married one of the daughters of a wealthy Sultan who traded in uniquely woven rugs. Rebecca's exotic features were her mother's gifts and her temper her father's. She also had a strong sense of reciprocity and loyalty, demonstrated by her actions that afternoon.

There was a knock on the door to the chamber. The mistress sent one of the students to investigate who was knocking. A man with a face full of welts peaked in and asked to speak to the mistress. It was one of the unfortunate members of Rebecca's escort. The mistress stood and went to the door. He asked her if they could speak in private and so the mistress looked back at the classroom and then stepped out. The moment the mistress stepped outside the door Rebecca got up quietly, walked to where the spare paint buckets were sitting, picked up a bucket of black paint, slowly walked behind Alice, and spilled the entire contents of the bucket on Alice starting at her head. The paint poured down the sides of her head like ebony waterfalls. There wasn't a part of Alice that was not covered in black paint. Alice tried to scream but the amount of black paint running down her face was such that she could not open her mouth; when she tried paint streamed past her lips causing her to choke. By the time she let out a panicked yell, gasping for air, Rebecca was already back in her seat acting as innocent as could be.

She smiled at Katrina and then gave a deathly cold stare at the rest of the class as a warning. When the mistress rushed back in Alice was still gasping for air, choking, and crying from the rage at having been embarrassed in such a way in front of the whole class.

"You miserable Green Eyed Devil, I'll get you," she screamed.

No one else said a word. The mistress looked at Katrina and then walked Alice out of the chamber. There were a few giggles that slipped out of tightly clenched lips, but no one dared say a word. At that moment Katrina and Rebecca secured a bond they hoped would last forever.

The next day in the school yard awaiting the start of the day, Katrina and Rebecca talked for the first time.

"Your robes are so beautiful, where are you from?" Katrina broke the ice with the first phrase.

"Don't you want to know my name?" asked Rebecca.

"I don't think there is anyone in this prison that doesn't know your name Rebecca," Katrina said.

"I suppose that is true, Katrina," said Rebecca sarcastically sending a challenging remark.

They looked at each other for a second, squinted through the slits of their eyes, and then laughed.

"I'm actually from here. I was born in Paris and then my family moved out here. I want to thank you for helping me the other day. I don't think you realize that you might have saved my life. There is a sickness in my family that makes us extremely vulnerable to insect bites. My great-grandfather and a distant cousin died from bee stings. I don't know if I have the disease, but I don't want to find out either. My mother is a Persian Princess and this is why I wear these robes. They are made with the textiles my father sells at the market. I imagine I will see the same fabric on furniture and drapes one day," Rebecca said and then laughed.

"Sorry to hear about your great-grandfather. That is a frightful thing. I'll make sure to keep you away from flying insects. How did you end up here?" Katrina asked.

"Here at the school?" Rebecca clarified.

"Yes, here at this school," answered Katrina.

"I believe my father is dealing with the Huguenot prince and so I guess all this is for my protection," replied Rebecca. "I believe it was the same with me," Katrina retorted.

Their friendship continued through the years. They finally gained some prestige among their peers and though their bond grew tighter, there continued a rift between Katrina and the Banshees. Alice and her crew were getting tired of Katrina always busting up their schemes and ambushing the one or the other in some embarrassing trap. It happened so often that Rebecca was starting to call Katrina her little witch. She would not have tolerated that from anyone else. It came as a complete shock to Katrina when one day Rebecca was talking friendly to one of the

Banshees in the school yard before class.

"Katrina, this is Audrey. We were talking and you should see how much we found out we have in common," Rebecca said as Katrina approached.

Katrina stood blank faced and stunned at the sight of one of her rivals frolicking with her best and only friend in the Academy. She could tell the girl was hiding something but could not sense anything in particular. She couldn't make out what it was. The frustration similar to coming to an impasse while solving a jigsaw puzzle must have shown on her face.

"Oh, come now Katrina, let by-gones be by-gones. We don't have many friends and Audrey is well connected in society here. This could be the chance we've been looking for," Rebecca told Katrina full of early teenage excitement.

"I don't think it's a good idea Rebecca. I don't think she's being sincere," Katrina said quietly, trying to warn her.

"Well, I refuse to choose. You two might not get along, but I can be both your friends. Maybe one day we can all be friends," Rebecca sadly replied and walked away with Audrey.

"I'll see you later?" Katrina asked as she watched Rebecca walk away.

"Yes, of course, at midday recess," replied Rebecca.

For months Katrina watched as her friend was driven away from her and into the clutches of the 'Banshees.' Rebecca was always kind enough to spend her recess with her, but the mornings and evenings were spent with Audrey. Eventually, the rest of the 'Banshees' ingratiated themselves with Rebecca. They attempted to poison her relationship with Katrina, but Rebecca did not give in; she remained a good friend to Katrina and never did her any wrong.

"I don't trust them," Katrina told Rebecca.

"You don't trust anyone," Rebecca replied.

"You didn't trust them once either. You shouldn't trust them now," Katrina warned.

"I don't know what evil you see in them, but they haven't done anything to me, and they say nothing but good about you. Tell me what it is that repels you so!" Rebecca challenged.

Katrina struggled between keeping the secret of her abilities and the need to keep the friend she felt drifting away. She did not answer.

"So be it. I will not abandon you, but don't ask me to abandon my friends," Rebecca said angrily as she walked away.

A few days later Rebecca was met at the gate by Audrey.

"Rebecca, Katrina told me to ask you to meet her at the gazebo in the center of the topiary maze. She said it was important," Audrey told Rebecca.

Rebecca found it odd that Katrina would send a message through Audrey, but how else would Audrey have known about their secret meeting place?

Rebecca ran through the maze remembering the trail just as they had first discovered it and used for so many midday romps in the garden. She arrived at the gazebo and called out to Katrina, but there was no answer. A strange noise startled her instinctively forcing her to turn around. The shock was so great she could not scream.

Katrina was met at the gate by Alice. "Your best friend is waiting for you at the Gazebo," Alice said with disdain.

"You bitch, you don't know what you have done," replied Katrina as she pushed Alice aside and raced through the maze to her best friend's aid.

Katrina arrived at the gazebo and was stunned by the sight of Rebecca's feet protruding through the door way from the inside of the enclosure. She ran to the steps and her heart sank as all hope of assisting was crushed by the sight of the wasps buzzing around the nest lying on the floor by Rebecca's head. She knelt down and lifted Rebecca's head with her hands as tears ran down her face.

"Why, why did you do this to me?" Rebecca asked in a low raspy voice struggling to push the last words she would ever speak from her body.

"No, it wasn't me; I could never do this to you. You have to believe me!" Katrina yelled to Rebecca as she shook her trying to spark some life from the badly swollen wasp-stung body. Her tears streamed down with increased fervor as she sensed the last thoughts that ran through her friends mind and felt her pain in death. A pain multiplied by the fact that her best friend died believing she was responsible for this evil act. She sobbed and cried out in anger and frustration. Her cries helped those that had been searching for them find their way through the maze. The Head Mistress along with a few other school Masters rushed to her side with a crowd of gawking children fast behind them. Grandmother Arias made her way through the maze at a slow pace as she followed. From among the crowd of children Katrina heard the giggling of the Banshees as they ran up to the Gazebo anxious to gloat at their handy work; the prefect prank. Their faces and thoughts expressed it all when they realized the awful outcome of their joke. Katrina was enraged.

"Are you happy now? Is this what you wanted?" She yelled at the Banshees focusing her stare at Alice.

"Katrina, you can't blame them for this!" said the mistress.

"Shut up you blind cow! Can't you see they planned this whole thing!" screamed Katrina a maelstrom of rage churning in her gut.

Katrina then fixed her stare at the Banshees and at that moment the wasps rose from their nests and surrounding nooks and crannies, and then hovered around the crowd. Everyone looked on as the wasps swarmed in increasing number swirling around the crowd like an approaching storm. Some panicked and ran, others stood in shock, but everyone feared what was coming next. Katrina dropped her stare, cried her last lament for her lost friend, and the wasps poured their terrible vengeance on the Banshees. Chaos ensued as the girls ran in every direction trying to elude the fiery sting of their tormenting marauders. Everyone tried in vain to deter the wasps and assist the Banshees, but nothing helped. The girls fell to the ground convulsing from the amount of venom in their system. The relentless attack went on until Grandmother Arias arrived.
      "Licentia is locus, Metatron," said Grandmother Arias in a barely audible whisper.

As the swarm faded away and disappeared into the forest the mistress noticed that no one else was hurt. The Banshees were the only ones who were even touched by the wasps. Not even those who tried to help the girls were stung as they swatted and flailed their arms in an attempt to scare off the swarm. The Head Mistress went to Katrina's side and picked up Rebecca's body. The gardener arrived at that moment and assisted her. Katrina clung to her friend's arm and wailed. Grandmother Arias took Katrina by the shoulders, turned her around, and walked her away in an embrace. As they passed a group of girls that had gathered around the school mistresses trying to help the Banshees, one of the little girls looked up and said, "witch!"

A physician was able to arrive in time to assist the Banshees. None of them died as a result of the swarm attack, but they were left in near catatonics from the fear that now gripped their souls. Every now and then they were heard calling out "Metatron," but never louder than a whisper.

As a result of the incident the topiary maze was cut down and the gardener was tasked with eliminating all the wasps from the grounds. The school mistress resigned her position and was never heard from again. Rumors abound that she had joined a sect of witch hunters. The Head Mistress took a more active role in the social interactions of her students and even instituted chaperoned visits to the boy's Academy that opened up later at Wassey-Sur-Blaise in Champagne. Katrina never returned to the Academy. She and her grandmother were happier for it.

New World
Chapter Three

Years later, Antoine like many of his colleagues, as a result of the rising violence against the Huguenots and the growing pressure from the Vatican on the King of France decided to send his daughter away to the New World. Grandmother Arias was to accompany her and they would be called back when the times were more favorable. Katrina was completely against the decision and fought ferociously with her parents. She did not want to be separated from her family. Least of all, she didn't want to leave her forest friends behind. Estella, understanding the urgency and hoping that the end would justify the means, broke one of her most precious of rules. She used her talents against her own daughter. Through the influence of her mother Katrina not only accepted the situation but exhibited an excitement for the adventure that lay before her. Grandmother Arias was not happy.

"How could you do this? Should I have charmed you away from that worthless husband of yours when I was against the marriage? No offense my boy, I've come to love you like a son, but it was no secret I was dead set against this marriage. What have you got to say for yourself? Have you no control of this woman? My lord! This house has gone mad. Me, an Arias, in the New World! I suppose we're traveling on a ship full of riffraff."

Antoine had silently held his tongue at first, chagrined; he turned to look out the window. He had learned to keep his mouth shut when the old woman fired off her tirade of scathing rhetorical assaults. He stifled a sigh before returning his gaze to the older woman.

"With diplomatic charters granted by Queen Elizabeth I acquired through a colleague," replied Antoine.

"Oh my lord, a British ship?! You're going to send me across the ocean on a rat infested bucket of filth? I see now how little you value me." She sneered at Antoine, cursed, and then turned to yell at Estella.

"Don't you dare try those tricks on me! I might be old but I'm still more than a match for even your highly developed powers of persuasion!" she blasted at Estella. Folding her arms, she harrumphed a moment then grudgingly agreed to accompany Katrina on her journey. The ladies departed France traveling under the name of Arias to throw off any potential followers. Once in England they joined an expedition to colonize the New World in the Virginias under the command of Sir Walter Raleigh.

At first, they enjoyed some notoriety when they arrived on the ship due to their diplomatic affiliations. This was, however, short lived and through the course of the journey across the Atlantic their popularity with the English waned. Labeled as snobs and aristocrats by their travel mates, they secluded themselves in their cabin and rarely came out accept for the occasional meals with the ship's Captain or to take in some fresh air when the ship's stifling aroma became intolerable. Out there, despite the vastness of the open sea, such close proximity to the other passengers fostered a relentless assault of the voices in Katrina's head. At times, it felt as if she could hear other people's thoughts, though she dismissed the notion as ridiculous.

How could anyone think such vile thoughts? What a wild imagination.

Grandmother Arias' irritable demeanor made the voyage even more unbearable. She had no sympathy for the plight of these travelers. They were escaping one form of oppression to impose one of their own on others and she knew it. This was compounded by the fact that Grandmother Arias was far more sensitive to the energies projected by thought waves than her fledgling telepath granddaughter. The ocean was not her favorite place. Two places grandmother learned to avoid in her many years were cemeteries and the ocean. To her, they were one in the same. The constant complaining, bickering and conspiring of the living was bad enough without the rhythm of the dead's laments in the background. It was enough to drive any normal person insane, but for grandmother it was an irritation that made her temper extremely short.

"At least French pigs enjoy gourmet slop!" snapped Grandmother Arias to the astonishment of what passes as a sue chef on this ship, who happened to be holding out a plate of that afternoon's indescribable stew in her direction.

Everyone else in line stared with the same blank look of astonishment. Katrina gave everyone an apologetic look and quickly dragged her grandmother away from the line.

Katrina had diversions that she kept very secret. They were her occasional rendezvous with the ship's lower form passengers; the rats. They had stowed away on the ship trapped in the crates and barrels carrying the ship's supplies and provisions. She was utterly disgusted at first, but as the days went by and she became lonely for companionship the little rodents sort of grew on her. They weren't nearly as nice to look at as the wolves from the forest outside her chalet, but they were just as entertaining to watch. At least they helped to pass the time aboard the ship.

Finally, on July 22, 1587, the ship reached the coast of Virginia at the established colony of Roanoke Island. The remnants of the previous attempt were still visible. The settlers walked about the ruins of the makeshift town and peered into the cabins with some trepidation. Katrina strayed from the group and walked about the area looking through all the ruins. There were signs of a battle and the soldiers that escorted the ship found some weapons and ammunition, but no sign of combatants. As she walked about the town Katrina couldn't shake the feeling that she was being watched. As the other settlers inspected their new town, Katrina made her way to the edge of the village and stood staring through the trees at the forest beyond with great curiosity. Her curiosity got the best of her and she stepped through the trees and into the forest.

Katrina was in her own little slice of heaven, new fragrances from trees and flowers she had never seen before; beautiful sounds from song birds she wasn't familiar with; the dramatic view of meadows like islands in an ocean of trees scattered across the forest. It all transported her to a world of fantasy. She wandered farther and farther away from the village losing herself with each step drawn by the allure of the wild and the attraction of a familiar sensation. A feeling she thought she had left in France and would not ever experience again. The sensation was the same, but the feeling was much stronger. She was surprised and excited to feel that the Darklings were in the New World. Still, much like in her beloved France, she could feel them but not see them.

Katrina continued to walk through the dark shadows of the forest entranced by the euphoric overload of her senses. She arrived at a clearing that was filled with flowers. A few butterflies flitted about, visiting each pistil in search of their nectar. She followed them and teased them with her finger as they fluttered through the air. Through the pleasant, almost mesmerizing, sounds of the forest the whimper of a wounded animal broke through the deep darkness of the woods and woke her from her euphoria.

She then came to the harrowing realization that she was lost. She had strayed so far from the village that she did not know in which direction to begin her return. Euphoria turned to fear as she heard the low pitched troubled breathing of an animal in pain approaching. She stood motionless in the clearing hoping it would just pass by. For a moment, she even closed her eyes to fight the panic that was rushing through her body. The sound got closer. She could feel the beast's breathe on her face in rhythm with the sound that pierced her soul. As she summoned up the will to open her eyes she found herself eye to eye with the biggest wolf she had ever seen in her life. She gasped and trembled in shock as her body struggled to move but her limbs would not respond. The wolf took one step closer causing her to jump back in fear. She was then eerily calmed by the feeling that the menace standing before her was also nervous about the encounter. She looked deep into his eyes and as if guided by his feelings, made her way down his leg to his paw and with her hands pulled out the thorn that was lodged between his two middle toes. The wolf let out a sharp howl then licked her face. He sat and stared into her eyes as she stroked his coat. She sat down next to him stroking his back and scratching his ears. She then started talking to him.

"What happened to you, big boy? Did I scare you? I bet not half as much as you scared me. I have many wolf friends in my lovely estate, but none as big and handsome as you. I was starting to feel a little like Little Red Riding Hood. Ironic, I know. Here I am, lost in the woods, I run into a big wolf, and I end up helping you."

She chuckled then looked around straining to recognize her way back.

"Well, I've gone and done it now! I am completely lost. I need to get back home before my grandmother misses me. I'm sure she must be worried after all this time." At that moment, the wolf slowly got up and started to walk away. "Hey, where are you going? You can't leave me here all alone. I helped you, doesn't that mean anything?"

The wolf stopped, turned as if urging her to follow, and then continued to walk away. She did not move. The wolf came back and tugged on her dress, then walked away again. Katrina followed this time. They walked a long way and ever so often the wolf would stop and sniff the air. He would stare out into the wilderness and stand very still. He would then continue through the forest. Finally he stopped and Katrina could see the village through some trees. He had led her back to her people.

"You are a remarkable animal. How did you know?" she remarked.

Just then one of the settlers noticed her and called to her. She turned away to acknowledge them and when she turned back to say goodbye to her new friend, he was gone. She walked through the trees heading back to the village.

"How curious," she said as she looked back towards the forest and strolled into town.

A New Town
Chapter Four

While the women and children waited aboard ship a small village of cabins was erected under the leadership of John White, a close personal friend of Sir Walter Raleigh. A makeshift town hall and court house was set up. A charter was drawn up and signed by Raleigh, and the village was officially dedicated for the Queen of England. The settlers were all assigned to cabins and of course, Katrina and Grandmother Arias were appointed to the farthest cabin at the edge of the forest. This didn't bother Katrina much, she preferred it that way. Town attitudes towards Grandmother Arias slowly changed, especially once everyone realized what a great cook and seamstress she was. Grandmother Arias set up shop in a small portion of the cabin; and due to the vigorous nature of the daily routine she had a lot of business. Another enviable talent, an extremely peculiar one for an aristocrat, was Grandmother Arias' baking. For these delectable treats, Katrina would gladly scavenge through the forest for berries and wild grains that grew near the village. A monetary system had not been established yet and the coin of the realm, even though widely accepted, had little purpose so the barter system was in full effect.

Katrina would spend her day rushing through her chores helping Grandmother Arias. She spun yarn, hung candles and other tedious work, then she would escape into the woods and explore the strange and mysterious settings beyond the edge of the forest. The men were given chores by the constable, each according to their trade or skill. There were carpenters, blacksmiths and farmers. Then this very large man, who seemed to be friendly with the constable, took the rest and organized a sort of militia. He was an interesting man, but something about him was off. He drilled them and taught them the proper way to handle a knife and musket then set up a schedule for patrols. Katrina watched the whole affair and laughed. She didn't think any of that was necessary.

Men and their games.

Katrina knew most of them were just doing this to impress the few single women in the village. She then noticed a group of men that were getting their muskets and bundles together organizing a hunt.

Now this is going to be interesting.

Katrina watched them act so serious. The expressions of determination and boldness imprinted on their faces seemed even more ridiculous to her. She followed them into the woods, but kept her distance fearful she may get shot. She took the opportunity to gather some berries for her grandmother. She watched as they fumbled around the forest as the animals darted away. She was so amused by the spectacle that she almost spilled her basket of freshly picked blue-berries. She followed the line of berries through the woods taking in as much of the scenery and ambiance as possible. Before she knew it she had once again strayed. She lost site of the hunting party. She walked back along

45

the line of berry bushes that led her astray then was startled by an animal in her path. She then recognized the beast from the other day.

"How do you know when I'm lost?" she asked. "I wonder what kind of wolf you are. You've got to be the biggest one I've ever seen. The ones back home were never as big as you. I also never saw one alone."

She started to look around and an eerie feeling came over her as if she was in danger. Something wasn't right. She stood motionless among the berry bushes staring into the forest, searching for the source of her apprehension, but could not see anything beyond the trees. The animal looked at her for a few seconds then turned away and ran for the woods. Katrina somehow regained her bearings darted off to the village spilling berries along the way. She ran quickly and made it to the village tripping over a root as she cleared the tree line tumbling to the ground along with all her berries. She looked back in a panic as she saw something moving towards her through the woods. As it charged out of the forest, Katrina held up her basket in a defensive posture to strike her assailant. A raccoon came into view, ran towards her, snatched a few berries from the ground in front of her then darted back into the forest with as many berries as it could carry. Katrina sat and laughed for a moment. Then she realized that her grandmother was not going to be amused at the empty basket and decided to go back for more berries.

The sun was quickly setting. She rushed to try and get as many berries as she could. She hoped to make it back to the house before it was too dark for her to find her way. Every time she thought she had enough, she ran across a new bush of exquisite fruit and couldn't resist taking a little more time to pick them. By the time she sensed the Darkling watching her from the trees, she could barely see the berries through the gloom. This was a familiar feeling, but this time she sensed no fear or apprehension from the Darkling. She started walking quickly in the direction she hoped was home. She quickened her pace, but the Darkling followed closely. The feeling this time was so intense that she felt as if she were watching herself through its eyes stumbling in the darkness, trying desperately to get away.

She called out, "What do you want? I won't tell anyone you're here. I promise. Please leave me alone."

His intentions were now clear to her. She tried to run as fast as she could to get away. It was too late. After her next step the monster at her back knocked her to the ground. Katrina struggled to turn and fight while on the ground. She managed to face her attacker but could do nothing to knock him off of her. In the light of the moonlit sky, she could see it was a savage. The type she had read about in descriptions of the New World. She fought with the Indian brave confused about what she was sensing. This couldn't be the same thing she sensed deep in the forest of her home. This could not be the same creatures that shied away when she spoke. Finally, the brave grew tired of her struggling and before she was aware, it struck her across the head and rendered her unconscious.

When she came to, the first thing she saw was the eviscerated corpse of the Indian brave laying a few feet away! She screamed and sat up coming eye to eye with her wolf friend who was completely covered in blood. The shriek she let out startled the wolf away and drew the attention of everyone in the village.

Within a matter of seconds there were villagers with torches all around her. A couple of militia boys helped her to her feet. She was still a little groggy from the blow to the head. At least the voices had stopped. She only heard the groaning and the treble-heavy sound sparked by the villagers' whispers as they walked by. As soon as they got to her cabin the interrogations started.

"What were you doing out there all by yourself?"
"What happened to that Indian?"
"Are there more of them out there?"
"Did you do that to him?"
"God protect us. They're going to come after the village now when they see what happened to their friend."

There were worse things left unsaid. Grandmother Arias heard them, but remained quiet, as the mob outside her door grew more and more panicked. She remained quiet, because she knew someone was coming, someone whose presence made her uncomfortable.

"Leave her be," a deep voice was heard above them all, which sounded almost like a harsh growl.

"You and you, go to the spot where the Indian is laying, dig a hole, burn the body and bury him. Make sure there is no sign of him. Tomorrow I want a militia patrol to venture into the forest. Widen your search, engage no one and report everything you see to me," commanded the man.

"Excuse me mademoiselle Arias, what can you tell me about what happened? Do you remember anything?" He asked her doing his best to seem sympathetic.

"A wolf," responded Katrina just as she passed out once more.

The man slowly turned and stared out into the darkness of the forest outside the cabin. At that moment Grandmother Arias' suspicions were justified. She knew there was something odd about this larger than life man. He was Canis. His thoughts betrayed him. She now also knew that the Indian brave was Legion and that there were probably others. Still, she said nothing.

When everyone left, she put Katrina to bed, undressed her and washed her with a cloth. She barred the doors and windows, pulled out a dagger her father gave her as a young woman and sat in a chair in front of the door. She was too exhausted to stay awake all night and shortly fell asleep. Katrina woke before the sun the next morning, got dressed, grabbed another basket and walked out of the cabin without disturbing Grandmother Arias. Katrina walked past a few astonished villagers towards the home of the village farmer. She called out but no one answered. She opened the door to the barn and found that no one was there. She called out again and waited a few minutes but still there was no reply. As she walked she noticed a few skinned rabbits hanging from a post. She looked around then snatched one and dropped it in her pouch. She ran out of the barn and headed towards the forest once more. As she ran away the farmer neared the barn, saw the door open and went in to investigate. He came back out and stared at Katrina as she ran deeper into the woods.

Katrina arrived at the site of the attack the night before. She looked around at all the blood and found some tracks. It looked like the tracks of her wolf friend. She walked around the area slowly as she pieced together the event, reliving the moments in her mind. She smiled because she felt she would be safe as long as her furry friend was around. She then wondered why the Darkling attacked her.

She paid no attention to the latter and continued on to venture into the woods for more of the troublesome berries. This time she hoped to run into her friend. She walked further into the woods and found a meadow with a pond in the center. The edge of the pond was surrounded with large cattails and high grass. She followed a path in the high brush and stood at the edge of the pond. It was quiet and beautiful. It looked so inviting on such a hot day. She walked on and reached the largest huckleberry bush she had ever seen. She picked as many as she could reach and almost filled the basket when she finally noticed her woodland friend.

"There you are!" she said full of excitement. "Where have you been? I've been so anxious to see you. You saved my life! I'm sorry I scared you away. I was just so horrified by what I saw that all I could do was scream. I'm so grateful you came along. God only knows what that savage's intentions were." She reached into her pouch, pulled the rabbit out and dropped it right at the wolf's paws.

"Are you hungry?"

He smelled the carcass and with one bite split the rabbit in half. They walked together and sat under a tree. He finished the meal-- bones and all-- while Katrina told some stories to pass the time. She was talking to this animal as if he understood what she was saying. Every now and then he would look up and perk up his ears which gave the illusion that he knew what she meant. When she noticed that her friend had completely finished his small meal she stood up.

"My name is Katrina; Mademoiselle Katrina Le' Giroux, but I prefer Katrina," she said throwing a regal pose. "Damn it's hot! I saw a pond earlier. Do you think it will be safe for me to bathe in it?" she asked, looking at the wolf as if waiting for a reply then continued. "Oh I'm glad you think so."

She turned and ran away giggling. The wolf got up and chased after her. They ran through the brush surrounding the pond and stopped short of the edge of the water. Katrina laid down her basket. The Wolf walked over to the bank of the pond and looked all around and across. He looked into the water and searched the whole area. Katrina pulled her boots off, walked over to where the wolf was, hiked up her dress and said, "Is it safe?"

She dipped her toes in the water and startled the wolf as she jumped to get her foot back out. It was colder than she thought it would be.

Ouch, that was cold. Still on a hot day like this it's going to feel just great after a few minutes.

She walked over and hid among the cattails behind a tall shade tree. She completely undressed and walked slowly into the water. She swam back and forth enjoying the cool clear water. She splashed the wolf trying to coax him in but he didn't budge. He just sat and watched her intently. As the sun began to sink into the horizon the wolf barked at her.

"Okay, okay I know; the night will come soon and grandmother will be worried. My grandmother would be proud of you. You make a good chaperone."

Katrina walked out of the pond; squeezed the water out of her hair and dried off with her cloak. She got dressed and started walking towards the village with her new companion by her side. The wolf again stopped short of the clearing at the edge of the forest and watched her as she ran to her cabin. Katrina turned to watch him run away into the darkness of the forest.

"Have a good night my woodland friend."

Katrina stepped into the cabin and found her grandmother already asleep. She walked over to her side of the cabin, as she put away her clothes she realized there was something missing. She lit a candle and looked around the room. While she searched Grandmother Arias awoke.

"There you are. How was your bath?" she asked.

"It was fine," she responded before realizing what happened. "The water was a little cold, but it felt great in the heat of the day," she continued playing it off.

"That's just great honey. I think you left something at the pond by the tree," replied Grandmother Arias before nodding off to sleep again.

Grandmother had a tendency to talk in her sleep. Some of her best premonitions developed in her sleep. This was, at times, a curse.

Katrina wrapped herself up in her cloak and walked out the door. She managed to find the path in the darkness added by the light of the moon. The noises of the night-time forest were strangely soothing and drove her initial fears away. That was until she entered the darkest part of the forest and spooked an owl into screeching.

She managed to make it all the way to the meadow with the pond. She traced her steps to the place where she entered the pond, then walked slowly to the shade tree. As she got closer to the tree she was stunned by the shock of seeing a naked man rise from the base of the tree and run away. This wasn't half as shocking as what she saw next. The man transformed right before her eyes into a wolf as he ran away. She stood there motionless as the wolf looked back, stopped running, and then turned around. The wolf walked slowly towards her and sat right in front of her. They stared at each other for what seemed an eternity to Katrina. She was staring at the wolf that had become her woodland friend and for the first time she was afraid.

A New Friend
Chapter Five

Katrina trembled in fear wondering what would happen next. She slowly turned and started to walk away. She took a few steps and heard, "I think you might want this back."

She stopped, stood as still as she could and stared out into the darkness of the night. She gasped as she slowly turned around and saw a naked man standing there holding out her handkerchief.

"I already saw you. I figured I should return the favor," he said with a smile on his face.

"That was really you; I'm not having some sort of episode?" she replied, still trembling from the shock of the situation. "You are the wolf."

"I'm more than just a wolf," replied the man standing in front of her. "Does that frighten you?"

"I think it was more of a shock than fear. I have always dreamed of goblins, fairies, witches, vampires and werewolves. At times I even thought I communicated with them, but I never thought I'd be standing face to face with one," she said, still shaking from the shock of what was happening.

Katrina took her cloak and tossed it at the man.

"I was wondering how long you were going to take advantage of the situation," he said with a smile on his face.

"Well, how long did you watch me bathe?" she replied, smiling with a face flush with embarrassment.

There was an awkward moment of silence then he said, "I hope you enjoyed it as much as I enjoyed watching you."

She smiled and asked, "What happens now?"

"I guess I'll have to kill you."

She looked deep into his eyes searching for a sign of humor, but there was none. Somehow she could tell he was just joking.

"You will marry me or I shall have to kill you," he continued with his ruse.

She just looked at him with a smirk on her face signifying her disbelief.

"It's the law. Only my wife, family and immediate friends may know my secret. It's a secret they must take to the grave."

Katrina looked right into his eyes and said, "Kill me,

then, for I shall never marry you." They laughed and came together in an embrace. They spent the night in each others arms. Before the dawn, the man transformed to a wolf once more and escorted her back to her cabin.

As he was about to turn away and run back into the forest for his daily activities, she called to him, "Oh my God, I never got your name. What is your name?"

For a moment he rose from the ground shedding his animal form and replied, "Bruno, I'm known as Bruno."

With that he turned and ran into the forest disappearing into the darkness.

They met the next day, while Katrina finished her daily chores that took her into the woods. He ran to her and they walked about the forest picking berries for Grandmother Arias. As they wound their way through the thick woods, they heard the clanging of armor and weapons. They quickly hid and watched as the town militia walked past without noticing them. Katrina giggled as they passed and then broke out into full laughter once they were gone.

She thought they looked so ridiculous. Stalking the militia became a part of their daily excursions into the forest. Bruno would lead Katrina on deer and rabbit hunts. Katrina and her grandmother always had fresh meat for supper. Some of the villagers made it a point to stop by their cabin in the evenings in the hopes of being invited to the table.

For the next few days and nights they spent their time in much the same manner. The whole time Katrina could sense that not far away the Darklings were watching. She sensed their fear and reveled in the protection Bruno could offer. She delighted in the pleasures of their interludes among the animals, the birds, and the trees. She drew great pleasure in giving herself to him under the light of the moon as she sensed the Darklings watching them. Even then, the Darklings did not dare provoke the Canis.

Witch Hunt
Chapter Six

One afternoon, Katrina had just completed her chores when she decided to repay the farmer by replacing the rabbits she had once taken. She walked over to where Grandmother Arias had left the hares hanging and pulled a couple down. She walked over to the barn, she called out and once again it seemed like the farmer was not home. She knocked on the barn door and there was no answer.

"Perfect, I'll just leave the two bunnies here and he need not know," she said to herself as she entered the barn.

She walked across the floor to the farthest end of the barn where the farmer hung his pelts and fresh meat to dry. As she reached to hang her hares the line broke and the meat came crashing down. She frantically searched through the stack of hay for the hook to replace the line. It was difficult to see the hook. She began to trace the line looking for the end. She then got the feeling that the farmer was watching her from the door of the barn. She turned to see him looking at her with a very angry look on his face.

"Pardon me Sir; I was trying to replace some meat I borrowed earlier. You were not home and I needed it badly," she was interrupted before she could say anything else.

"You little thief," he growled as he lunged at her.

Katrina tried to run, but there was no other way out. She had to go through the farmer. She backed up and then tried to quickly run past. He caught her and tossed her to the ground throwing all his weight on top of her. She whimpered from the pain of the force of his weight on her body. Katrina could see his intensions and frantically tries to fight back. He rips her blouse and pulled on her corset exposing her breasts. He wraps a hand around her neck, rises up with all his weight on his hand and fondles her breast with the other. He leans in and kisses her face, her lips and her breast. Katrina kicks, screams and tries to push him off to no avail. She is nauseated by his breath and fights back the urge to wretch.

"You're going to pay for your thievery," he said as he reached for her dress.

Katrina, knowing she could not fight this large man off goes limp and accepts her fate. The farmer rips at her clothes, reaches under her dress and invades her body. She lays motionless under the farmer's weight and offers no response. She drifts away as if in a trance attempting to pass this ordeal with minimal injury. The farmer angrily attempts to elicit a reaction from his reluctant lover, but she just lays there like a corpse. Infuriated by the lack of emotion and response, he drives himself between her legs, forces his member into her. She gasps from the pain. Just then a familiar sensation came upon her. A feeling she had not experienced since she was a little girl; an indescribable sense of joy. At that moment she felt the weight of the man lift off her and she rolled to her side. It was as if the man had been carried off by a strong gust of wind. A strange glow filled the barn then quickly went away. She scanned the barn in every direction looking for the farmer, who she quickly located lying on the ground next to her. His eyes were wide open and fixed on the ceiling, blood was pulsing out of his chest, and the spikes of a pitch fork protruded from his body. Katrina grabbed her clothes, got up, and ran out of the barn screaming. As she got passed the barn doors two women saw her and came over to help. She struggled to get what was left of her clothes on and sobbed in their arms. A few of the men from the militia arrived and the constable was close behind. They looked into the barn and saw the bloody corpse of the farmer lying motionless on the floor. Katrina was in hysterics; she lost control of her senses and began to speak.

"I didn't kill him. There is nothing I could do. You can't call me a whore. My grandmother raised me right. Don't you say anything about her," Katrina yelled out not realizing she was answering the thoughts of the villagers around her. The people around her quickly backed away. One of the matriarchs began to whisper the words that would change Katrina's life forever, "Witch."

The constable ordered that the militia place shackles on her wrist and take her away to the jail. In her panicked state she managed to see her wolf friend watching from the edge of the forest. She could sense his anger and helplessness as he watched her being dragged away. At the jail she was thrown to the ground in one of the cells. One of the town's matriarchs went into the cell with her. Katrina's wrists were shackled to the bars. The old woman then pulled out a weathered Bible and began to quote scripture. She then ripped what was left of Katrina's clothes and she continued to quote scripture as she inspected every inch of her skin.

"There, I found it," yelled the woman pointing at a mole above Katrina's left breast.

"This is the Devils gate to her soul," she hollered to the two women sitting outside the cell. One of the old hags handed the matriarch a silver dagger with a gold cross on the pommel. The woman raised the dagger to Katrina's face, quoted some more scripture and slashed the mole from Katrina's skin. Katrina writhed in pain as the blood ran down her breast and streamed to her feet. Searching for a release from the pain, she drifted into another trance that brought visions of her Grandmother Arias. She calls to her, but grandmother ignores her and continues to mill the grain for the evening's bread. She is shaken out of her trance by the matriarch quoting more scriptures from the Bible.

"Confess your sins to the Lord. Ask Jesus Christ to forgive you. Release her Satan!" The old woman screamed, but Katrina gave no reply; she whimpered and sobbed in agony. The matriarch then motioned for the two old women to join her in the cell. They pushed Katrina down to her knees. She hit her head as she fell to the ground. She felt a warm stream of blood race down her face from a cut on her forehead. Her tormentors then added insult to injury as she was subjected to a most intimate form of inspections. One woman pushed Katrina's face to the ground; her hands were still shackled to the bars. She moaned in pain as one of her shoulders was dislocated from the contortion of her arms. Another woman forced her legs apart dragging her knees across the floor. The Matriarch then inspected.

The woman recoiled in disgust and yelled, "Unwed seductress! Temptress, adulteress, fornicator, confess or burn in hell with all your demons!"

Katrina again gave no response. She hung from the bars of the cell whimpering in pain, completely humiliated from the indignities that had been thrust upon her. The old women looked at her with disgust for a moment then stepped out of the cell. The Magistrate stepped into the holding area.

"Put some clothing on that wench!" he exclaimed.

One of the old women threw a tattered gown over Katrina to cover her body. Katrina looked up and saw the man standing in front of her through the bars.

"Has she confessed?" He asked the matriarch.

"This one is strong willed my lord. She refuses to even speak. I'm afraid she is too far gone and the devil has already taken her soul," said the old woman with a look of repulsion.

"How do you know she has anything to confess?" asked the Magistrate with his usual suspicious blank stare.

The matriarch pointed to Katrina's chest and said, "She has the mark."

"What mark are you talking about exactly?" replied the Magistrate.

She walked over to Katrina, reached between the bars and pulled away the blanket exposing her blood smeared breast.

"And she has fornicated with demons in the forest," continued the old woman.

"Bring her to the next cell. I'll continue the inquisition," he said with a very pious voice.

The shackles were removed from Katrina's hands, the two old women dressed her, escorted her to the cell next door and they dropped her to the floor. This cell was different from the other. There were no bars, no windows and the cell door was made of heavy wood with a peep door at eye level. In the center of the room was a wooden bed with shackles at both ends. Katrina trembled in fear as her mind was bombarded with the most despicable thoughts from those around her. Even her mind was being tormented by her captors. She cowered in the corner of the cell whimpering and sobbing as the tears streamed from her eyes. She wondered if her wolf friend would come to her rescue this time. She wondered if he even knew what was happening. The Magistrate stepped into the room and he motioned to the two old women and they pulled her up off the ground to her feet and onto the bed. They raised her arms over her head and shackled her wrist to the bed frame. Then they did the same to her legs and shackled her ankles to the other end. Deacons from the church arrived and brought some tools and instruments of the trade; there was a cross, a tub with water, some coal and some fire brands in different shapes. As they were setting up, her mind reeled with images from their lecherous hearts invading her thoughts. They sparked the fire and stoked the brands until they glowed bright red. The Magistrate ordered everyone out of the room accept for the priest. The women left under protest. The Magistrate locked the door and closed the peek gate.

"You have been much too troublesome for such a young woman," he said with a low guttural voice.

"The farmer you killed was my brother."

The Magistrate took the first fire brand and held it to her face. Katrina could feel the heat of the red hot glowing brand stinging her flesh. He waved the brand mere inches above her flesh, stinging a trail to her left breast. He held it over the spot where her mole used to be.

"I think I need to purify your soul before we can accept your confession," said the Magistrate with a sneer on his face.

"Sir, this is not acceptable. This is barbaric," said one of the deacons.

"If you don't have the stomach to fight for your Lord in the face of evil then maybe you should leave," replied the Magistrate.

The deacon looked at his colleague, looked at Katrina, swallowed in disgust, and slowly walked past the Magistrate to the door. At the door he glanced back with a compassionate gaze and shook his head as he walked away. Katrina's screams could be heard through the thick wood of the door; the sounds waned as he traveled down the short hallway. The deacon left the jailhouse with tears in his eyes.

Katrina screamed until she passed out from the pain. The Magistrate had her dowsed. The deacon that remained poured water on her face from a copper pitcher, it streamed down into her nostrils and filled her mouth until the body naturally reacted and she woke. She gasped and choked as her natural reflexes expelled the water from her body. She was awake but barely conscious.

"Confess your sins and the gates of heaven shall open to accept your soul," said the Magistrate.

"Confess!" He insisted angrily.

Her eyes were glazed and her breathing labored, but the Magistrate pressed his inquisition. His inability to elicit any response from his prisoner caused his frustration to get the best of him. He slapped Katrina and he ripped her gown exposing her breasts. The deacon winced at the violence of the Magistrate's slap.

The Magistrate looked up at the deacon and ordered him to assist him in turning Katrina over. They undid her hands and twisted her onto her face leaving her torso contorted. Katrina once more screamed from the pain as her muscles stretched beyond their limit and her ligaments ripped from her ribs. The Magistrate watched for a moment as Katrina moaned, very near to passing out from the pain of this position. He then reached over and undid the shackle on her left leg allowing her some relief. The deacon released the other leg allowing her to fall into a natural face down position. The Magistrate shackled her ankles into position. She lay motionless hoping that was the end of her torment. It was not to be. The Magistrate reached into the tool box and pulled out a straight blade dagger. He pointed the tip of the dagger to the vertebrae at the base of her neck and pierced the skin at every bone, working his way down to the center of her back. Her whimpers fell on deaf ears as the hair-thin slices trickled blood. At the vertebrae at the center of her back he stood the dagger on end and slowly pierced her skin.

"Confess," he said over and over as he continued to press the blade against the bone. She gave no reply as she writhed in agony, grimaced, and struggled to absorb the pain. The Magistrate growled in frustration and kicked the tool box knocking it over.

"Get out," the Magistrate told the deacon as he unbuttoned his tunic.

"Sir, I am with you in whatever you require," replied the deacon.

"You have served our Lord well my friend. It is time

for me to go beyond the calling and tread where the holy should not venture," replied the Magistrate.

The deacon excused himself, took one last look down at Katrina and shook his head as he walked out the door.

The Magistrate looked down at Katrina's battered unconscious body and took his scarf off from around his neck. He reached down and strapped it across Katrina's face putting it over her mouth and tying it on the back of her head. He picked up a piece of her ripped gown and blindfolded her with it. He moved down to her feet and undid the shackles from around her ankles. He pulled her feet swinging her off the bed and let her fall to the floor. He then picked her up by her waist and pushed her onto the bed. She was face down on the bed once more with her body bent over her arms while her hands were still tied to the bed rails at her waist. He ripped what was left of her gown leaving her completely nude. Her legs just dangled to the floor limp from exhaustion. She saw what happened next through the eyes of her assailant as if in a smoky dream.

The Magistrate stepped behind her, put his hands on her back, and stroked her. He ran his hands down from her neck to the small of her back and back up again. He kneaded her hips and squeezed her flesh until it was rosy pink. He put one hand on the center of her back, pushed her face into the bed, and cut a trail on her lower back with the tip of the blade from his dagger. The blood slowly oozed to the surface in the wake of the blade, cutting a path through the skin in the shape of a "W" inside of a circle.

Katrina slipped in and out of consciousness as waves of pain rose and waned ravaging her body. She strained against her bonds to scream in release, but the muffled whimpers held no satisfaction. Her mind was then filled with voices as if the whole town was shouting at once. The sounds in her head only added to the torment as it seemed all her senses were overwhelmingly stimulated. The metallic taste of her own blood burned her throat and numbed her tongue as she continued to strain against the rags that bound her. Her body crumbled under the pain at the touch of the blade. In the silence of the moment she could here every thought in the village. Though she was blindfolded, she could see the brutality as if through the eyes of her attacker.

He looked at her limp figure bent over the rail of the bed with such distain. He wanted to kill her. His frustration rose and he fell to his knees in a fit of rage and beat her with his fist till his arms fell exhausted to his side. Katrina, barely conscience, could see everything unfold like a nightmare bathed in fog. She sensed his rage, felt his pain, and knew what he intended to do next.

Katrina knew she would never walk out of this cell alive. She beckoned to the gods to help her, she called to her Canis friend, she even prayed to God, and then from the abyss of her mind's eye something came into sharp focus. A pale skinned man asked one question, "Do you want to live?"

She gave no answer as she saw the Magistrate rise to his feet. He looked at the bruised wretched lump of flesh before him. He reached down and tied one leg to the rail then the other, went to the door, and locked it. He walked around to face Katrina, pulled the gag from her mouth, pulled the blindfold from her eyes and said, "I want to hear you scream!"

He walked back behind Katrina, undid his buckle, and let his pants fall to the ground. He ran his fingers up and down the mound between her legs, fondled with the other hand, and prepared to thrust into her. He wanted to do this not out of lust or desire, but as a last act of vengeance and humiliation. He spread her open with each hand and right when he was going to push a voice called to the Magistrate saying, "Don't damn yourself any further over one such as this." The Magistrate was startled; he looked around the room, having seen no one, shook his head and continued with his course of action. Before he could achieve his despicable goal Katrina screamed, "I want to live!" The room filled with a blast of light and a force as strong as a cyclone threw the Magistrate to the ground. Sluggishly he stumbled to his feet in a daze and found Katrina standing in front of him with the shackles and rags that bound her lying at her feet. He was frozen in shock, trembling with fear, and yelled, "Witch!" Katrina collapsed to the floor. He quickly pulled his pants up ran out of the cell, locked the door behind him, looked through the peek gate, and ran out of the jail in horror.

The Trial
Chapter Seven

That evening Katrina woke in her cell to the sensation of someone touching her. She quickly scrambles to her feet, cowering in a corner, and finds two village matriarchs attempting to dress her. Standing at the door with their backs turned are two guards holding shackles in their hands. One of the matriarchs rushes over to Katrina and puts a hood over her head.

"Don't look into her eyes or she might enchant you with a spell," said the old crotchety one with a fierce despising look.

Katrina didn't put up a fight. Even if she wanted to she was too exhausted to retaliate. After she was fully clothed the guards walked into the cell and wrapped the shackles around her wrists. She fell in and out of consciousness and stumbled to her knees a couple of times along the way as she was walked to the makeshift court room. The soldiers at her side simply yanked her to her feet. The guards took the hood off her head when they entered the great hall.

The candlelit chamber was full of people but their faces

were unrecognizable due to the irregular shapes caused by the mix of shadows and candlelight. The view seemed surreal from Katrina's perspective. It was as if she was being offered as that evening's dinner at a feast of demons. The dancing light continued to play tricks on Katrina's eyes and mind. For a moment she thought she sensed the presence of a Darkling. That didn't make sense to her; she dismissed the feeling as fatigue then finally just stood in the center of the chamber while the Magistrate barked out the charges brought against her.

For the first time in a long time she noticed the voices in her head were silent. The visions, which at times confused her were also gone. She slowly looked around the room desperately trying to find a friendly face. She hoped maybe at the very least a sympathetic expression, but there was none that night.

"...Murder by witchcraft and consorting with unclean spirits. For refusing to confess your sins before the Lord your God, lying to a Magistrate of the Queen and her appointed commission. For attempting to seduce an official of this court by means of mysterious enchantments and finally for the blatant lack of remorse for all these actions, I condemn you to be hanged by the neck until your death, burned, and then have the ashes scattered to the wind."

She was still in a daze when her senses surged jolting her out of her lethargy. Right behind her, more guards stepped in pushing a strange man into the courtroom. This man, though very good looking, seemed to have gone through something terrible. His skin was pale, his hair matted and his body bruised; he looked more dead than alive. He was hunched over as if suffering from a terrible stomach ache and his eyes, flushed red and bulging, made him look demented. He stood there peering into everyone's eyes as if he were looking into their souls. There was something familiar about his presence or in the things she felt about him, but she couldn't quite nail her thoughts down long enough to think on what it could be.

The Magistrate finished his dissertation of charges against Katrina, said a short prayer for the men appointed to carry out the execution and then said, "Hang 'er!" The two soldiers at the door stepped forward to secure their prisoner and then, to everyone's surprise, the strange man let out a terrible howl like an animal in pain. The crowd inside the hall looked on in awe as the once seemingly debilitated man broke his chains, knocked one of his captives across the room, and while lifting the other in the air ripped his throat out with one bite. Blood flowed from his mouth and ran down his chiseled chest.

Almost instantly and right before everyone's eyes, the bruises disappeared from his skin and his whole body seemed to heal. The man was in a complete rage. The people who were so eager to see bloodshed that night had had their fill and scurried about panicked by fear as they tried to find a way to escape. The panic only grew once they realized that the only way out was in the direction of the deranged man in front of the door.

The maniac shred through his victims as they attempted to escape their inevitable demise. The walls of the chamber were splattered with the blood of the carnage left in his wake. The salty smell of blood and gore filled the air as the screams of terror deafened the moment. In the confusion, the Magistrate had slipped away leaving Katrina paralyzed by fear in the center of the room.

The madman slowly approached. Like a rabbit gripped by the fear of an eminent strike from a snake, Katrina stood and watched as this thing closed in for the kill. Katrina's breath began to fail her, her heart beat faster than ever, and her skin began to crawl. Though she tried, she could not even scream. As the man drew near and his face met hers, she closed her eyes and said one solitary word, "Aeacian!"

The beast stopped directly in front of her and stared deep

into her eyes and replied, "What did you say?"

"Aeacian, you are Aeacian," replied Katrina still held motionless by fear. She had felt the presence of his kind for years. She had dreamt of them and experienced them through the vivid images of her mind's eye and many times wanted to be like them. The man did not give her a second thought as he lunged at her throat.

She pulled away and said, "Don't kill me. I will give you what you crave if you will do something for me."

The man did not listen. He pushed her down to the ground and threw himself on her. Katrina grabbed a knife that was on the floor and stabbed the man in the arm as he landed on her. It was as if he felt no pain. He did not even flinch. He lunged at her neck, but she quickly moved around and he bit her on the shoulder. He fed on her blood with such intensity that he did not notice her drinking from the blood spilling from his wound. As she drank she began to realize, there was something else. Something she did not expect, but it was too late to fight now. Her body convulsed in pain that ripped at her from the inside. Blood spilled from her mouth and then her body went completely limp as she fell into a trance.

"They'll burn me at the stake for this for sure," she heard a voice bring her back to consciousness.

The man stood there looking much more like a normal person than moments earlier. He looked around at the devastation he had just brought on the town then they both realized at the same moment that there was someone missing. He made his way passed the podium to an adjoining room. Katrina followed. The stranger found the man cowering beneath his desk.

The Magistrate started shouting insults at both of them.

"Demon, diabolical spawns, what do you wish from me?" He said, as he trembled at the sight of his former prisoner looking down at him drenched in blood.

Katrina stepped forward, startling the strange man, looked at the Magistrate, and said, "You shall be my first victim. With your blood I shall consummate my evolution into darkness."

She reached down, grabbed the Magistrate by the neck, raised him to the air, and slammed him on top of his desk. She plunged her fangs deep into his neck and began to drain him of his blood. He struggled under her grasp, turned, and looked up to the stranger. There stood the man that just moments ago he was ready to condemn. Unable to speak because of the wounds inflicted by Katrina he stared and reached out pleading for help that would never come. The man watched as Katrina exsanguinated the Magistrate; who gasped for air, choking on his own blood as Katrina finally released him. She leaned over to the Magistrate's ear and said, "Now prepare to meet your Lord whichever one he might be."

She stood up and watched as death surged throughout his body with slow waves of tremors and violent convulsions swept over him. The convulsions and tremors then waned as life slowly slipped away. His eyes fixed on the ceiling, his face flush with a deep look of surprise as if peering into his fate, and then nothing. She felt strangely weak, barely alive; it was not what she had expected. For a moment she even felt faint. The convict walked up to her and asked, "Who are you?"

"I am an oracle; I have sought your kind for all my life. I wanted to be what you are!"

"I don't even know what I am anymore, how could you know?" replied the young man.

"You are Aeacian, you were born of a human blood slave. You are a very rare creature. You were born a Vampire. Stay with me and I can help you uncover all your secrets."

"No. I was bitten; I haven't always been like this."

"Think; search your memories, you know this is true. I'm sure you have questions that can only be explained by what I am proposing."

The room then erupted with the sound of screams, blades clashing and gun fire. Her first thought was of her grandmother. She ran out of the courthouse and straight to her cottage. There were two beasts standing in the center of the cottage looking down upon her grandmother, who was cowering on the floor. The shocking scene must have been too much for Katrina because she fainted as she tried to protect her grandmother and fell to the floor.

The next thing she remembered, she was in a cold dark place. There were blurred visions of figures flashing passed her. They howled as they ran up to her and struck her. One by one they took turns slapping her on her head, poking her in the back, or slapping her on her behind. She could feel herself fading out of consciousness. Two dark figures rushed to her and pulled her arms apart. She was on her knees and her face was pressed against the ground. She felt the damp cold air travel between her legs as her clothes were ripped from her body. She didn't have the strength to struggle. She felt the weight of two strong hands grasp her hips. Another pushed down on her back between her shoulder blades. The hunger that ravaged her body intensified. She was feeling nauseous. She then heard a loud hiss that toned down to a low growl. Instantly her assailants released her. From the darkness a voice called to her, "You are dying. Do you want to live?"

"Give me… life," answered Katrina delirious from the pain inside her.

A pale figure approached from the darkness and she felt the now familiar salty metallic taste of blood rush passed her lips and down her throat. The pain became stronger as the new blood attacked the old and the darkness seeped into her soul. Visions of past centuries coursed through her mind as she picked up on the experiences imprinted deep in the blood by the spirit of darkness that now possessed her body. In an instant, through her unique abilities inherited from her ancestors, she relived the history of the Nyxian spirits going back to the pre-creation wars. Once the pain had passed, she rose stronger than she had ever felt before. Her vision was sharper, her senses enhanced, her muscles more powerful, but her heart did not beat.

"But, I was already a vampire," she said.

"Ah, is that so? You took the blood of an Aeacian. This might keep you walking that thin line on the edge of death. You might exhibit strange tendencies, blood lust, and erratic behavior, hear and see things you've never seen before, but once the blood dies you die with it. This gift, ability, or curse must be granted and accepted. It can not be taken. The mere act of taking the blood from a Legion does not a Legion make," he told her.

Katrina tried to read the man's thoughts, but she could not.

"You now have the blood of the House of Dracula surging through your veins. Consider yourself privileged among the Legion. You are the newest member of the most elite house in all of our empire. I have many names, but to the modern world I am Vlad Tepes III," said the pale man.

"I have wanted this for a long time. How did you know? I told no one," she said.

Vlad did not answer. He looked at her with stern eyes as if trying to communicate and waiting for an answer. When nothing happened he turned away disappointed.

"I have hunted your kind for ages. I was lucky to find you here," replied Vlad.

Vlad ordered the group of Croatoan braves who stood over Katrina to bring in some wood from the forest. Katrina was surprised to find them to be a mix of sorts. There were light and dark skinned men, some had blue eyes, some had light hair, and there was even one with red hair. All of them had tattooed their faces with distinct symbols or patterns. The braves fashioned a large wooden case and placed it deep in the darkest region of the cave.

"The sun will be up soon and you look like you need some rest," Vlad told Katrina.

He took her by the hand and walked her to the spot where the makeshift sarcophagus was laid. He opened the lid and helped her climb in.

"Sleep well, tomorrow is your first night in a new and marvelous world," said Vlad as he closed the lid and walked away.

Captive
Chapter Eight

The next night Katrina was lifted in the air while in her coffin and dumped to the ground. The box was slammed from cave wall to cave wall with her still in it. She finally fell out of her small sanctuary when it splintered into a million pieces. The pain was unbearable but she managed to slowly rise. She could not see anyone around her. Then the hardest blow she had ever received in her life knocked her back on her ass, an extremely rude awakening.

"Welcome to the world of the Dragon," a voice said in the dark.

She slowly tried to get back on her feet and was immediately blindsided and thrown back to the ground. She was starting to panic and searched the dark for her assailant. She realized that there was no light, but yet she was able to focus her sight through the gloom. A blurry figure streaked across her view, followed by another, by the third she was able to bring the flashes sharply into focus, and almost slow down what she saw. It made no difference; she couldn't fight the onslaught that fell upon her. She was beaten down and slashed across her face. Vlad appeared through the blur of the blood tears that welled in her eyes. He grabbed her by the neck, pulled her up, and lifted her in the air. Katrina kicked, struggled, then gave up and let herself fall limp. Vlad was enraged.

"Use the power within; I can see it in you. Use it!" He growled at her.

When he failed to illicit the proper response, he flung her across the threshold and slammed her against the rocky side of the cave. Katrina slumped on the ground bleeding, battered and bruised. She had not fed and her body was slow to recover. She rose, looked at her battered body, and charged in a swift violent attack. She flung herself upon the man in front of her and dug her fangs deep into his neck. They fell to the ground and she sucked his blood into her mouth with a feverish fervor. She could hear the man's heartbeat, she felt his pulse quicken, and then he collapsed and breathed no more. She jumped to her feet and stood ready for the next attack. Her cuts closed, her bruises faded, and her bones mended seemingly in an instant. She then spun around and thrust her nails to slash at her next attacker, but Vlad blocked her blow. He held her by her wrist and slammed her to the ground.

"What have you learned?" he received no reply.

"Tell me, what you just learned?" he insisted.

"I don't understand what just happened," Katrina was in a Neomorph fog.

"You have just cracked the shell of the powers you possess. When you have finished your training here, none shall rival your abilities, and you shall use them to serve me," Vlad said.

"I serve no one," she replied.

"Ah, the adversarial nature I admire so much surfaces, but you will serve me, or I'll phase you," Vlad answered.

He looked at her and walked away. Out of the darkness a few braves emerged. They helped her to her feet. She could not understand what they were saying, so they signed to her beckoning her to follow them. She followed the men outside the cave and into the forest.

The group joined another and together made a hunting party of ten braves plus Katrina. They formed a circle; one of them crouched in the center, rubbed his hands together, ignited a log with his touch, and started a fire. They danced, chanted, and moved in an almost trancelike state. The pace built in tempo and the rhythm became steadier. It continued to build in speed until it was all a blur, then they swept out of the circle peeling off in single file, practically flying through the forest. The troupe moved swiftly underneath the canopy of the forest cutting through the darkness of a moonless night. They reached the edge of a rival tribe's camp.

First they set up in positions around the campground just beyond the wood line, and then they began to howl, yell and scream like a pack of wild animals. The startled men of the camp ran out of their shelters with weapons in hand, ready to defend their homes. It was to no avail; Vlad's Native American Legion fell upon them slashing throats, ripping at their flesh, and bleeding them all dry.

Katrina could not resist the frenzy, killing and feeding as viciously as any in the hunting party. She swam through the human wave of slaughter; blood drunk from the amount she had ingested. Her body began to enter her first blood glow and the intense feeling of lust was only subdued by the horrific realization that the one she was feeding on was a young baby girl of no more than three.

She immediately dropped the lifeless toddler to the ground in disgust. Repulsed by what she had just done, she ran into the forest at a blind frantic pace, reached a clearing, and collapsed to her knees.

"What have I become?" she screamed at the top of her lungs, scaring birds out of their roosts for miles around.

Katrina regretted ever envying the Darklings that roamed the forests outside her home back in France. She wondered if she was being stalked by them so many years ago, and what kept them from exacting their fiendish plan. She collapsed from her kneeling position, landing face first on the ground, and cried. A deep sorrow filled her cold dead heart as she replayed the actions of the past few minutes in her mind and saw the faces of those she had destroyed; men, women and children... lots of children. When she was finally subdued by the extreme strain of her grief and the loss of blood from her tears, she looked up to find Vlad standing over her.

"When you feed, try to avoid the frenzy of the blood lust or you will go into what we call the blood glow. It is a physical state that effects your body, bringing back all your human attributes, but with a heightened sense of feeling. The touch is extremely sensitive, smells are enriched, the sight may blur from reaction, and your taste is sharpened.

It's your emotions that will suffer the greatest affects. Depending on your mood during blood glow, you will feel it to its awful extreme; anger to rage, love to lust, fear to panic, and pain to despair. Ingest just enough blood to heal, refresh and repair.

Then again, if your intention is to indulge in the feelings of your past, some have even been able to walk in the sun for a short period of time. I myself will feed to watch the sun rise or set depending on my mood. It is also the only way you will be able to ever have sex again, but when you do, you will feel it like you have never felt it before.

All of this contributes to the danger of falling into the trap of addiction to blood glow. It could lead to your destruction. There is much more to learn, but I see the exertion of the night has taken a toll on your Neomorph body. Make sure you feed again before the night is done and get plenty of rest. You will need it for the next evolution of your training." Vlad walked away and left Katrina in the clearing surrounded by the braves of her adopted clan.

One brave signaled another member of the clan, that brave approached her and helped her up off the ground. He led her through the woods slowly allowing her to take in the sounds, smells, and other sensations of her environment. The rest of the braves stayed in the clearing and watched them walk away. As soon as they were out of sight, the troupe headed back towards the cave.

In the serenity of the forest, Katrina's panic and apprehension dissipated and she was once more able to pick up the familiar voices carried by the thoughts of those around her. She didn't even know she had missed it. With her psychic power restored, she felt slightly more at peace. She was now able to decipher what the brave was trying to tell her, and at the same time begin to learn their language.

They walked for a long time watching the animals as they went about their business. He taught her how to stalk her prey using normal human techniques and then showed her how to enhance her success using Legion skills. He stalked a buck, killed it, and they fed. He taught her that animals are useful for their blood, fur, and to make weapons from their antlers, hooves and bones.

He gave her a chance to practice what she had learned by allowing her to stalk and follow a doe that was drinking water at the edge of a stream. She saw the doe in the distance, approached using the brave's techniques, and got close enough to hear the animal's heartbeat. It never moved. She was going to reach out and touch it, when something else startled it. Katrina sensed it too. She could hear the thoughts of the two sentinels from a neighboring Iroquois village making their rounds.

She hid and waited for them to approach. The Croatoan brave signed for her to take no action. There was no need, Katrina had already sensed his wishes, but she wanted to test her new skills on a higher form of prey. She waited till they were close enough to touch, flicked them both on the ear, and then flashed passed them like the wind. The two sentinels were left puzzled, searching in the night, and rubbing the pain away from their ears.

Katrina and her companion ran all the way back to the clearing at Legion speed and then fell to the ground laughing. She thought she would never laugh again and was relieved to feel the urge once more. They got up and returned to the cave.

Once back at the cave the rest of the clan was preparing for the end of the night. They all sat around the flames of a small fire and talked about the actions of the night, the needs for the camp, and the requirements for the next night. Vlad stepped into the center of the circle.

Four survivors from the raid on their rival's camp were brought forward; a brave and three squaws were dragged to the center of the group tethered by a rope. The three women were tied between two poles close to the fire. Vlad walked over to the man, ripped into his neck with his fangs, and left him standing upright as his body convulsed and warm waves of blood spilled from his neck down over his body. The squaws were terrified; they screamed in panic and struggled violently against their bindings. Vlad then pushed the brave knocking his bloody corpse down to their feet. Three Neomorph clan members rushed over and dismembered the corpse as they fed on its blood. The three squaws were out of their minds with terror. Blood rushed from their wrists as they thrashed about trying to break free.

Katrina felt an urge welling up inside of her the likes of which she had never felt before. It was as if a great hunger burned deep inside of her flesh and an unquenchable thirst was buried within her soul. She remembered Vlad's words and fought the urges as she watched the spectacle unfold.

Vlad motioned to one of the Neomorphs to attack the first squaw. The brave jumped up and violently ripped at her throat and fed on her blood nearly to the point of her death. Vlad stopped him just as the squaw started to fade. He said something to her that Katrina could not understand with her ears, but from his thoughts she heard, "Do you want to live?" The squaw nodded, but Vlad angrily told her to say the words. She let out a scream and answered. Vlad pushed the brave aside, slashed his wrist, and placed the wound in her mouth all in one blindingly fast motion. The squaw drank from the wound slowly at first, and then more vigorously. Once in blood glow, she was set free and the brave was allowed to do with her as he pleased.

The second squaw was resistant to the ritual and even managed to kick the brave off of her on his first attack, but when her life was slipping away she gave in, and uttered the words of submission.

The third squaw was speechless from the horrors she had experienced. She remained defiant beyond the point of her attack. Vlad knew she would never willingly turn, so he pulled the brave off of her, allowing her to live and then set loose the Neomorphs who were still under the effects of their full blood glow. They ravaged her in every demeaning manner imaginable. She was left tied to the post by the fire and every brave that reached blood glow had his way with her. Vlad turned his back and walked away. He took Katrina by the hand. Katrina was still struggling against the urges that had been welling up in her soul.

"Blood glow addiction can be used against those you want to control, if you learn to control the urges within yourself. These savages would do whatever I ask of them, even to the point of their own destruction once taken to the level of addiction that they are in now and they don't even know it," he said to her as they walked into the cave. He took her to her new sarcophagus, bid her a restful slumber, and disappeared deeper into the cave.

Katrina fought the temptations for the rest of the night as she experienced the events unfolding just outside the cave through the thoughts of the victim and her attackers. The squaw could be heard whimpering and pleading for death throughout the night. She was left hanging between the poles. When the braves woke up the next night they found that the squaw was gone.

"Someone came and took her during the day," said one of the Croatoans.

"Not someone, something, look at the tracks in the area. Those are giant wolf tracks, or more likely, Canis tracks," replied Vlad.

"Shall we hunt him down?" asked the brave.

"No, not yet, go about your business, but be watchful of the beast. I think our strange marauder has not left our area yet," said Vlad.

"Why do you call him strange?" asked Katrina.

"Because he never ventures into the cave, has never attempted to phase us, even though he has had plenty of opportunity, and he's the one who brought you to us," Vlad answered.

"He is definitely a strange one," commented another brave.

"I thought he would have left by now," said Vlad.

"What makes you think that master?" asked a brave.

"Mathias has left the area, I assumed he would go with him since they travel in groups," Vlad answered while looking at Katrina.

"I wonder what he's after," Vlad commented still looking at Katrina.

Katrina just looked away and wondered the same thing.
"This doesn't matter at the moment. You have much more to learn," Vlad said and pulled out a strange curved shaped knife.

He brought her to a spot in the cave that is used as both quarry and foundry. He showed her where to find and how to harvest steel. He instructed her on the art of forging a strong blade from a lump of steel, sharpening, honing it to a killing edge and binding it to any material for a strong hilt. They practiced the steps over and over throughout the night. Using her psychic powers she absorbed all the knowledge Vlad had to offer. When the night was over he handed her two square plugs of Asian steel; part of a set offered to him as a gift by a Samurai several lifetimes ago.

"By the end of the next night I want you to make me two blades of this style so that I may offer it to a special dignitary," Vlad tasked Katrina.

Katrina took the steel and went to rest for the day. She climbed in her box, laid the steel plugs by her head, and went to sleep. Just before the sun was about to rise the howl of a wolf resonated on the walls echoing throughout the cave. Vlad and a few of the clan rose from their coffins ready to take on whatever stepped through the opening of the cave, but nothing showed itself. When it seemed the danger had passed they all returned to their chambers and continued their rest.

When the sun went down Katrina went to the foundry

and began to work on the blades. She called the brave with the fiery hands to light the furnace. She stoked the flames until the fire rose to the proper temperature, then she fired the steel, hammered it, and folded it again following the ancient techniques as taught by her new master. She did everything as instructed, except the hilt and pommel, which she forged from the same piece of steel and carved the symbol as she remembered it from his thoughts. When the night was over she had created two masterpieces of cutlery that had not been seen in ages.

Vlad appeared just as Katrina was done polishing the blades. She presented the two knives to him in the same manner as the ancient sword-smiths presented their work to their patrons. Vlad was impressed; he held them up and inspected the edge, the shine, and their balance.

"The balance is exceptional, the pommel design is exquisite, but how strong is it?" He said and then swung them inches away from her head with all his might striking the sides against the anvil near the bellows. The blades withstood the impact without a blemish; a deep tone resonated through the cave from the blades. Katrina was surprised, but pleased that her work seemed to meet his expectations.

"These are good but what did you learn," he asked.

"I learned from a master how to bend the metal to my will," Katrina answered.

"Besides fashioning trinkets of death, what did you learn?" Vlad puzzled her with his reply.

"I learned how to absorb information using all my faculties," she replied.

"And you did so without trying to pilfer the answer

from my thoughts now; very smart. I'm impressed," Vlad encouraged his disciple.

The sun was about to rise. Vlad took the blades, bowed to Katrina in respect for her skill and her efforts, and disappeared as always deep into the cave. Katrina walked to her resting place and settled in for the day.

The next night Katrina rose and found it eerily quiet in the cave. She walked throughout the lair and could find no one. She stepped out of the cave and found that the fire was not lit. Her senses began to search for signs of life. She walked through the forest and finally picked up the panicked thoughts of humans under attack. She arrived at a clearing to find her adopted clan feeding on another rival tribe. She even saw Vlad and joined in the feeding frenzy that had developed. She fed, had her fill, and then pulled herself away. She dropped her victim to the ground and wiped her mouth as the chaos around her continued. As she fought the urge to continue feeding and slowly walked away, a sound she had never heard before froze her in her tracks and put a quick end to the frenzy. It was the howl of Canis in the woods.

Immediately, the Croatoans scrambled and gathered at the center. Vlad pulled them together and prepared them for an attack. The Legion were waiting for the inevitable onslaught. Katrina could sense them, coming, but was unable to decipher any thought process; she just got visions of them running through the forest. The clearing exploded into a battle so intense it shook the ground. Many Croatoans fell to the power and savagery of the Canis attackers.

Katrina met her attackers head on and was beaten down to the ground. She stood up and tried to match power with power against the behemoth that mauled her. She managed to get the upper hand and drove him down to the ground. The Croatoans then started to evade the Canis and run for the security of the cave, so Katrina turned to run, but was grabbed by the throat as she turned.

A Canis slammed her to the ground, stunned her, and carried her off through the forest. She fought but was no match for the monster that held her. They arrived at another clearing and the beast slammed her to the ground. When she jumped up, expecting to fight her last stand, she found Vlad and a crew of Croatoans standing there laughing. The Canis looking down at her then changed right before her eyes.

"Katrina, let me introduce you to Wanchese, Chief of the Croatoan Nation, and our daytime protector," said Vlad.

"This is not the strange one," replied Katrina.

"No, he isn't, but he is like him," said Vlad.

"This one is a minion, what is the other?" asked Katrina.

"Wanchese and his men are not minions they are our ally. Their people consider them avenging spirits of the forest. The ancients believed that those who ate man flesh would be possessed by spirits that would transform them to animals and they would vanquish their enemies. Many have tried in vain to bring forth these spirits by blood ritual and incantations, but it wasn't till the northern coasts were raided by men from the sea that the spirits appeared. Among the invaders were men that fought, sounded, and looked like beasts. The white invaders called them the Wen. Some know them today as berserkers. Wanchese and his clan are survivors of a vicious encounter with these beast men. Wanchese ate the heart of a vanquished berserker stealing his spirit. His people call him, and those like, him Wendigo. The other is a rival, a cunning adversary and probably the most dangerous opponent I have. We must be vigilant, this one and his Sucanis threaten everything," replied Vlad.

"Why is he such a threat, and what is a Sucanis?" asked

Katrina.

"He's an old adversary, one that has vanquished many of our kind. Sucanis is the cursed human survivor of a Canis attack. They are every bit the were-wolves of legend; controlled by the phases of the moon or the whims of a Canis. They are wild beasts with one sole drive - to kill. They are part of what makes fighting a Canis so dangerous. One must either kill the Canis or become its subordinate; a Su-Canis," Vlad answered the question with a blank expression as if recalling some distant memory.

The braves walked back to the cave. Katrina went to join them.

"Wait!" said Vlad, snapping out of his trance. "You are to stay here and complete the next evolution of your training. Chief Wanchese is going to mold you into my secret weapon. Learn everything this creature has to teach and learn it quickly. I will soon have needs for your special talents."

"The sun will be rising soon, where am I to rest?" Katrina replied.

"That is part of your training. I suggest you learn quickly your life depends on it," Vlad answered.

"Life, what life? I'm already dead," Katrina answered sarcastically.

"Oh, this is life, it's just not the one you're used to," replied Wanchese.

"Well said my friend. Teach her well, your life may one day depend on her and the skills you pass on," Vlad told Wanchese as he disappeared into the darkness of the forest.

"Training starts now," Wanchese told Katrina.

Wanchese and his clan ran into the forest. Katrina followed close behind. They stopped at the banks of a creek that ran through the middle of the forest. They dug a trench near the edge of the creek.

"Take your clothes off," Wanchese instructed Katrina.

"I beg your pardon. I'm not undressing in front of you and all your men like some sort of strumpet," Katrina replied offended by the suggestion.

"The sun will be rising soon. There is no box out here for you. There is no cave. We can teach you how to survive. It will be painful, but you will live," replied Wanchese.

"This vampire existence is getting more and more tedious," said Katrina.

"No, not vampire, you are Legion!" answered Wanchese.

Katrina took her clothes off completely embarrassed and offended at the humiliating circumstances. One of Wanchese's men went over to Katrina and motioned for her to paint her body with mud. He picked up a handful from the ground and rubbed it all over his chest. He then gestured to Katrina. She followed his instructions. The sun was starting to peek over the horizon when Katrina got the last of her body covered in a think batter of mud and sod. They walked slowly to the pit and then laid Katrina in it.

"We shall watch over you. If the sun starts to penetrate your cover we shall come to help. Make sure you close your eyes or they will burn. Also, remember, you are not completely covered, so you will feel some pain," Wanchese told her.

"Don't worry, pain and I - are old friends," replied Katrina.

"I'm sure you have never felt pain like this before. At least that is what they tell me," Wanchese answered.

"Well they are not me," said Katrina with a tone of arrogance.

That is when the sun finally showed its face over the horizon. The pit was well dug and placed in a spot where the sun would not be completely over it. It was deep enough to keep Katrina in the shadows of the walls for most of the day. She tried to rest. At mid-day the sun was at its highest in the sky. The mud began to dry and cracks formed in her earthen armor. The limited light that seeped through began to sting Katrina's skin. Wanchese watched as she squirmed in her shell.

"Don't move or the mud will crack open and the sun will burn you," he said.

Katrina kept as still as she could under the circumstances. The pain, even in these limited areas, was becoming unbearable. She could not believe how hard it was becoming to just sit still. Then the worst thing that could possibly happen occurred, a piece of her mud case dried, cracked, and fell off her leg. That was more than she could stand.
The sun seared a trail of pain down to the bone that made her jump up. Instantly her skin ignited in a giant ball of flames. Wanchese and his men frantically poured water and dirt filling the pit quickly. Katrina's muffled screams could still be heard through the dirt.
When they were sure she was secure, Wanchese sent

a messenger to let Vlad know what had happened. She would need blood as soon as the sun went down in order to recover. When the messenger ran off, Wanchese jumped and his heart skipped a beat. He noticed in the distance, across the creek, just passed the field, in the wood-line, a Canis attentively watching them.

"I wonder how long he has been there," Wanchese told his companions.

"What should we do? You want us to go after him?" asked one of the men.

"Let him be. I'm not sure what he's up to, but I know I don't want to tangle with that one. There is something about the strange one that unnerves me. If he meant us harm, he would have done it a long time ago," Wanchese replied.

"So we do nothing?" asked another.

"Just watch him. I don't want to be surprised by that one," said Wanchese.

The men went on a hunt for a meal. A couple stayed behind and fished by the edge of the creek. Later that day, they had a meal of venison and trout. The stranger in the forest had long gone and had not been seen or heard from thru the rest of the day. Shortly after they were done with the meal, the sun went down. Wanchese and his men dug up the pit once more and pulled Katrina's charred body from the ground. Even her eyes were burned. She could not open them. They placed her on a blanket by the creek.

A few minutes later Vlad appeared with an Iroquois squaw. He dragged the woman next to Katrina's body, ripped open a wound on her wrist with his fangs, and squeezed the blood into Katrina's mouth. Slowly she began to regain her strength and parts of her skin cleared up. She then rose up and attacked the woman. As she fed her body regained its original shape and form. Once fully recuperated she leapt up and slammed Wanchese to the ground then struck him across the face.

"You bastard; how could you allow that to happen!?" Katrina was enraged, driven by emotion and the amount of blood she had taken in order to recuperate.

She pounded on this man until his face was bloody and yet no one did anything. When she was done beating on him, he simply stood, and said, "Don't worry, it won't be the last time you burn."

He then walked away and tended to his wounds.

"You shall do as he says if you want to live. There is a lot you will need to learn from him. He is the key to your success. If you can't adapt to the situation, you are useless to me," Vlad told Katrina and once more walked away.

Wanchese approached Vlad as he passed. "Master, I think you should know that our woodland companion was watching us most of the day. I think he's up to something. I've also noticed that he's been taking interest in our Neomorph," he reported.

"I suggest you accelerate the training. She's going to need to learn how to defend herself quickly," replied Vlad.

Wanchese signaled to a few of his men. They rushed into the forest and disappeared. He then walked over to Katrina and said, "You must now learn to fight."

"It's about time, I'm ready for this," responded Katrina with enthusiasm.

Apprentice
Chapter Nine

Wanchese picked up a stick. He approached Katrina slowly and then wacked her on the thigh with it. She winced in pain and snapped to a combat ready position. He approached and slapped her again; this time, on her other leg. She was getting annoyed at the fact that she could not anticipate his moves, even while trying to read his thoughts. She concentrated harder and got another walloping for her troubles.

"What the hell is going on? Why can't I pick up your intentions?" she said, full of frustration.

"I'm not thinking about what I'm going to do; I'm going purely by instinct. This is how the Canis fight. It is why they do so well against the Legion. There is no apparent logic in their actions except in the aftermath. They seem chaotic yet they fight as a cohesive unit. Your best chance against them is when you face one alone, but even then they are formidable opponents. I suggest that if you face one before you become proficient with your skills that you run. At least, they are no match for our speed." Wanchese instructed her in the basics.

"When do I get a weapon; a rock, a stick, whatever?" Katrina protested.

"First you learn to strike with your hands, then you learn with a stick, and finally you wield a blade. You do this so that your blade eventually becomes like your hand and strikes with the same deadly result," Wanchese explained, though growing tired of the talking.

He put her through a series of exercises designed to help her learn to take advantage of her new skills, especially her speed. He showed her special stances to optimize her balance, generate power, and increase mobility. He handed her a blade and showed her the proper way to hold, slash, and strike with one. He then showed her where to strike at her opponents; Canis or Legion.

He pointed his blade to the regions that would immobilize

an opponent and those that would deliver a swift death. He then slashed at them forcing her to protect herself; he struck faster, and faster until Katrina struck back, burying her blade deep in Wanchese heart.

Wanchese grabbed the hand holding the blade, fell to one knee, let out a gasp, then rose back up to his feet and pulled the blade out. He looked at her intensely as he slowly turned the blade towards her face. She fought with all her strength to hold the blade away. Wanchese reached up with his other hand, placed his wrist against hers, transformed, leveraged against her wrist, and pulled the blade away from her grip slicing her across the thigh with one swing. She buckled to the floor and then stood back up ready to continue.

"That was excellent; there is just one thing you must remember. The blades must be silver plated to do any permanent damage to the Canis," Wanchese said laughing, as he gasped for air, completely out of breath.

"Why silver?" asked Katrina.

"Silver is poisonous to the Canis. It is like snake venom to humans only faster; the closer to the heart you strike, the deadlier. You would have definitely killed me if it had been a real fight with a silver blade," Wanchese replied.

"What about the Legion?" asked Katrina.

"The Legion can be irritated by silver; it all depends on the Legion. Some have no effect, some might get sores, some lose power to heal, but there are those rare ones that will die just like the Canis," said Wanchese.

"How do I know which one I am," asked Katrina.

"That will come later. Right now, I think you need to feed, the sun will be rising soon and there is another part of your training you must complete before we move on. You are doing well," answered Wanchese, as he walked away from the clearing.

Katrina was alone, but with a new sense of confidence she set out to find sustenance before the coming day. She walked into the forest and her senses came alive with the thought waves of humans at a distance. She quietly traveled through the shadows of the woods, avoiding detection the whole way to the outskirts of the village. She waited until the thought waves turned to those familiar scene's created when humans dream. When she felt comfortable that most of the people were asleep she approached the village. She found a wigwam near the edge of the forest. She snuck up close to the entrance. She looked inside and found a woman sleeping on the ground curled up in buckskin blankets. She worked her way inside and wedged herself between the woman and the side of the wigwam. As the woman slept she fed. When she had had her fill, she snuck out of the wigwam, made her way to the forest, and traveled swiftly back to the clearing. She found the Croatoan braves waiting for her.

The braves took her to a spot by the river and motioned for her to dig. She already knew what was coming and dug the trench quickly. She undressed, and then covered every inch of her body with a thick layer of mud. She jumped into the pit and lay at the bottom. The sun rose just as she fell asleep. This time she made it through the day without panic or incident. Her skin tingled, but there were no burns. After the sun went down and she woke, she climbed out of the pit and went to the river to wash the mud off her body. As she came out of the water, Vlad and a squad of braves were watching her.

"Did you guys get a good show, once again at my expense?" She asked, more than just a little perturbed.

Vlad and the braves just laughed.

"Come now, follow me, it is now time for you to learn to fight like a dragon," Vlad said to Katrina.

"I thought Wanchese was my combat instructor?" replied Katrina.

"He teaches you to fight animals. I will teach you the skills I have learned through my vast journeys from civilization to civilization, living among them, fighting with them, and killing them. Of all the people I have encountered in this world, there is one that I most admire. In a remote section of an island empire across the great sea to the west is a village nestled deep in a forest. I was in exile there for a while and during that time I learned to meld their techniques with my talents to create a system of deceptive close quarter combat," said Vlad.

"Does your system have a title?" Katrina asked.

"I have given it no name. If it has no name, it is that which cannot be identified. If it has no name, it is easier to keep secret. If it has no name, it can only be passed on through expression and therefore only learned through expression," replied Vlad.

"I've learned so much, there isn't a human that can take me on," Katrina said tired of all the training.

At that moment Vlad disappeared. Katrina was amazed. It was as if he just vanished right before her eyes. There was no trail, no sound, not even a thought to guide her senses. She lunged with her arms at the spot where Vlad had been standing. She sensed something behind her; she turned to face it, and was slapped in the back. She rolled forward over her right shoulder to the ground and landed on her feet in an attack stance. Vlad appeared from the darkness of the forest.

"I'm not training you to hunt and kill humans, there are other things in this world that need extinguishing," Vlad said as he brushed passed her.

He then showed her how to use her surroundings to appear invisible even to vampire eyes.

"It's a slightly more difficult trick to pull off against a Canis; those bastards can smell you. With them it's about surprise. You might not be able to disappear before their eyes, but if they don't know you are there in the first place, it makes your job that much easier," Vlad explained.

Katrina practiced her invisibility techniques for most of the night.

To extend the lesson, Vlad created an obstacle course of sorts. He placed two pieces of steel on a barrel in the far end of the forest. He had Wanchese and his clan set up torches along the paths and told them to patrol the area. He then stood watch over the steel blocks in the small clearing. Katrina had until sunrise to steal the blocks. Most of the night was quiet. Wanchese's men knew Katrina was coming and grew bored of searching the darkness. The night passed slowly and a breeze broke the still of the night carrying a familiar scent. The Wendigo rushed to find the source of the smell. They were certain the Legion female was about. They searched frantically, each one hoping to be the one to please the master and capture the woman. Finally in the emptiness of the night a howl echoed through the forest followed by a boasting cheer of, "I found her!" Vlad rushed to the place his ears indicated to find a disappointed Wendigo standing over a pile of clothes, holding a shirt that had been draped over a tree, and wincing in anticipation of the master's wrath. Vlad just laughed. He quickly turned around and ran to the barrel. Wanchese and his Wendigo followed howling and barking in excitement. They arrived at the clearing to find the barrel and the blocks of steel were gone. Vlad called out to Katrina, but there was no answer.

"Come on now, you've won, the sun will be up soon we need to get back," Vlad continued to laugh.

"Maybe she is embarrassed to come out. She is running around the woods with no clothes on," replied Wanchese.

"A sound observation my native friend, she does seem to be too modest for a vampire does she not?" Vlad replied.

"No vampire, Legion," Wanchese corrected.

"Oh, yes, that is right we are Legion!" Vlad said as he laughed some more.

When they finally made it back to the cave the men found Katrina at the mouth of the cave, sitting in the barrel, and holding the two pieces of steel.

"Two steel bits for my clothes?" she asked with a smile on her face.

"Keep them, they are yours, and you'll need them for your next evolution. They are very valuable; I suggest you keep them in a secure place," Vlad replied.

He then held up her clothes and said, "What do you bid for these rags!"

The men all laughed and threw out bids ranging from pelts to blood slaves. The men whistled and cat-called until they all rolled on the floor laughing. Katrina, tired of being the center of ridicule, picked up her barrel and walked to her den.

"I better have a fresh coffin to sleep in," was all she said as she walked away completely indignant.

"Sleep well Mademoiselle Le Giroux," Vlad called out and laughed.

The next evening Katrina woke early hoping to find her clothes. Instead, she found a new set of clothes of a very queer style. It was made from some sort of silk, almost like a robe, and colored in black. It had quilted pads for the shoulders, a hood, and lots of straps. There was also a pair of strange looking sandals that made her laugh when she tried them on. She had never seen anything like it before.

"I see you're getting acquainted with your new assassin's garb. Stick your great toe in that part there," Vlad said pointing to the sandals.

He pulled out a set of his own and showed her how to don the outfit. He pointed out how to use the various straps and indicated how to hide things effectively using various pouches. By the end of this lesson, they were both dressed exactly the same.

"Now, follow me out of the cave. We must not be seen. The next phase of your training is the most secretive and sacred. No one must ever know of its existence or its ritual. Bring the steel blocks," Vlad said.

They made their way through the cave and passed all the Croatoan, Legion, and Wendigo without being seen. They kept themselves hidden throughout their journey. They climbed high above the tree-line along the side of a mountain until they reached the summit. At the summit was the entrance to another cave. This one was hidden at the base by the roots of a giant tree. One needed to be skilled indeed to notice this cave. Katrina slipped in as Vlad watched the forest. Then he jumped in after her.

They dropped down a few feet before landing on the soft earth below. It was musty and humid in this cave. The smell of wet dirt filled the air. They walked through the narrow corridor for almost half a mile. There were many passages that crisscrossed the trail they were on, but Vlad just kept going straight.

Katrina noticed that the ground became harder and felt almost like cobblestones. She adjusted her eyes and realized it was a brick path. The passage led into a great chamber with marble floors and eight great columns supporting the ceiling. Statues of figures dressed just as they were and holding swords lined the walls in between each column posed in different defensive and offensive positions. At the farthest end of this chamber was a set of hammers, a pile of wood chips, a trough, an anvil and a fire pit. There was a stone slab table with different types of silk strands and silver trinkets. Near the table was a steel box with a lock on it. Next to that was a second bucket full of some sort of muddy water.

"What is this place?" asked Katrina.

"This is where I make the tools of our trade. It is not only where I forge the blades for combat, but forge a bond with my students that can never be broken," replied Vlad.

An Ancient Skill
Chapter Ten

"Many years ago, my master in the art of Shinobi showed me how to take raw materials and forge these great weapons," Vlad said as he drew both his swords from the scabbards on his back.

He then pointed to some items and described their name and function.

"This stack of wood chips is hand split from specific trees. I use pine; it is the best wood for forging swords. The larger chips are used in forging - the Kitae. The smaller chips are used in tempering and quenching or Yakiire. This process is called Sumiwari. A student usually spends at least three years learning the Sumiwari process. You will do the same, but for now you will assist me in making two complete swords. Watch the process carefully and do not deviate from my steps. The blades we make are tried, tested, and true. They will kill the Canis. The process produces the two blocks you hold in your hand - the Tamahagane. One is Kawagane; high carbon very tough steel, the other is Shingane; low carbon softer steel. The Kawagane will assure strength and sharpness; the symbol of the master. The Shingane is softer, more malleable allowing the blade durability; the symbol of the apprentice."

He disrobed and put on a strange smock and then wrapped his head in a wet rag.

"Take your clothes off and put this on in the same way I just did. The heat in this cave will be unbearable," Vlad said as he handed her a bundle.

Normally, Katrina would have complained at having to disrobe once more in front of this man, but this seemed different. Vlad wasn't even paying attention to her. He almost seemed to be meditating as if calling on his ancient master for guidance. She disrobed then sat across from him on a mat already in position.

Vlad lit the fire pit, took a long flat piece of steel and placed the Tamahagane on the steel. He stacked wood chips around the steel and wrapped it all in a special paper. He then took water from the bucket and poured it over the paper. Finally, he covered the whole thing with burnt straw.

"This is the process of Tsumi-wakashi; the stacking. The burned straw or Aku keeps the temperature uniform while the Tamahagane is in the hearth. This prevents contamination from other impurities and stabilizes the carbon content inside the Tamahagane. The heat in the hearth is raised and the Tamahagane are placed in the fire."

Once the Tamahagane was heated and the steel was glowing Vlad pulled the Tamaghagane out of the fire.

"Now we work together. I'll use this small hammer, the ko-zuchi, to lead your blows with the big hammer, the o-zuchi."

They worked together hammering slowly at first and then

increasing in rhythm as Katrina caught on to the routine. The steel was folded transversely and longitudinally 15 times. It was quenched and heated again between folds strengthening and purifying the steel. Vlad forged the metal into the shape of a long rod and then cut it into small sticks. He then stacked the sticks crossing one layer over the other and heated them again. He took the stacked steel and hammered it creating the Tamahagane that would replace the ones he granted to Katrina. He then placed them on the wall on a shrine erected to his master, who auspiciously did not have any identifiable name or Japanese character. There was only the painting of his master and a list of the steps in the process. He then turned to his apprentice and asked her for her Tamahagane. She gave him the two blocks of steel. He held them up and spoke.

"These are Tepes Kawagane and Giroux Shingane. Alone they are nothing; together they are a powerful implement of death and destruction to be used for the better of the Legion. We are ready to hammer the steel again, but this time we are going to heat, quench, fold, and hammer to stretch and shape the steel into a blade."

They worked night and day without stopping. Hammer after hammer, soaking after soaking, and firing after glowing firing the steel was transformed. He held the blade in the air and said, "The dragon now has teeth."

He brought the steel box with the lock on it to the hearth. He went back and carried over the bucket of silt.

"Here is the secret of our deadly blades. This mixture of clay was created according to the recipe passed down to me by my master. It was sent down to him from his ancestor. I added my own touch years later. Mixed with the silver powder in this box the clay that coats the blade for hardening also makes it deadly to the Canis."

After mixing the clay and silver slurry he laid in the pattern for the glaze and adds his distinct markings that will strengthen the blade and prepare it for sharpening. He then takes the blade and heats it again making sure to watch the temperature. Once it reached the required temperature he quenched it in a specially prepared trough that was kept at a prescribed temperature. Once the blade had cooled he checked the blade for imperfections and found none.

"Take it, feel its balance, gather its weight, and absorb its extension. Follow my instructions precisely so by your hands shall it gain its polish. The glaze is special; it shall polish to the pitch black color that distinguish our clans blades," Vlad tells Katrina handing her the blade.

The sword was finished with the special signature or mei written in Japanese by Vlad. He named it youji-doragon, baby dragon, and marked it with his own special symbol. The tang, or nakago, was covered with the two tiles made from the femur of a slain Canis and then braided with a silk cord. Vlad took the katana, stood in the center of the chamber then called for Katrina. As she approached, Vlad drew the katana with his right hand --the blades edge facing up-- spun it towards her face, passing it just off her cheek down to her left foot, spun quickly dragging the blade across her body up towards her left shoulder, back down across her abdomen, and then quickly sheathing it all in one quick motion. Katrina stood awestruck by the action as Vlad knelt, bowed his head, and offered the katana. Katrina took the blade, knelt and bowed her head as her new master stood.

"Rise my new apprentice, welcome to the Lamia Imperium Potestas," Vlad said as he helped her to her feet.

"Thank you master, how may I be of service," replied Katrina.

"Your time shall come soon," Vlad answered.

They changed their clothes, put out the fire, slipped into the darkness of the forest, and returned to the Croatoan cave.

The Assassin
Chapter Eleven

When Vlad and Katrina rose the next night, the Croatoan had captured and prepared a meal for their masters. A pair of Spanish foot soldiers had wandered from their campsite looking to get lucky with the lonely native girl picking berries. The soldiers fell in the trap Wanchese had laid for them and were now food for the beasts. Katrina was famished. The three days in the cave sucking smoke and toiling over the fire had sapped her energy. She approached the first man that was tethered to a stake. The man was nervous but aggressive towards everyone that came near. Katrina shocked him into a completely passive state by disrobing in front of him. Like a rabbit mesmerized by the viper, the man awaited what was coming paralyzed against her entrancing walk, piercing eyes, and sultry form. Vlad had long dispensed with the theatrics of the feed and merely took his victim by the neck and ripped into his flesh devouring every drop of the crimson nectar that sustained his existence.

"There is a Canis among them," Katrina said as she sucked down the last drop of blood from her victim's body.

"Is it the strange one?" asked Vlad.

"No, this one is different. He is younger and appears to be of some importance; possibly an envoy from a reagent. I can't make out anymore. It just fades," replied Katrina.

"Your service to the Legion comes sooner than expected. Find this envoy, capture him, and bring me his head," Vlad ordered.

"Don't you want to find out who he is and why he is here?" Katrina asked, puzzled by his request.

"I don't care who he is and I know why he is here. There are those in the Holy Roman Empire that aspire to colonize the New World with Canis. This will not happen while I am here. At least not on my territory," replied Vlad.

"The Wendigo will go," said Wanchese.

"The Wendigo will guide you to the site, but you will deal with the Canis alone, quietly, and quickly," Vlad said annoyed at Wanchese for interfering, but restraining his anger because he knew how valuable this Wendigo was.

"As you wish," said Katrina and she quickly ran off to get her equipment.

Katrina returned dressed in her black silk garb, her khukri on her waist, and katana at her back. The Wendigo led her into the forest. As they traveled through the pitch black night, Katrina used her senses to home in on the creature she must destroy by sorting through the thoughts of those around her target. Once in range of the village, she began to move ahead of the Wendigo and led them straight to the Spanish encampment. At the edge of the camp, the guides blended into the forest and disappeared in the darkness. It was dark, there were about six shelters made from area foliage and drift wood. Katrina quickly identified the command hut as the one with the upside down boat for a roof. She crawled in the shadows of the forest and drew within feet of the first sentry. She lay still for a few minutes as she gathered the thoughts of her targets searching for the Canis. As she suspected, there were a couple of men talking to a third at the command tent, but she could not sense that third person at all.

That's him, it's over.

Katrina slid across the ground keeping to the shadows in the camp made by the fire at its center. She found a hiding spot right next to the command hut among the piled tarps that covered some boxes. She waited till two others had fallen asleep. She assumed the one she sought would also be sleeping. She opened a slit in the side of the hut with the Khukri blade and slipped in. To her surprise there was no third person there. She crawled from one to the other and read their dreams. She then stood at the opening of the hut and peered out. There he was, sitting by the fire completely alone. She knew it was him. The Canis had his back to her and she couldn't resist the temptation to slice the head off the unsuspecting mongrel. She hunched down to an almost sitting position and slowly walked with her hand on her blade ready to release its deadly fury.

"Now, that's not very sporting! Wouldn't you prefer a chess match?" he said, surprising her by not even turning around to face her.

Katrina froze. On the ground between his legs was a chess board with all the pieces set up for a match. She looked around slowly, halfway hoping he was expecting someone else who had not yet come into view.

"I'm talking to you. There is one thing about us Canis

that the Legion always seem to forget; our extraordinary sense of smell. I'll admit, you were pretty good, I would have heard you coming long before I smelled you had you been anyone else. To most, leaving the hut with the back exposed to the ocean would seem fool hearty, and so like most you fell into my trap. I'm sure you have figured out by now that moving around the back of the hut put you upwind and carried your scent straight to your demise. So, do we have a match or do we just kill each other?" the Canis said with the calm of a man who has had one too many experiences with these types of situations.

Katrina charged, the Canis transformed and faced her, but it was too late. With her left hand, Katrina reached into her sash, pulled out a pouch, and threw the entire content of silver dust in the Canis' muzzle. The Canis instantly froze from the pain, unable to even scream. Before he could take another breath, Katrina slashed her katana in a figure-eight and chopped both his hands off. In the same motion she slashed straight across the top, severing his head at the neck. The Canis body collapsed to the ground and blood spewed everywhere.

"Welcome to the New World, bastard," Katrina hissed as she grabbed the severed head. She picked up the chess board and slipped back into the darkness of the forest before the sentry could return.

The Wendigo were still hiding in overwatch when Katrina flew past them in a blur.

"Let's go boys, things are going to get ugly here in a minute," she called to her cohorts as she ran through the woods.

The Wendigo broke into a dead sprint and gave chase all the way to the safety of the Croatoan cave. Katrina entered the cave holding the head of her first Canis kill raised high for all to see. The cave erupted in cheers as she passed by the Croatoan braves. When she reached Vlad she knelt and held the head up in offering.

"Your loyal servant offers this prize of victory," Katrina said respectfully, but full of pride.

"So, you have taken another step towards the metamorphosis of the warrior I need you to be," Vlad said as he proudly displayed the severed head to all in the cave.

Vlad asked Katrina to stand. He then presented her with another katana. This one was longer than the one she watched him make for her. It also appeared to be much older and worn. She was so overwhelmed by his award that she reached out forgetting about the chessboard she had tucked in her robe. The board fell to the ground scattering pieces all over the floor of the cave.

"What is this?" Vlad asked humorously astonished.

"The Canis had it when I found him. He probably could have surprised me, since he sensed me long before I approached, but instead he challenged me to a chess match. He seemed very calm and not the least bit threatened," Katrina replied with a puzzled look on her face.

"So, what happened?" Vlad asked, almost as puzzled as she.

"I threw silver dust in his face and cut his hands off," she said.

"That seems a little harsh. What did he do to deserve that," Vlad said sarcastically.

"I don't know how to play chess," she said.

Vlad could be heard laughing across the entire cave.

"Remind me to teach you. I want my assassins to be ready for anything," he said barely able to contain his laughter.

"So I may keep the chess game," she replied.

"Of course; now, show me what you did with the silver dust, that seems very interesting," Vlad answered just barely maintaining his composure.

The Wendigo stood guard that night on high alert. They were certain the Spaniards would try to track them down and retaliate. In the morning, part of the pack went to the Spanish encampment to finish off the rest of the invaders, but found the camp had been deserted and the boat was gone.

The Raid
Chapter Twelve

Katrina spent the next few nights training with her new katanas testing their limits and learning new ways to slice through her opponents. She trained with the Wendigo to learn as much as they could teach about close quarter combat with a Canis. Vlad and Wanchese were gone for most of that time searching for allies in the impending battle for control of the New World; the night they returned everything changed. Vlad woke Katrina from her lair and rushed her to her feet.

"Get yourself together; we have business to attend to. Today we raid a village with people that refuse to join us. We cannot allow these cowards to threaten the emergence of the House of Dracula in this land. We cannot wait for them to attack us as we sleep. We need warriors and squaws to swell the ranks of the clan. I will not relinquish my foothold on this land to the Spanish, the French, the English, and least of all the Church," Vlad instructed.

"Stealth will not be needed tonight," he said angrily as he tossed Katrina her buckskins and a pair of Khukiri blades.

While she dressed, the Croatoans built a small map using sticks and rocks showing the layout of the village they were going to raid.

"The assault cohort will approach from the east. I want the security cohort to form on the north side of the village. Once formed, we wait for the villagers to change sentries. They will be groggy from just waking and the others will be tired from the shift on guard. The assault cohort will attack the village, killing everything in their path until they get to the outer edge. Once at the west edge of the village they will signal the security cohort. The security cohort will then dash across the village kill any remaining humans and then set up a line of defense at the south edge of the village. The Wendigo will then take over security while we feed. We will take any warriors captive that we can. We will swell our numbers with their best. I will lead the security cohort. Lady Katrina will lead the assault cohort. The Wendigo will join the assault cohort; the sight of charging Wendigos should be enough to shock the villagers into a panic. Lady Katrina, be ready to fight, they might panic, but they are not going to just surrender, they are proud Issa and fierce warriors. Move out!" commanded Vlad.

The cohorts moved out swiftly carving a path through the forest. Just as planned, they arrived moments before the sentries were relieved by the next shift, but something wasn't right. Katrina's senses told her something wasn't right, but she could not tell what it was. Before she could scan further the signal was given. The assault cohort launched to action. Katrina and her cohort slashed their way across the village. Everything in their path was skillfully mowed down by blade or claw. Suddenly, a loud howl was heard from the west side of the village. The sound even stopped Wanchese in his tracks.

"What the hell is that?" Katrina asked.

"If you can't tell me, that can only mean one thing; the Canis are here!" Wanchese replied.

"What the hell do we do?" Katrina started to panic.

"We fight!" Wanchese roared.

Out of the woods, a Canis in full feral transformation charged the assault cohort. A war party of Issa braves followed wielding English axes and swords; some even had armor. They rushed forward killing with great skill the first Legion they encountered. Katrina snapped out of her initial shock and attacked as she remembered everything she had learned from Wanchese. She lunged forward at her first attacker, ducked under his blade on his right side as he hastily struck at her neck. She drew her katana, sliced her adversary behind his right knee severing the leg, then spun around, and dropped all her weight behind the blade slicing his head clean off his shoulders. Vlad saw the Canis and sent in a few of the Croatoans to assist the assault cohort. He led the rest of the Legion around the edge of the forest to surround the Canis and his group. As Vlad attempted to circle around, the Canis was wreaking havoc on Croatoan Legion.

The beast ripped through several braves before coming muzzle to muzzle with Wanchese. Wanchese struck first. He ripped a large gash into the Canis' abdomen and blood streamed from the wound. The Canis howled in pain, then launched himself at his assailant, buried his claws into Wanchese's chest, and knocked him to the ground. He slapped Wenchese across the snout, jumped up, and grabbed a Croatoan by the neck as he passed by and slammed him on top of Wanchese. With one swing of his claws at the end of his massive arm he nearly decapitated the brave. He stood, looked down at Wanchese, and growled.

Vlad and his Croatoan Legion then charged out of the forest catching the Canis and his Issa by surprise. The Canis grabbed Wanchese by the neck and crotch, lifted him off the ground, and tossed him at Vlad, knocking him to the ground. Wanchese rolled off his master and Vlad jumped up ready to fight. He found himself face to face with the Canis. Vlad swung his blades, but the Canis ducked underneath one, caught Vlad's arm with his, and spun behind Vlad locking his left arm around Vlad's left arm then slammed him to the ground landing on top of him. Katrina leapt to action and knocked the Canis off of Vlad's back.

Wanchese suddenly realized what was happening; the Canis was just stalling while the women and children of the village escaped into the east side of the forest. The Issa protected them as they fled. Wanchese was slowly getting back to his feet when the last one was disappearing into the woods. He rushed to give chase and was met by the Canis at the edge of the forest. Wanchese leapt and landed on top of the Canis as they fell to the ground. Wanchese reared back then slammed his claws down hard on the Canis' chest and ripped it open. The Canis howled in pain, grabbed Wanchese by the throat, and slammed him off his chest. The Issa moved quickly and pulled the Canis up before Wanchese could recover. They dragged him into the woods and quickly disappeared into the darkness of the forest. Katrina signaled to the members of the assault cohort and started to chase the Canis and his tribe of Issa.

"Wait! Never follow a Canis into the forest. Let Wanchese and his pack give chase. We need to find our meals elsewhere, and get back to the cave before the sun rises. Wanchese, if you catch up with them, bring the Canis back alive, and kill the rest," Vlad commanded with an expression of despise and frustration.

Katrina watched as Wanchese and his Wendigos disappeared into the forest. She wished she was going with them.

"They are far better equipped to handle this situation at the moment than we are. We are battered and famished; we must feed; something tells me we are in for a hell of a night tomorrow," Vlad explained.

Katrina followed Vlad and the Croatoan as they followed the scent to another village. It was a small village further west into the wilderness. They had not ventured this far west before. The Legion took out their frustrations over the failed attack on the villagers. They slashed, ripped, and bled everyone. Those who were awake put up a fight, others were killed in their sleep, but everyone in that village died that night. Katrina began to feel herself lose what little was left of her humanity with every drop of blood that passed through her lips. The torn flesh no longer held any horror, the gore presented no shock, and the whimpers failed to elicit any sympathy. They killed and fed well that night.

"Set the village on fire. We must not leave any evidence of our existence here. Soon we will take this land too, and they must not know what is coming for them," Vlad told his Legion.

They left the village in flames and raced back to the cave. Once at their lair Katrina could sense something odd, but she couldn't make out what was wrong. They began to settle in for the night. Katrina arrived at her resting place and instantly her skin began to crawl; alerting her to the danger hidden in the darkness. From the gloom in the darkness she could see a pair of large yellow eyes staring at her, she froze.

Vlad too sensed something was not right in the night. He went to the mouth of the cave to find Wanchese crawling up the hill battered and broken. He was covered in blood that poured from the wounds on his body. His arm and legs looked deformed and broken. Vlad walked up to help his friend.

"The Canis is here!" Wanchese managed to say as he gasped through the blood that poured out of his mouth.

Vlad turned around quickly and was blown over by the force of the Canis running right through him. The beast had Katrina on his shoulder as he ran into the forest. Vlad started to give chase and was blinded by the sharp rays of the early morning sun breaking through the trees as it cleared the horizon.

"I'll rip your heart from your chest and show it to you as you die!" Vlad screamed in anger, pain and frustration as the monster fled deep into the woods.

The sun's rays started to sting Katrina's skin, she screamed as the beast continued to run through the forest. She panicked and struggled then fainted. Katrina woke up to find herself in another dark cave. She sat up and looked around. The daylight sun's rays were sneaking into the cave at the end of the shaft. She looked around but found no one. The chamber was empty. She sat in the farthest end of the cave. She could here the sound of water flowing through the walls of the cavern. The drone of the water trickling passed lulled her to sleep.

That night she woke to find an Indian tied up lying next to her. She bit into his shoulder and fed. The experience of the previous night had left her extremely thirsty and in need of healing. She fed frantically trying to heal up and gain strength to make her escape back to the cave. She sucked down as much blood as she could get in her mouth and lost herself in the frenzy, falling quickly into blood glow and then rage.

Her senses alerted her to the presence of someone else in the cave; she turned to find the Canis looking at her from the end of the cavern. She attacked with everything she had. He just simply slapped her down to the ground. She got up again and swung her claws at him. He reached up and held her by her shoulders. She struggled against his grip but could not shake herself loose. He held her suspended in the air and then transformed.

"Bruno?" she asked.

He did not say a word. He brought her close and they embraced. The embrace led to a kiss, which led to another. They fell to the ground writhing in their desire. Her clothes are ripped from her body by the claws that embrace her. Together they explored the most erotic regions of their flesh and were lost in their passion. Katrina, fully engulfed in the blood glow let go all of her inhibitions and accepted him fully. The world they live in and lives they lead are left behind in the wake of their sensual maelstrom.

Through the rest of the interlude they answer only to the primal instincts that drive them to climax. They race to their release and reach it to the sound of their efforts echoing through the cave. They roll over and lay on the ground at arm's length exhausted from their encounter.

As the ecstasy wears off, Katrina's Legion blood resumes control and she remembers what the Canis did to Wanchese. She realizes she has been kidnapped by this beast. Rolling over onto Bruno's stomach, she buries her blades deep into his chest.

"You fucking monster!" She yells out.

Bruno howls in pain and tosses her off his chest. He slowly gets up and pulls the blades out then throws them away. His senses dulled, but yet alert, he's aware of the braves that approach the mouth of the cave. He turns to run deeper into the sanctuary of the cavern, but runs into Vlad.

"Well done my pet. I am so pleased to see you come

around so nicely," said Vlad as he applauded her actions.

Bruno transformed, turned, and ran towards the mouth of the cave. He knew he had a better chance with the braves than to get held up tangling with this Legion and then have to face the approaching savages. He blasts past Katrina and charges the mass outside. Katrina looked at Vlad inquisitively, and then gives chase.

"Don't bother, he's probably already killed them," Vlad calls out.

Katrina didn't believe him and rushed to assist her new family. She was not prepared for the scene of blood and gore that awaited her. A trail of crimson led off into the woods so Katrina followed. The trail left a winding path of blood through the forest. She finally arrived at a clearing where she caught up to Bruno. He was bathed in blood and holding the last of the Croatoan pursuers in his claws.

"Haven't they taught you not to chase a Canis into the woods yet?" Bruno sarcastically told Katrina.
"You're a fucking monster! Look at what you've done," Katrina replied.

Bruno could see Vlad approaching past the trees in the forest. He quickly transformed back to his animalistic state and said, "Things are never as they appear," and ran away.

"You were smart to let him go. He might have feelings for you, but he will kill you if you press him. Trust me; I know that kind," Vlad said in a cocky tone.

"How many are dead?" asked Katrina.

"Well they're all dead, but we still have a few walking among the living as it may be said. I think our efforts to start an empire in the New World have met with a major setback," responded Vlad.

"He's just one Canis," commented Katrina.

"You don't yet understand, I had hoped this Canis was gone. You've seen what he's capable of. Imagine what he can do with a Canis force behind him," answered Vlad. "The other one is still around, but I can handle that one," Vlad said with a little less cockiness and sarcasm.

"Which one are you talking about, I thought he was the Canis that tormented us," Katrina replied.

"I have an old nemesis the Legion call the Vindicator. I knew him as Mathias of Hapsburg. He was the beast that would have killed you in your village. He has hunted me for years, but that is a tale for another time. We need to get back," Vlad told Katrina and then led her away through the forest returning to the cave.

The next night, Katrina was awakened by two braves. They bowed in respect and led her to the mouth of the cave where the tribe awaited sitting around the fire. As she approached everyone stood and bowed. Vlad stood by the fire, bowed, and extended his arm inviting her to join him. Katrina walked up and turned to look at all the Legion bowing to her. She was overwhelmed.

"Welcome Madame Katrina Arias Le' Giroux, now I have a new assassin; a final solution for all enemies of the Legion. Last night you earned the last tools I can offer, the Silver Khukuri of an assassin in my service. Accept these blades, remember what you have been taught, and hunt well," Vlad announced.

The moment Katrina took the blades in hand the tribe

raised their blades and let out a great shout in unison. Then Wanchese appeared. He stood at the edge of the woods and howled. He then turned and ran into the forest. The entire tribe followed. The hunt was on. As they ran through the dark forest, Katrina could sense the excitement in all their hearts as they searched for signs of the Canis and his pack.

They ran most of the night and found nothing. Finally near dawn Katrina stopped. She sensed something was not right. She started running back to the cave and everyone followed. As they neared the entrance they could see flames billowing from the mouth. The Croatoan stood and watched in horror as standing silhouetted by the light of the flames was the Canis dressed in ancient armor and holding long sharp blades in each hand. Bruno raised his swords clashed them above is head and howled. He pointed at Vlad and then ran off. Katrina burst forward and ran past the flames into the burning mouth of the cave. Everyone was surprised by her actions and ran to stop her, but none reached her. A few seconds later she emerged holding the Katanas, her chess board, and Vlad's battle armor. The sun started to peer over the horizon. Katrina tossed the armor to Vlad and handed him his swords. The Legion scrambled to reach cover. They all feared the coming day and the prospect of possibly being exposed to the sun by the Canis and his men. Katrina ran to the spot she had last dug her pit, covered herself in mud, and buried herself inside the hole as best she could. Throughout the day Katrina heard the screams of those that were dug out of their shelters and left to fry in rays of the midday sun. A few times she heard rapid footsteps rush near her hole; they stopped, walked around, and then continued. It was a terrible day. When the sun finally dropped and the darkness of the night blanketed the forest, Katrina rose from the pit. In the darkness she found Vlad standing over the mangled mess that was Wanchese. As a result of the events of the past day, they were the only two Legion survivors that remained.

"I'm sorry my lord. We tried to fight them off, but he

was every bit the monster you warned us of. He cut down my Wendigo like blades of grass before a raging fire. His men searched and phased everyone they found. Strange though, twice his beasts stopped at your hole and that of miss Katrina, but he did not let them pull you out. I don't understand why," Wanchese struggled to get the words out of his battered body.

"He wanted us to feel the horror of coming so near to death and feel the helplessness of hearing our comrades' fall at the hands of our enemy while we could do nothing," replied Vlad as he knelt holding Wanchese head up.

It was the last time Bruno was seen in those parts. Vlad was angry. Over the span of one day and part of a night this Canis had destroyed his hopes of starting an empire in the New World. He would not forget this.

"What do we do now?" asked Katrina.

"We do as we have always done," Wanchese replied.

"Recruit, rebuild, and avenge," said Vlad.

That night Katrina and Vlad hunted for their meal together before their daily rest. Wanchese prepared a new resting place for them in a cavern that he found near the coast. He watched over them during the day. When the sun went down the next night, Katrina and Vlad woke to the sound of voices in the distance. They walked out of the cave to find Wanchese peering off into the horizon passed the waves. A Spanish Galleon had anchored in the cove and a small boat was battling the waves trying to make its way to shore.

"I think fate has granted a new beginning to our empire," Vlad said.

Road Trip
Chapter Thirteen

The story continues after the events at the end of Chronicles of the Damned.

A few centuries have past since the day Katrina became a Legion assassin. The New Minority had secured certain rights for vampires, and with the discovery of the Canis, some negotiations are expectantly planned in the legislature this coming session. At least she doesn't have to worry about being hunted by angry villagers anymore. Those days are gone. She even expected this wretched war to have come to an end, but the Legion doesn't seem to want to let go of old grudges.

Her skills increased and enhanced exponentially, made evident by her continued survival despite the countless missions against all enemies of the Legion. A few of those enemies have put unofficial bounties on her head, but so far there hasn't been anyone proven good enough for the task of claiming the bounty. She gained much control over her senses since the early days, yet they seem inexplicably different. What little control she had over them at the time felt good, almost enjoyable. They had become more taxing on her these days and sometimes downright stressful.

She was still angry about having to leave her home in Miami, because of the position the New Minority had put her in. She didn't understand how her superiors could order her to assassinate her maker, mentor and official leader of the New Minority, especially when he's supposed to already be dead. Well, dead again, one might say. Borrowing from a famous American writer - "the circumstances of his demise have been greatly exaggerated" on more than one occasion, but being beheaded and buried underneath a pyramid by the El seems fairly final.

She struggled to understand what was going on, but wouldn't put anything passed the vampire that made her. Okay, Legion. After all these years, she still can't get used to that title. Obviously some sort of reference to the ancient Romans. Vlad Tepes III was a great leader, a caring mentor and a good friend. The thing that bothers her most is that if he is still walking among the living, why hasn't he tried to contact her? These midnight runs across the Everglades in her black Camaro relaxed her and allowed her moments of levity which she seemed to need more and more these days.

Relaxing, of course, until the flashing blue lights from the Miccosukee Police cruiser crept up behind her and robbed her attention. She quickly reached behind her and threw a blanket over her new charge, hoping Gabrielle wouldn't wake up. After her latest encounter with Mr. Casta, she needed blood and it would get real ugly if she were awakened. She pulled over to the side of the road careful not to run over an unsuspecting alligator and waited in the car for the inevitable speeding ticket. The patrol officer stepped out of the cruiser and walked towards the Camaro.

Wonderful, it's a woman. I hope this one doesn't have a chip on her shoulder. Maybe she'll let a sister off the hook.

"Excuse me ma'am I need to see your license, proof of

insurance and registration," said the police officer.

How original.

Katrina pulled the paperwork out of the center console for the officer.

"Stay in the vehicle, I'll be right back," the officer said as she walked back to her cruiser.

Katrina realized what was happening. The policewoman stepped out of her car and walked over to Katrina's window.

"Excuse me Ma'am I need you to step out of the vehicle and put your hands on the hood please," said the officer.
Katrina did as she was told hoping to avoid any serious problems.

Too late, here comes back up.

"Look officer, the registration is expired, it's not like I stole it," said Katrina being careful to keep her hands on the hood.

The other patrol car pulled up in front of Katrina's Camaro. An extremely large Native American gentleman with broad shoulders, dark piercing eyes and hair tied back in a ponytail stepped out of the vehicle and walked towards her. He was also extremely confident judging from the fact that, unlike his colleague, he did not wear a bullet proof vest.

"Still Ma'am, it seems like it actually has been reported stolen," replied the officer.

Sure, but don't you think it's a little late?

"There must be some mistake," replies Katrina.

"Ma'am it says here that the car was stolen in 1984. It's been a few years, but we need to check this out anyway just cooperate and we'll straighten this all out," assured the officer trying to be polite and defusing the situation. Katrina already knew what their intentions were.

Okay, enough with the nicey-nice. I guess this is how the Protectorate wants to play it.

Katrina spun around and jammed her elbow into the officer's face as he neared the car. His nose exploded in a gush of blood and he bent over to the floor in pain. The female officer reached for her weapon and before she could take aim Katrina slapped it out of her hand and swung her around to the top of the car by the neck. She buried her fangs deep into the woman's neck and almost bleeds her dry.

"Sorry officer...," Katrina looked down at the name plate on the woman's uniform, "Maderas. I guess this just isn't your night." Katrina threw her nearly dead body to the ground.

By then the other officer had recovered and drew his weapon. Just as he fired the first round she landed on top of him and pushed him down to the ground. She ripped into his neck and drank him into a coma then tossed him to the ground.

Let's see what that does for the New Minority's precious truce with the Nation you fucking bastards.

Katrina referred to the long standing peace treaty the Legion had signed with the Native American Counsel of Nations which secured an uneasy pact of coexistence during the struggle against white expansion into the American wilderness. A treaty the Canis friendly Nations despised, but tolerated for the sake of a peaceful existence.

Katrina walked over to her car and got in. Gabrielle was still knocked out. The encounter with that Canis must have left her in worse shape than actually appeared. Still a few more hours of rest, some blood and she'll be back to normal.

Ah, what a way to start a night.

Katrina settles in to the seat of the car, turns the ignition and lets the V-8 rumble to life. Buckling her seat belt she leans back as the car goes through its warm up cycle, the tone of the exhaust deepens the rhythmic thunder of the classic muscle car as it awakens. Katrina loves the sound her car makes as it idles.

Nothing sweeter, except...

She pushed the Hurst shifter in to first and pounded her foot down on the accelerator. The Camaro Z-28 lunged forward, tail wagged slightly to the right, tires spitting gravel as she screamed across the pavement. The tires gripped the road and Katrina smiled in near ecstasy as she was pushed deep into the seat back.

Ahhh, yeah, nothing sweeter.

She drove off heading west towards Tampa. She can't wait to see the look on her minions faces when she arrives at the Castle. She's sure they've been taking advantage of her long absence and turned the place into a dive.

I don't care much for the bar, it's a business, but the Invidia better be in tip top shape or I'll skin them and stake them out in the sun.

She sped across the Tamiami Trail with the windows down to let in the night air. Having just fed, the blood flowed freely through her body giving her skin the life and sensations she missed so much between feedings. The effects don't last long, but they are always memorable. Her skin tingled as the night breeze caressed her skin and caused goose bumps to erupt and sent chills up her spine. The hairs on the back of her neck stood on end as she blushed from the thoughts that raced across her mind.

There's never a man around when you need one. Then again, there might be more around if I didn't have to kill every other one I met.

She raced past the Butcher Gallery.

Is that man still alive? I tell you; sometimes I think he's a Canis. He just hasn't come out of the closet yet. I know there isn't a vampire around that would stop at that place. Something just isn't right about that little old man with the grey beard. He's just too lovable.

Speeding along she finally reached Naples. Her dashboard fuel level indicator light flashed on as she approached the outskirts of the city.

Oh no way. You better make it across this hell hole. I'm not stopping here for any reason; way too many furry bastards here. It's like a great big Canis retirement resort. Let's go baby don't let me down.

Katrina was well aware that this place was not friendly to her kind at all. She hoped to have it in her rear view mirror as quickly as possible; preferably without incident. The Z was showing signs of not wanting to cooperate with Katrina's plans of escape.

Damned V-8's, love the power, but you pay for it in so many ways. Come on baby, just a little further I see the gas station just up the road.

The Z sputtered out just a few yards from the gas station entrance. She got out of the car, gave it a stern look and yelled, "There goes the Mobil One oil change I promised!"

She opens the door, grabs the steering wheel and starts pushing. She peeks into the car checking to see if Gabrielle was awake or not. No sign of life. At first she thinks of waking her to help push, but then quickly decided against it. A few cars pass by none pay any attention to her, but then a pickup truck slows down as it approaches. Now she's glad she didn't wake her.

Please don't stop, please don't stop, I don't need your help.

Katrina used all her powers to influence the good Samaritan and deviate their intentions, but it didn't work.

"Hey baby, having trouble?"

"Oh gee, what ever gave you that idea, Captain Obvious?" She replied without even looking up.

"There sure is something exciting about watching a woman pushing a car on the side of the road," said another from the back of the pickup.

Wonderful, more than one asshole.

The pickup truck pulled over cutting her off. Three men get out of the truck and stumble over. The only sober one appears to be the driver. As soon as he saw her face, he knew she was not someone they would want to mess with.

"Never mind bro, let's get out of here," the driver tells his buddy as he pulled him by the arm.

"What? No way man; we can't let this poor stranded young lady push her car all by herself. What kind of men would that make us?!" insists the other drunk.

"How about live ones," replied Katrina.
"Let's go man," said the driver. "She's Legion, bro, let's get out of here."

"What are you talking about they don't come around here? They like Miami," replied the man, too excited by the shape of Katrina's ass and too drunk to see the truth. Katrina opens up her jacket exposing her blades and flashes a fang filled smile. The men stop dead in their tracks, hastily turn around and head for the truck. They speed away leaving a dust cloud in their wake. Katrina pushed the Z faster and quickly reached the pump. She then realized this backwards ass place doesn't have card swipe pumps and had to go to the window to pay.

"Are you okay there lady? Were those guys messing with you?" The attendant asks with genuine concern.

"I'm okay, but if you don't hurry up with this transaction I'm not responsible for my actions when those guys come back. So, unless you want a blood bath incident on your shift I suggest you forget about me and hurry up with the gas." Katrina was in no mood for conversation at the moment.

The station attendant set the pump. Katrina paid the man and ran to the car. She watched the numbers slip by on the gas pump as the fuel poured into the tank. In the distance she could here the roar of several V-8 motors heading towards her on the road.

Great, more redneck fur balls. That's all I need right now.

She threw the hose down spilling gasoline all over the ground. Katrina jumped in the car as the trucks pulled into the gas station. She starts the engine and pushes her foot down hard on the accelerator. The car responds with a roar and the tires chirp two lines of black rubber onto the asphalt as she speeds away. A small red glow hurls out of the dark night air and lands on the spilled gas directly in front of the pickups. Instantly the high octane fuel catches on fire. The trucks brake hard and break left to avoid the swirling flames. The station attendant runs out as fast as he can and tries to reach the red emergency cut off button on the wall, but it is too late. The flames reach the pumps and the night sky is lit up with the orange-yellow flames of a large gasoline explosion. The attendant is blown back by the blast into a pile of tires sitting on the side of the building. He gets up, brushes himself off, and flips the bunch of rednecks watching from the side of the road the finger.

"Lucky thing I'm a Canis!" yells the attendant.

Katrina watches as the flames rise up through her rear view mirror. She speeds away ignoring any speed limit signs.

Enough of this shit I just want to get home. Z, you piece of shit, you do that to me again and I'll poor liquid glass down your oil pipe and turn on the ignition. Fix you real good. Just give me another excuse and see what happens. Great, what is it they say about talking to inanimate objects...

Gabrielle finally wakes up and slowly leans over.

"Oh well, finally. You think maybe you could have awakened just a little bit sooner?"

"Did I miss something?" Gabrielle said waking slowly in a groggy stupor. She dives head first into the passenger seat and sinks into the smooth leather.

"I just passed Naples."

"Oh, wonderful, I'm so glad I slept through that. I'm thirsty as hell. When do we feed?"

"Might as well lay back and go to sleep. I'm not stopping till Tampa," replied Katrina.

"Ah man, you're killing me. I'd settle for some road kill right now."

"I've got New Minority premium grade blood slaves waiting. Take another nap."

Gabrielle drifted away salivating at the thought of premium grade. Katrina wanted to keep her thirsty so she would be too weak to try anything. Gabrielle might be acting like a helpless little girl, but she's a highly efficient killer and a member of the Dragon Praetoria which makes her extremely dangerous. Vlad doesn't select just any vampire for his personal guards.

The Castle
Chapter Fourteen

Katrina arrived at the bar on the fringe of Ybor City. The parking lot was as full as always on a Friday night. Between the college students and local party animals the place stays busy on bar nights. She pulled up to her designated parking space and found there was someone already parked there. A shiny black Nissan GTR occupied her Camaro's space. She's annoyed, but knows it's been a while since she's been around and doesn't make a big deal about it. She just simply parks the Z-28 behind the car in her space. A brawny line-backer type bouncer the Pittsburgh Steelers would be proud to have on their roster ran towards her.

"Hey, lady, you can't park there! You're blocking that car."

Gabrielle woke up and was ready to jump out and split the guy in two, but Katrina held her arm out and eased her back into the seat.

"Wait in the car. Make sure this meathead doesn't wreck the Z. I have some house cleaning to do, so keep an eye open for trouble," Katrina tells Gabrielle as she stepped out of the car. "And do me a favor, don't bite this guy."

Gabrielle just furled her lip and rolled her eyes as she pouts in disappointment.

"Excuse me- lady! I don't know who you think you are, but you can't leave that car there," the bouncer continued to bark out orders.

"Yeah, sure-sure, call Celeste and tell her I'm here and to get that piece of shit out of my space before I decide to blow it up. And Meathead, here; park my car, when it's clear. Also, Sergei, make sure you don't put a scratch on it or that pretty young thing sitting in the front seat is going to rip your throat out," Katrina commands her unwitting employee without a hint of emotion as she threw him the keys.

Sergei called his boss over the blue tooth headset not even flinching when Katrina called him by his name.

"There's some vamp bitch here giving me a hard time. She said to tell Lady Celeste that she's here and to get that 'piece of shit' out of her space. Lady's crazy; she's driving some old fucking Camaro and calling the GTR a piece of shit."

Katrina just walked past him towards the front door. Celeste appeared in the doorway. By now, everyone knew Katrina was there and started scurrying around like ants in an ant pile. She made her way through the crowd that was swaying to the sounds of Linda's voice, soothing the grinding guitars and pumping bass of Phoenix Nebulin on the stage. They have drawn a good crowd tonight. Too bad the party had to end.

"It's Katrina," the whispers flow through the air and fill the space. The music and dancing stops in a slow wave, the lights come on, and the bouncers bow at the door as

Katrina stepped onto the dance floor. Those that know, bow, the others look on puzzled, but curiously intrigued. She was finally home. She won the place in a poker game years ago during her pirate days, before she got tired of taking people's money in such a fiendish way. It's hard to lose when you can read their cards through their eyes. Still, there were some people she just couldn't read. She doesn't know why and there doesn't seem to be anything special about them. It was as if they were immune to her abilities. Those were the best games she ever had. It's like finding a mark that she can't track with her special senses. The hunt then becomes that much more thrilling. The kill becomes that much more satisfying. Those little pleasures have been few and far between.

Winning the bar was one of those occasions where she won the game by skill alone, making it one of her most prized possessions. She named it the Castle. It had become a mainstay of Legion society, appealing to characters from all walks of life. It was a favorite hangout for vampire wannabes and preferred hunting ground for Legion looking for blood slaves. The Castle is where years ago, Katrina established her first home and harem in the Americas. The sun would be rising in a couple of hours. She was anxious to get to her other, most prized possession, but first she must take care of business. Celeste followed Katrina to the office. There was a stout middle aged man standing by her desk with a couple of ledgers opened.

"Close the place and call a staff meeting right now," she tells Celeste before settling in behind her desk.

Katrina scanned the ledger then stared right at the accountant standing by her desk.

"We've done well," she said blurring the line between statement and question. "I believe you're probably the most honest accountant I've run into in this business, Barabas."

"Could it be any other way, Madam?" He replied as gracious as he could.

She looked at him with a cold, calculating stare and just smiled.

Celeste stepped into the office, "The staff is assembled, Madame Le Giroux. They await your presence on the main dance floor."

"Tell all non-Legion personnel to go home, now."

"I have already done so, Madame."

"Good Celeste, Let's get this over with."

They all walked out of the office, down the stairwell, and stepped onto the dance floor. Katrina walked to the center of the dance floor, looked around at everyone. It had been a long time since she was at the Castle, but she saw their faces and instantly remembered each one of their names. Everyone was present.

"I want to thank every last one of you for the service you have all provided. After the demise of our leader and benefactor, there have been some organizational changes within the Potentate. I have been put in a position where I will no longer be working for the Potentate. So, it pains me greatly to say good-bye."

With those words fresh on her lips, Katrina struck a deadly blow at two of the staff members; pierced their hearts and bled them dry on the floor. The rest of the staff ran and jumped trying to get clear of their attacker. Katrina chased them down.

Celeste, an experienced hunter, joined in the bloodshed of the massacre that ensued, hoping she wouldn't be added to the list of victims that night. She threw her hand out and caught a fleeing vampire by the neck that ran by as she attempted to escape Katrina. She pulled the woman closer, showed her fangs as she hissed at the soon to be corpse and slammed her to the ground. Almost automatically she landed on the creature, buried her fangs into her neck and then just ripped the flesh spraying blood in every direction. They ripped through each member of the staff, destroying them like prey completely absent of emotion.

A cook got some courage in the face of the alternative, picked up a cleaver and knife, then charged. He swung the big cleaver at Celeste's head, then followed with a looping strike with his knife. She ducked the first strike, spun into the looping arch of the second knife, grabbed the cook's hand and pushed the knife into the cook's heart. She then spun in the other direction, grabbed the cooks other hand, snatched the cleaver away and with one move lopped his head clean off.

Katrina had finished off another two vampires. Celeste leapt to attack the last remaining victim as he ran towards the door attempting to escape, but Katrina knocked her down to the ground. Celeste prepared to defend herself from the strike that would follow, but it did not come.

"Barabas must not be harmed," she tells Celeste.

Barabas was relieved to hear those words and crawled to the nearest chair. He slumped into the seat, exhausted from a blend of fear and exertion. Katrina stood in the center of the bloodstained dance floor and stared out into the void as tears of blood streamed down her cheeks. Celeste approached slowly and asked, "Why?"

Katrina raised her gaze and through her tears her face cracked in emotion; then she said, "It had to be."

Celeste and Barabas looked at each other in disbelief. Not because of the events of the night, but because it was the first time they had ever seen her cry. Celeste walked up to her and handed her a fresh bar towel. Katrina accepted it and wiped the blood from her face. She invited them to sit at a table, walked behind the bar, grabbed a couple of bottles of Carpathian Blood wine and poured them a glass.

"Oh, forgive me Barabas. I forgot. Would some Merlot be alright?" She asked after realizing her mistake.

"Madam at the moment I will not argue with any recommendation you might be inspired to deliver," he replied.

"It is not as dire as that my old friend. I have some sensitive issues to discuss and a little libation might be in order to soothe the heart," she said trying to shed the emotion of the moment.

Katrina poured the Merlot into a wine glass. She noticed how well the bar had been maintained. She saw that all the glasses were in their proper station and kept to her standard of cleanliness.

"Our master is still around," she began. "Mark Twain's famous quote comes to mind at the moment. In this case it almost becomes a mantra for this man. I don't know yet what the end game is, but I was tasked with tracking and dispatching Vlad. I have resigned my so-called position and I'm now a target along with my master. What I have done here, is just one of many terrible things that I must do to protect myself and those like you that still count on me. Can I count on you? Can I trust you with my safety? You have both been loyal comrades, so I will give you the choice. If you choose to come with me, understand that we will now be considered rogue Legion and hunted by everyone. We can trust no one, especially Legion. I would like for you to stay, because I will need your help to find the master, but I can't force you to join me. If you choose to leave, do so with the knowledge that if I ever sense you again, I will phase you." Katrina looked at both of them with a stern look on her face.

Celeste leaned back in her seat and stared for a minute into the nothingness of the ceiling. "What will happen to the Castle?" She asked.

"We can run it as usual and keep up appearances," said Barabas. "The bar could be useful to you in many ways."

"That is true. We could recruit loyal Legion to our cause and monitor the activities of the Protectorate through here," said Celeste backing Barabas.

Katrina thought for a second, sipped on her wine and then said, "You have a point. I can't do this on my own. Where are we going to find Legion loyal enough to trust with our existence?"

"We can morph our own clan and I know a few fools, remnants of the House of Kharsag."

"We should start there. They have no loyalty to the Potentate and since they think Vlad is gone, their rivalry with us should also be gone." Katrina saw the potential for a new start.

"The Potentate will come after us. We need to appear as we are still loyal to them," said Celeste.
"What shall we do in the meantime, the sun is about to rise?" Interesting enough Barabas was the one to worry about the rising sun.

"We'll all go to the Invidia. I hope she's in the same or better shape than the Castle."

"Oh it looks just exceptional. It probably looks better than the first time you sailed it," said Celeste.

"How is it that you are so sure?" Katrina wondered.

"I've been on it several times this month. The hands keep that ship looking sharp awaiting your return," replied Celeste.

"Let's get ready to go. Do you have my car keys?" Katrina asked Celeste.

"No," Replied Celeste.

"Oh shit. Does that fool bouncer still have my keys?"
"Sergei is a good guy and a hard worker," said Barabas.

"Yeah, he is, and he wants to be Legion so bad. It might serve us well to make him a part of our new family."

"I want everyone to get one thing straight. I'm still in charge and any morphing is done by me or by my approval. Is that clear? If anyone has a problem with that we can go our separate ways now, anyone?" Katrina wanted to make sure everyone understood that there would be no rivals to her authority.

No one in that room dared to challenge her. Even if they did not agree, at that moment they weren't about to mess with her. They all got up and walked to the door. Celeste opened the door. It was still dark, but there were signs of morning coming. Sergei was still outside sitting on the hood of his car waiting.

"Lady Celeste, is the meeting over? Was it a good meeting? Do I still work here?"

"Hi Sergei, yeah, there's no problem. In fact we have to talk. Can you come with us to the ship?"

"Oh my god, I get to see the inside of the ship?" At first Sergei was overwhelmed with excitement, then he got nervous. "Wait a minute, are you sure I'm not fired? I've heard of people going in and never coming out. I'm not dinner am I?"

"My keys!" Katrina yelled as she suddenly appears through the front doors.

"Here you are Madam Katrina. Not a scratch, just like you said. I'm not fired, right? I really need this job. I'll do anything to keep it."

"That's good to hear, Sergei. I'll have to keep that in mind. I'm not going to fire you Sergei. It's actually more like a promotion."

"Promotion, what does she mean by that? What kind of promotion?" Sergei asked Celeste.

Celeste just pulled the keys away from Sergei, pushed him into his car and got in the driver's seat.

"See you in the evening," Celeste waved to Barabas as she pulled away in Sergei's 350 ZX.

Katrina watched as they drove away.
Freaking souped up rice burner.

Barabas waved as they drove by.

What the hell am I supposed to do with that mess in there?
Barabas had a long day ahead.

Katrina arrived at the dock before Celeste and Sergei. As she passed the gate the security guard called ahead. Katrina woke Gabrielle and they get out of the car. The captain of the ship greeted Katrina at the gang way.

"Good to see you again Captain. Cancel all charters and prep the ship for a long journey. We will be sailing at the end of the week. I have a few loose ends to tie up and then we're gone."

A very distinguished looking black gentleman stood at the end of the gangway on the ship. He wore jeans, a tight fitting polo shirt, and slip on vans with no socks. His muscles rippled underneath the shirt as he extended his hand to assist the ladies onboard.

"Madame Le Giroux, delighted to have you aboard once more. Young lady, a pleasure to meet you," said the captain turning to Gabrielle. "Madame Giroux, may I ask what will be our destination?"

"I'm not sure yet. I'll tell you in a couple of days. This is Gabrielle, she will be staying with us."

"Very well Madame, as you wish."

"Captain, for the coming day, lock down the ship completely and make sure our special security measures are in place."

"The wolves, Madame?"

"Yes Captain, the wolves. Tell the crew they can take the day off too. Have someone bring my gear out of the Z-28 and have it brought to my chambers. Also, I have some guests spending the day, make sure you let them on ship. Celeste will be with them she will need a hypo-chamber.

Captain, be careful, things have changed and we are no longer protected."

"Understood Madame, I guess it's back to the good ole' days then."

"Aye, the good ole' days."

The captain turned around and began barking orders to the crew. His delightful demeanor changed rapidly, a fire swelled in his eyes and his voice became like thunder. Katrina made her way through the ship. She gave Gabrielle the short tour. As she passed by, the crew greeted her and bowed as was the etiquette. She returned the greetings and even stopped to chat with a few of them. She introduced Gabrielle to the staff and gave orders to find her a blood slave for the night. The men are happy to see her back on the ship and a few expected to be called to her quarters for the day. Once she made it to her office she sat at her desk and contemplated what her next move would be. Gabrielle sat at one of the sofas quietly. A few minutes later the captain knocked on the door to her chamber.

"Madam Katrina, Lady Celeste and your guest are here. Lady Gabrielle, your chamber is ready and there are two escorts waiting for you in the hall. I did not know your preference so they are a male and a female," said the captain.

"Thank you very much Captain," replied Gabrielle. Then she raised her eyebrow flirtatiously and said, "What type are - you?"

"You flatter me, my Lady; I'm from the old country. My people are from Spain, descendants of the invading Moors. I am a Canis by nature, but a loyal Legion supporter. The lady sort of inherited me when she obtained the Invidia."

Katrina interrupted the conversation, "I know you're famished, but can you wait a little longer? I wish to introduce you to Celeste. You will be working together, I don't want any misunderstandings."

"I've gone longer without feeding. It won't kill me to hold off so that I may meet the Canis hunter supreme," Gabrielle responds in a sarcastic tone.

"Captain, show Celeste and her friend in, take them to the galley. Captain, the Invidia looks good," Katrina tells her long-time friend. She knew how much those compliments meant to him. "When you leave, make sure to lock her down," Katrina mentions as he turns to walk away.

"Yes Madame, I'm planning on getting off ship; will you be able to manage without me for the day?"

"I know; I think I can manage, Captain. How much night-time is left?"

"There are thirty or forty minutes left Madame."

"Then hurry, I wouldn't want you to miss your window of opportunity with that red-eyed vamp," Katrina replied with a smile.

"No Madam," the Captain responds, embarrassed at the thoughts he knew his mistress had read while they were crossing his mind. "I'll be on my way then. Good day to you Lady Gabrielle. Madam Le Giroux, with your permission," the captain excused himself, as he walked out the door. Katrina waved him away.

"Be careful my friend," Katrina advised. She walked out from behind her desk, and then directed herself toward Gabrielle, "Follow me."

Katrina walked down the corridor and stepped into the galley. Gabrielle looked around the ship taking stock of its layout as she followed Katrina into the galley. Celeste and Sergei were sitting at the table. Celeste stood up and asked, "Who's the Barbie?"

Gabrielle just sneered and blew off the comment.

"She's someone you don't want to mess with. How is Sergei doing?" replied Katrina.

"I think he's still a little nervous."

"Ladies, I'm right here. You can talk to me," said Sergei a little more nervous than he appeared.

"Can he be trusted?" Katrina continued, ignoring Sergei and talking to Celeste. Celeste stared at Gabrielle with a suspicious look. Katrina picked up on the sentiment. She was hoping to turn these two into her weapons of mass destruction, but before she could do that she had to get them to like each other and work together.

"Anytime you think you're ready for the ass kicking of your life, come see me. I'll be more than happy to oblige," Gabrielle replied, staring back at Celeste with the intensity of a cat stalking its prey.

"Gabrielle, you better take your leave and retire to your assigned quarters. Which one of the Plebeians are you taking?"

"I think I'm taking both. It looks like it's going to be one of those nights," replied Gabrielle.

Celeste furrows her eyebrows in confusion and looked at Katrina with an accusatory stare.

"Ladies, both of you know what I'm capable of and you have learned to trust me. I ask that you be patient and trust my judgment here. We'll pick this up in the near future. Now is not the right time or circumstance. Just be aware that you will work together and you will like it."

Gabrielle walked away and tauntingly waved at Celeste as she disappeared through the doorway and into the dark corridor of the locked-down ship. Celeste starts to say something.

"Don't even," Katrina interrupts, starting to lose her patience with Celeste's incessant challenges. "Let's get to the task at hand," Katrina barks as she turns her gaze to Sergei.

"Ladies, if you're trying to scare me, I just want you to know it's working," Sergei knew he'd put himself in a situation he could not control. He just hoped he wouldn't end up on a slab by the days end. The sounds of the Plebian Sucanis patrolling the grounds near the ship didn't help to placate his fears.

"Celeste, if you vouch for him, then I will accept him to our family. You understand he must accept the destiny we offer."

"I understand Madame, I wouldn't have it any other way," replied Celeste.

"Oh my God, what is happening? Are you talking about, Legion?"

"Sergei, settle down. You're about to experience something very few will ever even hear about and even less survive," Katrina soothed his nerves. It wasn't so much the words that worked the magic, but the psychic manipulation she had become so skilled at. Sergei is an intelligent fellow. Smart enough to be afraid of what was happening. It was his fear that made him vulnerable to her influence.

Her First Morphing
Chapter Fifteen

Celeste took Sergei by the hand and walked him to her appointed Chambers. There are candles lit for his benefit and a bed fitted with fine linens and pillows. The sway of the ship docked on the bay adds to the dreamy ambiance created by the décor of this room. She led him through the maze of dark veils that hung from the ceiling. She stopped at the foot of the bed and pulled him closer. They stand face to face. She reached up and pulled his head down towards her and kissed him deeply. They drew away from each other and stared into each other's eyes for a second. He opened his mouth to say something and Celeste silenced him with a finger on her lips. She turned him around and sat him down on the bed. She slowly unbuttoned his shirt and then striped it off his back. She undid the top button of her blouse and invited him to finish the job. As he continued with the following buttons she kissed him once more with same passion of the previous kiss. She pulled away when he reached the top of her plaid school girl style skirt and let the blouse fall to the floor. She stood in front of him and reached behind her back and unlatched her lacey bra letting it drop to the floor exposing her young voluptuous breasts.

Lady Celeste had the blessing and curse of having been morphed at a very young age. Though her actual age is unknown to many; some say even herself, she has the looks, complexion, and features of a seventeen year old young lady--an enviable quality that has been the ruin of many unsuspecting victims for many years.

Sergei sat at the end of the bed looking at one of the most extraordinary beings he had ever encountered. So extraordinary that he forgot about the girl waiting for him back at his apartment. He was mesmerized with her beauty; enslaved by her touch. She leaned and pulled him closer once more. He closed his eyes and submitted to the moment expecting another kiss. This time Celeste buried her fangs deep into his jugular. At first he was shocked at the exquisite sensations of pleasure and pain and then surrendered himself to the act. She felt his heart beat faster as the blood pumped into her mouth. She released her hold and licked the wound and it quickly coagulated. "Now we can continue," she said.

She undid his pant belt and unzipped the front. He lifted his hips to assist her in the task at hand. She pulled them down passed the knees and exposed his massively muscled sprinters thighs. She let the pants drop to the floor with the weight of the buckle. She pulled up his hands and put them on her waist. He worked his way around to her back and pulled down the zipper that held her plaid skirt at the hips. It fell to the floor leaving her with nothing on but black lace thong panties. He put his hand on her stomach right below her navel and caressed her skin. Her flesh was full of color from the blood glow; having just gorged on his blood her sensitive flesh reacted to his touch and sent chills of electricity up and down her spine.

They fell together in an embrace onto the fresh linens on the bed. They sucked and kissed each other in lover's play. They exchanged affections as they changed positions, flowing from one to the next like waves passing along the shore. The emotions flew as Celeste reached her most primitive level of ecstasy, her eyes glowed red with the fire brewing in her soul. Her temperature rose to a noticeable level and her fluids flowed freely as the blood surged through her body giving her life; or rather a vampire's illusion of life that returns temporarily in moments of arousal after feeding. She doesn't care, neither does Sergei. Reality or illusion, this moment will change him forever.

She rolled him on his back, straddled him, and they joined in the most intimate of embraces. They fell into that rhythmic dance lovers do, chasing the elusive satisfaction of mutual gratification. The pace quickened and their loins burned the closer they got to their fleeting goal but the chase continued. The ache for release increased and they released their tension in moans and pants of delightful agony. The anticipation of the moment built up higher and finally reached its peak. The tension was becoming more than each could stand. They clutched each other tight and with mutual screams of pleasure achieved ecstasy. At that same moment in time, almost as if she were timing the instance, Katrina appeared at their side. She buried her fangs deep into his neck and bled him to the point of death at which one would barely comprehend what was happening. It was in this moment when the victim got a small taste of death; after having been ravaged by the highest level of rapture, with senses still raw, most humans are vulnerable to the event that comes next.

"Do you wish life eternal?" Celeste asked as sensually as she could.

Sergei, was still lost in the emotions of what he had just experienced. His mind was clouded to everything around him and was not yet equipped to comprehend the weight of his response.

"I want to live…"

Katrina drained the life-giving crimson nectar from his veins. Piercing a deep wound over her breast with the nail on her index finger she pours her blood into her first morph's mouth. The mystery of what was happening was a secret to even the oldest of the existing Legion, but it has been done this way for thousands of years. The blood of Vlad Tepes now flows through the newest member of the Legion, but this one was hers. Sergei was now bound by a force he will never understand and shall forsake all others for the one who gave him second life.

His body trembled and tightened as the human life left his body and the Nyxian spirit that invaded it struggled to trap the soul within. The scene was macabre as his expressions ran from pleasure to pain and fear to ecstasy. He writhed in pain, screamed and laughed as if going mad. Then at the moment when the body, mind and spirits combined he fell unconscious in exhaustion. He will wake ready to feed and ready to serve. Katrina got up and walked towards the door. Celeste looked up at her with tears streaming from her eyes.

"Don't worry. He is my first morph, but he will always be your lover," Katrina assured her. "My love awaits somewhere else."

Celeste got up and pulled Sergei off the bed. She picked him up and laid him inside the hypochamber then lays down with him. The lid to the modern day casket slowly closed then sealed the two eternal lovers inside. The chamber churns to life with lights and the low hum of electronic noises as the casket fills with blood, New Minority Premium Grade.

Katrina walked down the corridor heading to her own quarters. As she stepped into the darkness, a low growl echoed through the hall; she stopped, and saw a pair of glowing yellow eyes peering through the gloom.

"Down big fella, it's your master," she whispers.

The creature grunts and turns away. She continued to her quarters, crawls into her chamber and seals the lid. She drifts off to sleep as the blood rushes into the tank. The weight of what she has done is fresh on her mind, her tears mix with the blood filling the tank.

They all rest peacefully as the day passes without incident. The captain arrived just as the last beams of sunlight creep across and fade into the horizon. He watched as the crew arrived. He barked orders prodding the staff and crew to prep the ship for a long voyage. Katrina will no doubt want to push off as soon as she awakens. The wolves are secured and transformed. After a few hours of rest they will join the crew and assist in the routine tasks that keep the ship afloat at sea. The supplies for the journey ahead are stowed away in the hold. Unlike other ships of that era, this one had a refrigeration system in the hull for storing essential food items for the human members of the crew. The plebes as they are referred to are wards of the vessel and guardians of its Legion during the day. They answer to the captain and follow any and all orders without question. Celeste and Sergei are the first to show up on the main deck. They watch as everyone scurries around like busy bees completely ignoring their presence.

"My Lady, we're having such a beautiful star-filled night. How did you rest?"

"Captain, I have rested better than I have in a long time," replied Celeste.

"Captain, I've never seen anything like this. How long have you been with the ship?" asked Sergei.

"Oh there is so much for you to learn my new friend. The Invidia is an old ship. She was one of the original ships of the Grand Spanish Armada. I have been the guardian aboard this vessel since its commission in 1584; it was christened La Magdalena. Madame Katrina had the ship refitted and renamed in 1588 after the defeat of the Armada."

"Captain, are you telling tall-tales again?" Katrina interrupted as she stepped on deck.

"Madame, you know there is no one prouder of this ship's heritage than I; and I won't pass on an opportunity to sing its glory."

"Well Captain, prepare to set sail for open ocean. We have a long trip ahead. There will be plenty of time for tales of glory," she laughed as she replied.

Gabrielle finally surfaced, last.

"Perfect, Gabrielle, we need to talk. Captain, I'll be in my quarters. Celeste, come with us; I need you, too. Captain, do you mind keeping Sergei company until he is needed? We have a lot of preparing to do for what lies ahead."

"Madame, it will be my pleasure to show the young man around while you carry on with your business."

"I'm sure it will," she replied sarcastically.

Katrina, Celeste and Gabrielle disappeared through the door of the hallway leading to the map room, which had been converted to a lounge. This is where Katrina preferred to take all of her meetings. Sergei watched as they walked away and wondered about what was so secret that he couldn't participate. His attention was quickly diverted by the interesting pistol at the captain's hip. It was like no other he had ever seen. The style was reminiscent of an old ball and powder smooth-bore pistol. The same ones you might see in modern pirate movies, but there was something different about it. The first sign of its uniqueness was the nine millimeter clip jutting from the bottom forward of the trigger assembly.

"Ah, you like guns, do you now?" the Captain said as he pulled out the modified 17th century Spanish flintlock.

"She's a beaute'," replied Sergei.

"Nothing finer at taking out overgrown vermin," said the captain with a gleam in his eye.

"You mean the werewolves," said Sergei.

"Them and other things," responds the captain.

"Wait a minute, I'm confused. Aren't you a Lycanthrope of some kind?" said Sergei.

"The correct term is Canis," snaps back the captain. "A Lycanthrope is a crazy person who thinks he's an animal. We are animals," he glared at Sergei then laughs letting him in on the joke. "I belong to a very different kind of Canis."

"Different? How so? Aren't all Canis the same," Sergei interrupted with the eagerness of an adolescent.

The captain's fierce yellow eyes pierced through to Sergei's soul as he transformed into the biggest, most handsome, yet fearsome animal he had ever seen; a black panther.

"I come from a rare species that originated in Africa. Our ancestors were the guardians and servants of royalty. Cleopatra herself had a pride of Canis at her service. Anytime you see a painting of a panther or lion alongside a royal it is most likely one of my ancestors. The most recent public evidence of our existence was the rogue pair at Tsavo in 1898. They were dealt with and not in the way the world believes. Let's just say we take care or our own justice. I've traced my lineage to Moors that remained in Spain after the Moorish occupation. I was born in Cordoba. Some call me a traitor to my kind for aligning myself with the Legion. I have a much different story to tell."

He morphed back to his human form put his arm around Sergei's neck and dragged him off joyfully.

"Come my boy, let me show you around and I'll elaborate on the woeful tale that binds me to the Invidia."

The captain left the preparations to set sail in the hands of the very capable and equally demanding first mate. After guiding Sergei on a tour of the ship from Bow to Stern and below all decks, he made his way to the bow of the Invidia where looking out into the bay he starts his tale. By now Sergei was completely enthralled with the captain's knowledge and hangs on his every word.

From Magdalena to Invidia
Chapter Sixteen

'It was sometime in February, 1588, La Armada, or as you may know it the Spanish Armada, was under the command of Medina Sidonia. King Felipe had formed La Armada to invade and occupy England. His intention was to suppress the attacks on Spanish territories in the New World. I was part of a special group of envoys from the House of Sixtus V on the Magdalena. It was a Spanish flagship responsible for the protection and transportation of treasure and dignitaries from the New World to Spain. My group and I were its special security force. After fighting our way through the treacherous waters of the Caribbean, returning from Cuba, we were ordered to join La Armada.

We met with the 130 ships of the fleet off the coast of France, bordering the Spanish Netherlands, at a place called Gravelings. We had just off-loaded cargo in Spain and the men were tired from the journey. We were to set sail for the coast of Flanders where we would rendezvous with the Duke of Parma's army of Tercios and carry them across the channel to invade England. The Tercios were an elite Spanish force comprised of mixed light and armored infantry. It was always ironic to me that Spain, who produced the best horses in the world, didn't have a formidable cavalry. The Tercios were the answer to this weakness. The armored infantry, surrounded by rows of skilled long pike men proved to be a formidable force against all opponents of its time. The men welcomed the rest, while the fleet awaited communication from the Duke. On the night of July 29th, we were attacked by English fire ships. The Spanish fleet ships scattered in panic. The Captain of the Magdalena saw an enemy ship on the horizon and gave chase. In the distance, one of the merchant ships that traveled with La Armada blew up after being struck by a fire ship. It must have been laden with black powder. The captain halted his pursuit in order to rescue survivors. The long boats were offloaded and we searched the waters for supplies and people. After an hour of searching, surprisingly undisturbed by the enemy, we found one survivor; a woman. I remember finding it curious that a woman would be aboard any of our ships. The men couldn't resist the urge to save her. She was dressed in white loose fitting nightclothes and soaked to the bone. As you can imagine it was quite the spectacle when she was pulled out of the water. Let's just say there was nothing left to the imagination. Her skin was cold as ice. The men were sure she was dead.

I watched as the members of the crew carried the woman to the captain's quarters. I had a feeling something was wrong. The ships physician tended to her and sent everyone away. The captain turned his attention to the enemy ship on the horizon. Shortly after we heard the sound of glass breaking and the blood curdling screams of a man in agony. Everyone on the main deck rushed to the sounds. As we approached the corridor to the captain's quarters out of the darkness sprang the woman; blood dripping from her mouth and hands. Her eyes glowed with a frightening look of rage that weakened lesser men's hearts. She ripped through the first three men as if they were wheat waiting to be harvested with the pair of Gurkha's in her hand. I and the other members of the special envoy quickly transformed. It was too late for one of my cohorts, she ripped his head clean off as she blew past us like the wind. She climbed the crow's nest and set a torch ablaze. Within seconds the ship was overrun by Legion. My comrades and I fought hard. We killed many of the Legion that night. I felt if we could just hold out long enough the sun would rise and they would have to leave or be phased. In the skirmish I was hit with a near fatal shot from a flint lock. The silver ball lodged itself in my chest near my heart and was doing its damage. I called to my comrades but they ran. We were completely over run by the shipload of Legion that had been sitting on the horizon just waiting for us to spring their trap. I cursed my men as I watched them jump overboard leaving me in the middle of a battle at the mercy of our most hated enemy. An enemy I had fought many times before and vanquished. An enemy we were always told was Satan incarnate. These beasts were different. They were almost naked and painted their faces. They wielded strange weapons that I had never seen before in my life. They were exactly like the descriptions I had heard of the savages from the New World. It was as if I were living my worst nightmare.

The Legion fell up on me and like sharks in a feeding frenzy battered me, slashed at me and bruised me. In the middle of the chaos, a pale man with long blond hair stood in the middle of the commotion on the ship and with one motion silenced the mob. I lay on the deck of the ship bleeding, battered and waiting to die. The Legion woman we had plucked from the ocean, walked up to me, looked down and then said something I could not understand to the pale man. He looked at me then stared at the woman and laughed. She reached down, pulled my head up and rested it on her lap. I then felt the most pain I have ever felt in my life as she dug her fingers in my wound and pulled the silver shot out of my body. Through the blur caused by the pain as I drifted from consciences I saw the name of the ship that attacked us, Elizabeta. When I came to, the Magdalena was adrift and I was alone on deck. It was as if I had been spared, but abandoned. I walked the ship calling out hoping someone could hear me, but I got no answer. All the long boats were gone. As I searched the ship I found plenty of provisions to sustain me on my lone voyage home. I just wasn't sure I could handle the ship on my own. I continued to search through the ship and aside from a few rats found nothing until I reached the farthest end of the cargo hold at the very bottom of the ship. There was a big black box adorned with silver. I remember thinking at first that it was a treasure chest; part of the shipment from the New World that was not unloaded. My curiosity got the best of me and I managed to pry open the box. To my horror it was a coffin and inside was the lady from the ocean. My first instinct was to reach in and rip her head from her shoulders, but I hesitated. I could not phase the only creature to ever show me mercy. I could not kill that which granted me life. It was on that day that I renounced my kind the way they had forsaken me. It was on that day that I aligned myself with my mortal enemy. I closed the casket and continued to rummage around the ship for something to eat. I found some salted pork and returned to the casket to await her awakening.

Shortly after the sun set, the lid to the casket opened, and the lady from the water rose from her slumber. She looked at me and with a smile on her face, in perfect Spanish said, "Saludos Señor Olivar, Yo soy Doña Katrina Le Giroux- Greetings Sir Olivar, I am Mademoiselle Katrina Le Giroux." The fact that she spoke Spanish did not surprise me as much as the fact that she knew my name. I was startled at first and chose my words carefully, but I soon realized there was no sense trying to deceive or hide anything from the lady. She read my thoughts and feelings as if they were written on my forehead. That night we walked the ship assessing the damage and planning the repairs. Together we got the rigging set up to set sail once more. We spent a week at sea. I would guide the ship by day and she took over the duties aboard ship at night. She soon got tired of this arrangement and decided to do something about it.

We sailed towards Spanish shipping lanes. The merchant ships were loaded with gold, silver and goods from the New World. Those ships were guarded by some of the best sailors and soldiers the Spanish Empire could produce.

Our third night out, Lady Katrina spotted a few ships on the horizon. She woke me and instructed me to wait for her signal. She set course heading straight for the ships. As soon as she saw them react to our presence, she set the ship adrift and let it flounder about. She then climbed the mast and hid among the sails. I watched from a porthole as the escort ship turned towards us and closed the distance rapidly. The cargo ship and other escorts sped away.

I heard voices as they called out to the ship. They even lobbed a canon ball over the ship as if trying to awaken any passengers. I could see the fear in the faces of some of the more superstitious members of the crew. There were others who were obviously excited to have found a derelict ship. They had thoughts of salvage on their minds, especially the captain. They threw their grappling hooks and pulled the Magdalena closer. When the captain saw the name, his excitement grew. There must have been a bounty on the lost ship Magdalena. They did not signal the other ships.

The captain ordered some more canons fired. In the distance I could see that the rest of the flotilla had no intention of coming to assist their comrades. The captain laughed and the rest of the crew joined him. The captain ordered some soldiers to board the Magdalena. They slowly and cautiously boarded. Once on deck, they walked the ship and searched around. I was sure I would be found.

I hid very well and moved from one location to the other as they cleared the different chambers of the ship. The man in charge of the boarding party then stood in the center of the main deck and signaled for the captain to come over.

The captain and his escorts stood on the main deck and proclaimed the ship captured in the name of the Spanish Crown. As soon as he raised his sword in victory, Lady Katrina fell upon him and took the sword. She dug her fangs deep into his neck letting the blood splash on his men. They were in shock for a second and then rushed her. Madame Katrina slashed with the sword at one soldier and then buried it deep in another's chest. She then signaled to me.

I ran across the main deck and transformed quickly driving fear in the hearts of the men causing them to panic, turn and run. I leapt over the side of the ship and across to the other ship. When I landed I was rushed by a few brave souls who lost their lives instantly at the end of my claw-filled paws. The others turned and ran in fear at the sight they had just witnessed. There were even those who chose to abandon ship. On the Magdalena, Madame Katrina killed many as she slashed and ripped through all her opponents. I ran through the escort ship and killed anyone who opposed me. Slowly many started to surrender and beg for mercy. Once I reached the main deck once more, I noticed the Madame was surrounded by soldiers bowing to her and others were kneeling in respect. I then realized what her intentions were. I, on the other hand, had no mercy for anyone on my ship.

Madame Katrina just laughed as I climbed back over to the Magdalena. She must have sensed my embarrassment. I was going to transform, but something told me to remain in full Canis form.

She had them all stand up and addressed the captured crew in Spanish. She gave them the option of living in her service or to die in loyalty to the King. There was one very brave and very loyal soldier who served to demonstrate the type of death that awaited any other brave ones. Madame Katrina threw him to me and I first ripped into his chest and ripped his heart out. I threw it down to the ground and pulled his head off with one bite. The head rolled straight towards the rest of the men making their decision.

The unanimous decision was swift after that display of a horrifically brave death. They would all be brave and loyal sailors in the service of Madame Katrina Le Giroux. She selected her crew and officers and dispatched their orders. She assigned the rigging masters to repair the damage to the sails and masts. There was a man who was a blacksmith. He was assigned to the canons. Madame Katrina then assigned me to get some rest and set up a schedule for the crew.

During the night a few members of the crew decided they might try to distract the Madame and escape. A couple of men cut a few sails and they came crashing down on the deck. Madame Katrina was trapped underneath the sails. Three men then jumped overboard with barrels and swam towards a nearby island. Madame Katrina cut through the sails, sliced through the neck of the nearest crewmember, grabbed a pair of grappling hooks and raced to the side of the ship. She stood on the edge of the rail, spun the hooks over her head a few times, and launched the hooks at the escapees. The hooks found their marks.

She pulled them on to the deck and tossed them to the floor. For some reason they thought they could actually take her down and lunged at her. She pushed the hooks through the bottom of their jaw and up through their skull. She threw the ropes up to the rigging and handed them to the crew members near her. She forced them to pull the escapees up and left them hanging. They kicked and shuddered most of the night causing the crew some uncomfortable moments. Just before morning, Madame Katrina woke me and I took her place. She gave me the objectives for the day and lay down in her casket. It was my job to watch the crew and also watch over her.

My day did not go without incident. At the end of the day, after all the assigned tasks had been complete, a group of soldiers came down to the cargo hold where the Madame lay in her casket. I don't know where they got the silver shot, but I got it right in the chest. It knocked me off my feet and sent me writhing to the floor. It didn't take much for them to strap me down. The men surrounded the casket and one lit a torch. I watched in horror as I tried to transform. There was too much silver in my system, I thought I was going to die. As I slowly drifted off I saw the flames rise from the top of the casket. I don't know how long I was out, but when I unexpectedly woke Madame Katrina was looking down at me, we were on the main deck and I was surrounded by men on their knees, in shackles with tears streaming down their faces as they shrieked in terror. Madame Katrina helped me to my feet and said, "Les fayó el cálculo del tiempo- their time calculations were a little off." I looked around at the men responsible for the actions of the past day. They looked so different now. They were so full of purpose that past afternoon, so intent on phasing us, and full of bravado. These same faces now looked so pathetic as I transformed and glared at my transgressors. Madame Katrina made the rest of the crew watch as I ripped their offending comrades to shreds. Not one was left alive. Not one was left in one piece.

Madame Katrina then ordered those who watched to feed their shipmate's pieces to the sharks that hungrily brushed up against the side of the ship. The rest of the tour went smoothly. After those two displays of power and retribution, there was no one left on the ship with heroic ideas. We raided several ships in the time we spent marauding the Atlantic. It was always done the same way. Many ships were sunk and many left floating adrift for others to find or as bait for our next victims. One day Madame Katrina ordered us to set sail for the New World. An area I was not familiar with.

We arrived at the shores of what is now Virginia shortly after sundown on the night of August 5th 1595, and dropped anchor. Madame Katrina joined me on deck and shortly thereafter a long boat approached and the Pale blond man boarded the ship again with a compliment of men.

I was not yet privy to the conversations of the masters

and so I sat and watched as they had a discussion. I heard Madame Katrina call the man by the name, Vlad. Even if I was allowed in the conversation I did not know enough of the language yet for it to make any sense. They spent most of the night talking and looking at maps. As they discussed their plans, the ship was loaded with more provisions.

That night, as they said their farewell, a young lady was brought aboard. She wore a cloak that covered her completely, but it was obvious to me that she was nude underneath. The cloak fell too close to the body outlining her form too well for it to be otherwise.

"Ven aqui Olivar," Madame Le Giroux called to me.

It was the first time I met Lady Elizabeth Shirland, one of the survivors of the Roanoke settlers. A crew member told me about what had happened, as he translated what the pale man said. She was raised by natives of the region. She had been captured during a raid on a Spanish ship. She had suffered much on that ship. The soldiers that had seemed to rescue her, raped her repeatedly. During the raid she managed to kill her sentinels and escaped only to land in the hands of the crew of the Elizabeta. Now she was being brought to Madame Katrina.

A couple of native females were brought aboard. They were directed by Madame Le Giroux to take Lady Shirland to the captain's quarters. A few of the natives that had beaten me senseless a week ago passed by as I glared at them. Lady Giroux laughed, no doubt reading what was going through my mind, and instructed them to carry a heavy travel chest to the lady's new quarters. Madame Le Giroux followed them to the room. I saw Madame order the natives to go down to the cargo hold. I stayed outside and just watched as everyone worked. There was some noise coming from below, a lot of sawing and hammering. My curiosity got the best of me and I went to see what all the commotion was about. I followed the banging noises and got to the end of the cargo hold. The men were building a wall with a door. It divided the hold in half. On the other side, another opening leading to the cargo hold was being made. Looking at the first chamber I deduced that it would be Lady Katrina's resting chamber. My assumption was confirmed when the two natives carried the black and silver casket into that room. Over the sounds of the men working on the room, I heard the distinct clanging sound of clashing sabers. I alerted the men working and rushed up the stairs, through the corridors and out to the main deck. In the night, I could see the two ladies swinging swords at each other. They were both dressed alike and it was hard to tell which was which. Then I noticed that Lady Elizabeth was about to strike a deadly blow at Madame Katrina with the point of her saber. I leapt into the air, transformed, pushed Madame out of the way and slapped the saber out of Lady Elizabeth's hand. Lady Elizabeth eyes grew to the size of saucers staring at the giant panther in front of her. She turned and ran away screaming and stomping like women do when they've seen a mouse. Madame Katrina was on the floor laughing hysterically at the spectacle along with just about everyone who was now on the main deck including the natives I had alerted to the danger. Madame Katrina sent someone after the young lady and again in perfect Spanish explained that it was a training session.

"La señorita tiene que aprender a defenderse si va ha viajar con nosotros - the lady needs to learn to defend herself if she's going to travel with us," she said between her fits of laughter.

The men laughed louder as I realized what had happened and transformed back. I felt completely humiliated. Madame Katrina must have sensed it because she then turned to the men and said, "Por lo menos se en quien puedo confiar- At least I know in who I can trust!" One could have heard a pin drop as she looked around the ship.

Just then one of the crew returned with Lady Elizabeth. I slowly walked up to her and handed the saber back. She stared at me and didn't say a word. I could tell she was still terrified.

Madame Katrina spurred everyone back to work and continued her exercise with Lady Elizabeth. I watched as they practiced and practiced the entire night. The last things I saw them use were those strange giant curved knives, the Khukuri. Today they are known as Gurkhas. Madame Katrina is deadly accurate striking with these and was giving Lady Elizabeth all she could handle. Lady Elizabeth was trying to ward off her opponent using a saber.

Throughout the night, men would finish their assigned tasks and gather around to watch the action. Madame saw an opportunity. She called me and told me to transform, she gave Lady Elizabeth the Gurkhas and instructed me to attack her. I toyed with the Lady and smacked her around for a few minutes, then got some good shots in after she let anger replace terror. Some good shots turned into near fatal blows and then it was on. We went at each other full force for about a minute, before Madame stepped in and reminded me that she was just a human. The group of natives had finished building the Madame's chamber and were also watching. Madame noticed their interest and must have sensed something she didn't like because she told me to stand down and called the natives to action. I watched as Lady Elizabeth struggled to keep up with the vampire natives, but she did well. The whole time I was chomping on the bit to get in that fight and avenge the bashing I took at the hands of these individuals. To my surprise, Madame Katrina gave me that chance. She suddenly called Lady Elizabeth to stand down. It was extremely humorous to see the look on their faces go from jubilation for having worn out the Lady to complete terror at the sight of me transforming to the deadly creature they once battered. I was so confident I could take them that I even let them attack first. I clawed, bit and bashed them till they were mere bloody piles of meat, but I would not phase them. I wanted them to suffer. I only stopped when the pale man appeared in front of me and knocked me on my back.

Judging from his speed and the force of his blow I was relieved when Madame Katrina stood between us to stop what was coming. They talked once more. The man announced something and everyone clapped and cheered. Madame Katrina knelt and kissed the pale man's hand in gratitude. He handed her a bottle of rum. Everyone gathered, walked past the Madame, congratulating her, and then all the crew and natives disembarked and rowed off to the shore. I was happy to see them leave. Madame Katrina then called to me and Lady Elizabeth and we walked to the bow of the ship. She stood at the rail and pointed toward the front. As I leaned over to see what she was pointing to I saw the name had been changed. She swung the bottle of rum and christened, "the Invidia." We heard the crew cheer from the shore.

Madame Katrina walked us to the captain's quarters and explained what had happened. The pale man was Vlad Tepes a leader among the Legion. He came to the New World to establish a new empire, but the expansion of the humans on this territory was threatening his seat of power. With this ship and others like it he would solidify his empire in the New World by raiding Spanish and English gold shipments and looting their ports. Roanoke was just the start and the raid on La Armada was a sign of things to come. I was to be first mate on the Invidia and entrusted with the security of the Madame during daylight hours. Lady Elizabeth would be the captain of the ship and carry out all of the Madame's instructions during the day. In order to do this competently the lady needed experience.

Madame Katrina arranged to have Lady Elizabeth snuck on a ship under the command of Sir Frances Drake. She was disguised as a young boy and traveled under the alias Eli Setterland. The lady used her time wisely and learned everything she could about, navigation, supply routes, port of calls and ship gunnery. The whole time her true identity closely guarded and safety guaranteed by the presence of yours truly.   She resented the assumption that she needed a - "nanny."

One day, Eli was securing the ties on the canons preparing for a night sail. A lonely sailor took a liking to the young boy that was less than appropriate for comrades at sea. His advances went unnoticed or overlooked by all except me. I kept an eye out for my charge the rest of the day and only worried about the coming night. Once night fell the First Mate announced the watch schedule and dismissed everyone to quarters. Some had earned shore passes, before the upcoming cruise. I was not on either list. I went to my sleeping quarters, stacked pillows under my blanket, threw a sleeping cap on a roll and set for a night of prowling on the ship. Eli drew mid-shift watch and was awake on deck when some of the men were returning from shore.   Among them was Eli's new admirer.   He was drunk and low on inhibitions.   His subtle advances turned less subtle.   He walked up to Eli and attempted to plant a wet sloppy kiss on Eli's lips and was met with a vicious right cross on the nose.   Blood gushed from his nose as the cartilage crushed under the force of the punch.   A couple of men stepped in and broke it up before it escalated any further.   The man swore and promised revenge.   I watched carefully from the shadows. Eli had only a few minutes left on the watch. Things seemed to have settled down until minutes before shift end. As Eli was doing the last security check things got ugly. The lecher was waiting for Eli at the bow. He pushed Eli face down on the stack of sails and ripped the pants open with a blade. The look of surprise on the man's face at finding a different type of equipment than expected was only matched by the look on his face when his head was ripped clean off his shoulder by a panther. I immediately transformed and began yelling the "man overboard" alarm. In the confusion that ensued Eli managed to get down below deck and change pants. The blood on deck was hard to explain, but the rest was no mystery since once they pulled up the body it had been chewed plenty by the ever present sharks. I took some lashes for having been away from quarters without authority, but the lady's secret was safe.

A few incidents of this type and others threatened that secret, but were met with equally swift and violent response. It was probably the largest rash of disappearances and desertions on record at the time. All this helped to strengthen the bond between the Command Cadre of the Invidia.

In the mean time Madame Katrina was busy overseeing the build of all the special features that made the Invidia the perfect Legion pirate ship. The ship had hideaway canons in the bow, hideaway canons at the stern, canon propelled grappling hooks, an incredible array of hidden corridors, trap doors and false floors in which to hide caches of loot or arms. Finally and the most ingenious feature was the hidden rowing ports in the haul. The ship could appear to be adrift with sails battered or down yet travel a controlled course and gain on fleeing ships. This was possible powered by the Sucanis at the controls to a hidden array of small paddlewheels on each side of the ship. The paddlewheels were submerged below the water line of the ship. The Invidia was equipped to become the most formidable warship in the Caribbean and the least known pirate ship of its time.

Finally the time came for us to part ways with Sir Frances Drake, Madame Katrina raided our ship with a crew borrowed from one of Vlad's Legion ships. We were taken captive in the chaos. Madame Katrina made sure to keep the fatalities and the looting to a minimum keeping this raid out of major attention. I'm sure we went down on a minimum of incident reports as random casualties of a common incident in those waters. With a new more than capable captain at the helm of the Invidia the next order of business was raising a crew. We set sail for the fertile waters off the Coast of Cuba. By order of King Philip all trade going to Spain from the New World was to assemble at Havana, Cuba and sail with escorts as one large fleet. This offered protection from most pirates, but against the Legion fleet of marauders it was a different matter all together.

Once we neared the coast of Havana, Lady Elizabeth raised the Spanish colors and we entered port. Once ashore, Doña Isabella disembarked with letters from the Spanish Court in Vera Cruz. Her entourage included Captain Thomas de Olivera and the casket of La Dama Katarina de Genoa. The Spanish guards were kept from searching the ship with warnings of a fever running through the crew. With fears of plague and scarlet fever it was enough to keep anyone off the ship at that time. It also influenced them to keep their distance from us. That night, while Doña Isabella was enjoying the company of the Capitan General at a lavish dinner and tour of the construction of the new Castillo de la Fuerza, Madame Katrina and I made our way to the more seedy parts of Havana and offered options to those that had none, with promises of a new life and wealth. El Matador cantina became our impromptu recruitment base. On the first night we recruited two navigators and a pilot among a few other key crew members. On the second night, Doña Isabella toured the linens of the Dock Master's bed and got our ship assigned to fleet, leaving the following morning. By then, Madame Katrina and I had recruited and outfitted the rest of the ship including cooks and carpenters. The Invidia was finally fully stocked and ready to set sail. In the morning, Doña Isabella broke a lot of hearts as she stepped foot onboard ship followed by La Dama De Genoa's casket and myself. We were set to embark on the true maiden voyage of the Invidia.

The first attack took place in an area that is now known as the Devil's Triangle. At night, Madame Katrina ordered the ship set adrift. On the horizon, a lone ship pursued the fleet making the Fleet Commander nervous. A Galleon was ordered to turn back and assist the Invidia as the rest of the fleet pushed on. As the Galleon drew close the canon grappling hooks were fired. The marauding ship on the horizon quickly approached and joined the Invidia in the attack of the Galleon. The men of the Spanish Galleon fought well, but they were no match for the combined forces of the Invidia and the Elizabeta. After the massacre at sea, Vlad came aboard the Invidia. He promoted the willing members of the crew and those freshly captured sailors that were spurned by the abandonment of their armada to full Legion that night on the deck of the Invidia. Of course, all this was done only after having passed Madame Katrina's inspection. Those who objected, showed signs of weakness, or betrayal were cursed by my hand to a lifetime of servitude as Plebian Sucanis of the Invidia. Others were left to become blood-slaves for the Legion crew and staff. So was the beginning of an era of wealth-building and recruitment to support the Potentate's agenda in the New World.

Using uncharted regions of the Bahamas and Bermuda as hideaways, the Invidia would attack by night and trade with ships and ports by day. Our biggest means of income was supplying the vast network of pirate ships and outlaw villages with gun powder, rifles, pistols and ammunition. The occasional scuttled ship brought in a nice size fortune and canons were always a premium high priced item on the special order list. Lady Elizabeth was the face of our operation and soon grew in fame as a ruthless, fearless and shrewd business woman. No one dared cross Cutthroat Bess. A name earned at the end of a perfectly wielded sword, known to end any and all disputes. All this of course, bolstered by the clandestine actions of Madame Katrina, against any and all opponents of the lady. It was becoming well known around underworld circles that it was best not to deal with Cutthroat Bess, but if a deal was proposed it was best to take it. She was also successful in keeping our operations secret from both the English and the Spanish as she consorted with both posing as a lady of each respective Court. Cutthroat Bess would bed her crew for pleasure, Lady Shirland would bed British royal court members for their secrets and Doña Isabella bedded Spanish noblemen for theirs. This all worked well until the burned Merchant incident in 1604.

The Invidia had amassed quite a treasure trove of wealth most of it going to the Potentate, but there was enough left to go around and keep the crew happy and wealthy. On the day in question, word got to Lady Shirland that a merchant ship, loaded with silk, gold and emeralds was heading to Spain under the protection of just one escort ship. This was a feeble attempt at disguising this ship's importance. Lady Shirland didn't want to pass up the opportunity to snatch this prize from the clutches of the Spanish Empire. Without telling Madame Katrina, she returned to Cuba as Doña Isabella and using some of her more enticing forms of persuasion managed to obtain the name of the ship and date of departure. We set sail to open water and waited for it to pass our way. The ship came into view in mid-afternoon. Lady Shirland became impatient and not wanting to lose sight of the prize ordered a full out attack on the Merchant. She pulled in behind the escort ship and let loose with all bow canons at once, disabling its rudder. Having put the ship out of commission she went after the Merchant. The escort ship stood by watching helplessly as we ransacked the Merchant and pillaged its cargo. Lady Shirland then, out of sheer disgust, pleasure or excitement, had the ship set ablaze. The days catch was divided among three ships from the Legion fleet. Vlad was generous that night and left the biggest portion for the Invidia.

Two weeks later Doña Isabella was using her usual charming ways to thank the man who had passed on the information about the Merchant, along with other tokens of her appreciation taken from the loot, and was captured by Spanish soldiers in the process. It turns out the man passed other information to the Governor betraying her to the Spanish authorities as a pirate. Cutthroat Bess lived up to her nickname and slit the man's neck and stabbed him in the heart with a blade she kept near as they dragged her naked body off the bed. The soldiers fell upon her and dragged her away. It was the last anyone had ever heard of Cutthroat Bess, but the Invidia continued its devastating campaign against all sea going vessels until the early 1800's when Madame Katrina settled in Tampa.

•

"So you see boy, you have just joined a tight knit family with a long history and proud heritage," the captain ended his story.

Sergei was enthralled with the tale he had just heard. He had always been fascinated by the legends of the pirates and buccaneers that sailed the waters of these parts. It was why he moved to Tampa. He hoped that somehow he could channel those adventurous spirits and live a life of excitement. After all the story telling by the captain he still had questions and couldn't wait to hear the answers.

"Captain, so, what happened to Cutthroat Bess?" he asked in a hesitant tone hoping not to annoy the captain.

"Well my boy, to some scholars and historical buffs of the subject, they know her as Cutlass Liz. There is a lot of confusion about her. That's exactly how the Potentate likes it. You know her as Celeste De Questa," replied the captain.

"Lady Celeste is the famous Cutlass Liz?" Sergei could barely control his excitement. "Wait a minute, how old is she? How did she escape the Spanish?"

The captain just laughed and pulled him to the main deck.
"Come now son, I think the Madame is ready for us and those are questions you should ask Lady Celeste," he told Sergei as they walked towards the center of the ship.

"Captain, enough with the stories, let's get this baby on its way," ordered Madame Katerina. "Set a course to Veracruz. There is a situation with a certain gentleman there that requires our immediate attention."

"Sergei, go with Lady Celeste. There is much to do at the Castle. Make sure all is ready by the time I return," she barked.

Celeste and Sergei watch from the dock as the Invidia pulled away to the open ocean. They get in the car and drive away.

"Hurry Sergei, there is much to do and the sun will be upon us before we know it," Celeste urged Sergei.

Lady Celeste and Sergei arrive at the Castle to find Barabas waiting at the doors. They pull up and park.

"We have a lot of work to do. Were you able to take care of the clean up?" Celeste asked in an almost sarcastic tone.

"It wasn't easy, but I took care of everything. We need to hire a new staff quickly. There can't be any irregularities to tip off the Potentate," said Barabas.

"Katrina said to promote the willing from the existing staff and fire anyone who is not. She will be back soon to bring them into the fold. Once she had done that then we will hire a new staff of plebes that meet with her approval. For now we make do with what we can get. I'll put up a sign tonight at the club, post on our website and you do the interviews in the morning. I'm sure we'll have plenty of applicants to choose from. Once word spreads, we'll probably get applicants from as far as Miami," said Celeste as she looked at Sergei and laughed.

Veracruz
Chapter Seventeen

The Invidia approached the coast of Mexico early in the morning. The sun was not up yet. Captain Olivar and his crew woke and immediately started preparations for the events of the day. Olivar, as usual, was the first on main deck. He walked past the remains of the previous nights feeding. Gabrielle strolled by him with an extremely satisfied look on her face.

"Another bunch of unfortunate souls cross our paths in the night?" He asked.

"Not this time. These were more of the misguided entrepreneurial type," she replied with a smirk.

"Ah, Pirates," said Olivar. "After all these years those condenados continue to maraud the gulf. Eh, serves them right."

Gabrielle went on her way and glared at a ship-hand who annoyed her by staring too much. The site of a near naked woman drenched in blood might have been too much for this young sailor. He got out of her way before almost being trampled. She laughed as she disappeared into the lower deck.

"Don't let her bother you," said Katrina startling the youth. "She just likes to show off."

Katrina appeared out of the darkness surprising everyone on deck including Olivar. He found it a little disconcerting how she was able to do that, but found it even more disturbing that unlike Gabrielle, she didn't have a drop of blood on her clothes. The lady didn't waste a drop.

"Olivar, make sure the men clean that mess up completely," said Katrina. "I saw a few sharks hanging around the keel. They should make it easier to dispose of the remaining evidence. Make sure the boat is sunk too. I don't want any issues with what passes as the coast guard around here." She continued then walked down below deck and disappeared.

Olivar ordered everyone to their stations to prep the ship for docking. He then told a few men to dispose of the carcasses by pushing them overboard. A couple of the others showed up at main deck with their wetsuits and scuba gear. One of them was holding an explosive device.

"Hey, what do you plan to do with that thing? Alert the entire Mexican Navy that we are here. Get a smaller charge!" He yelled at the frogman.

The one called Melchor shrugged his shoulders and stomped down the stairs to get a smaller device. Minutes later he came up and the two jumped overboard. Olivar ordered another group to grab mops and swab the deck to clean up the blood and gore. It seemed an impossible task, but a few minutes later most of the blood was cleaned up. As they continued to mop, they were startled by the sound coming from the blast at a distance. Within seconds, the well placed charges did their job and the boat sank into the sea away from view. Almost at the same time the two frogmen climbed over the side.

"What the fuck?" yelled Olivar pointing in the direction of the blast.

"It's an explosion, there's going to be some noise," replied Melchor, the cocky demolition man. "Besides, it's not like we can't take those Mexican Navy pussies."

"It's not that kind of trip this time. We need to blend in and not cause any disturbances," said Olivar.

"I apologize, Sir," replied Melchor snapping to attention and saluting with complete sarcasm. "Next time I'll be sure to pack the TNT silencer," he continued with a smile on his face as he turned and walked away.

"Next time I'll just snap your neck if that blast even makes a ripple in the water," said Olivar with as stern of a look on his face as he could muster.

The two men went back down below without even looking back. Olivar waited for them to leave then chuckled to himself.

They're good guys, can't blame them for having fun.

By then, the men were done mopping up what was left of the blood and carried the buckets down below deck. Years of experience turned what would be a nightmare job for anyone else into a quick breeze of a chore. Some resented having to clean up after the Legion like maids, but none dared complain. That usually never ended well for the one placing the complaint.

Must have been a hell of a party up here last night.

The ship sailed into port late in the afternoon. It drew a lot of attention from the locals as they woke from their siestas. The spectacle of a ship from that period seemingly so well restored and maintained attracted the stares of all the envious millionaire yacht owners playing ship captain in the port of Veracruz.

Olivar dealt with all the formalities of docking into a foreign port. His command of the Spanish language helped to smooth the road as they navigated through the bureaucracy and different levels of bribes.

Just like old times. Some things stay the same, no matter how much things change.

Once at their dock the ropes are tied, sails are stowed, and all the other menial things that make this look like a normal ship pulling into harbor are skillfully done by the crew. It was mid-afternoon by the time the sailors aboard the Invidia are done with all the docking procedures. On orders from the captain, the first mate draws up a guard duty roster and shore pass schedule. The men are anxious to hit the town and get a little taste of the local color. They are under strict orders to have fun, but keep their noses clean. There was no bail for anyone should an incident arise. There are three unlucky men who draw first nights duty and are among the security detail. Along with the guards there are also three Sucanis plebes in animalistic form under the control of the captain himself. They prowl the decks of the ship securing it from any unwanted visitors. These are relieved by the second shift once the sun goes down. There will be no need for plebes once the sun goes down. A dock security guard can't help but notice the giant dogs on the ship.

"Lobos?" He asked, but realizing the man at the end of

the leash might not understand he said, "Are they wolves?"

"Hybrids," replied the guard as politely as possible with his elusive reply.

"That is a really big hybrid. I never saw one so big. Can I touch him?" asked the dock guard.

"I don't think that's a good idea," answered the sailor as the hybrid growled and snapped at the dock guard.

"Oh, okay my friend. No problem. Keep him on that boat okay?" the dock guard answered, unnerved by the giant dog straining at his chains to eat him.

The dock guard finally got the message and strolls away to continue his lonely task. The ship was very well guarded and secured.

The sun sinks slowly behind the mountains. The guards seem a little more on edge and on alert. The canine sentries are taken away and locked in their chambers. Katrina stepped out of the gloom surprising the guards on the main deck.

"Has Gabrielle come up yet?" she asked.

"I...I have not seen her Madame," answered the guard barely recovering from his surprise.

"You, go make sure she's up. Wake her if you have to," replied Katrina.

A chill ran down the man's spine. The prospect of waking a Legion from its slumber especially this vampire had no appeal whatsoever. At that moment, to the relief of the sailor, Gabrielle stepped out of the darkness in the stairwell.

"No need, I was up wondering what I was having for

my breakfast," she said looking at the nervous sailor with a devious smile.

"We have some work to do, I'm sure we can pick up a meal along the way," replied Katrina.

"Oh, that is just perfect. Some free range local cuisine."

Katrina and Gabrielle walked down the gang way, off the Invidia, and disappeared into the dark passage ways of the port.

"Hey man, that Gabrielle is hot, but she's always looking at me like I'm a giant Rib-Eye," whispered one guard to the other.

"Maybe she's looking for some 'blood sausage'," he replied under his breath.

"I heard that," a voice from out of the gloom startled them to attention, tightly gripping at their weapons.

The cackles of her devious laughter filled the night air echoing through the alleys between the warehouses, cantinas, and villas at the edge of the city. Gabrielle and Katrina prowled the night following their senses, running down the signs of their elusive prey. Katrina filtered through the barrage of thoughts slowly filling the air as they entered the outskirts of the city. Finally it was their thirst that led them to their first objective, La Sombra de la Luna.

To the uninitiated this establishment just seemed like a highly exclusive lounge for the elite of the region. Two muscle-bound doormen sifted through the menagerie of hopefuls standing outside the doors just passed the velvet rope, like trolls standing at the gilded gates of Mordor, but what awaited the curious beyond those doors was much darker and sinister than they could ever imagine. Besides the exuberant price of admission, there was a larger bounty for becoming a member of this most selective club. Rumors abound about this hideaway, but nothing had ever been substantiated. This was probably due to the fact that those in a position to confirm those rumors fell prey to its subjects. The local authorities who were eager to investigate the night club lost their enthusiasm as the cash began to flow through the streets and made its way into their pockets.

Most of the locals ignored or avoided it. There was just too much that wasn't right with this place. The former proprietors of the Noble Hotel, where the club is situated, fell on a string of bad luck, causing the violent death of each of the family members. It was a complete surprise when the current owner purchased the property at auction. There was only one bid. It was so high, no one contested it. Either that was the case, or the muscle heads who accompanied the gentleman that night performed their duties of intimidation well. Whatever the circumstances, the Hotel Colonial was now in the hands of the Legion. Knowledge of this did not deter the tourist from staying there. It was almost an adventure or rite of passage to stay at the Colonial when visiting Veracruz, but La Sombra de la Luna was a completely different story. It took real cojones to visit the local Legion feeding ground.

"So, do you think the word has got around that you're a wanted fugitive?" asked Gabrielle.

"We're about to find out. Either way that's why I have you with me. No matter what we run into, I expect you have my back," Katrina said with a stern look on her face.

"I got your back, but I imagine you don't really need it with the captain lurking in the shadows. Did you really think I didn't sense him follow us?" Gabrielle said with a sarcastic tone.

"Just consider it an added precaution in case things don't

work out the way I expect," replied Katrina.

They reach the velvet rope, Gabrielle hands the doorman her ID.

"Welcome Madame Gabrielle. We are honored with your presence. It's always a privilege to have such a distinguished member of the Dragon Praetoria. I will let the boss know you are here," said the door man.

"Don't bother. I prefer to have a quiet evening with your best stock and I will be on my way," replied Gabrielle.

"Oh no Madame, it is no bother. Let me announce you and your guest Madame … ?" the door man paused awaiting a response.

"As I said, I don't want to be bothered and who I chose to spend my time with is none of your business. Let me by and if anyone comes near my table and isn't holding a tray, I'll personally take great satisfaction in splitting your veins open and watching you bleed out on the dance floor. Now, show me to my table and shut the fuck up," said Gabrielle looking up at his massive head sitting atop his massive frame.

The doorman sighed, looked at his partner then looked at Gabrielle, gestured with his head to follow and showed them both the way through the crowd to a table in the farthest corner.

"Will this be comfortable enough for you, Madame?" asked the door man trying to be as courteous as possible under the circumstances. "I'll tell the boss…"

"Eh-eh!" Gabrielle interrupted him in mid-sentence glaring under her eyebrows, pointing a finger at his neck, and her head tilted in a threatening gesture. The door man just turned around and walked away silently.

"That was brilliantly handled," said Katrina.

"It's all about attitude," replied Gabrielle.

"Well, don't be surprised when he doesn't do what you expect. I imagine the proprietor of this establishment will be paying a visit to our table before the night is through," answered Katrina.

It wasn't long before George, their host for the evening, stepped up to their table and asked their preference. The categories available read like a Chinese take-out menu; male, female, Caucasian, Black, Asian, type-O, type-A, and vintage. That was the most fascinating term; Vintage. Basically it was a degree of freshness. This ranked from Classic, or those who had been fed on so much it was an addiction, to Neophyte, the ones who had never been bitten, but were eager and open to the experience. Then there were the V.S.X.O (Very Special Extra Old) a group of blood slaves that were infused with enough vampire blood to sustain them, but not turn them. These were maintained on a strict diet and exercise routine to produce the best blood available. They were a delicacy that few Legion could afford. There were usually only two at most three at any given location and they were heavily guarded. The widely accepted best of class among V.S.X.O. blood slaves, or Sangus as referred to among the Legion, were those from the House of Dracula. No surprise there. They were even branded, a brand that the bearer displayed proudly. The difference between the categories was subjective, but separated by price. There was a broad gap between Neophyte and V ranking, but the product was basically the same; blood. It was really all a matter of taste, status and money.

"I'll have a Neophyte type-A male bound and gagged," ordered Gabrielle.

"Hold that! We'll have two type-O Classics," interjected Katrina.

"Oh, my! That is the worst. Just because we're in this predicament doesn't mean we have to lower our standards," protested Gabrielle.

"So, what shall it be Madame?" asked the waiter.

"I gave you our order," pressed Katrina with a cold piercing stare. The waiter rolled his eyes and walked away.

"We can't order anything as extravagant as what you would like. Every time someone orders from the 'top shelf' the Protectorate finds out. It's part of how they keep tabs on the Legion. We have to be careful what we do at every instance. For all intensive purposes, you and I are not to appear to be together if we are going to accomplish what we've set out to do," informed Katrina. Gabrielle seemed put-off by this little known tactic.

"Well, all I know is I'm starving and I would rather hunt down some human on the street than partake of a Classic," she said angrily as she rose from her seat to leave.

Katrina had to once again demonstrate her superior skills by swiftly slamming Gabrielle back to her seat with just a quick sweep of her foot.

"You will sit there, observe, enjoy your dinner and do it with a smile or I swear I'll bleed you where you sit," Katrina enforced her position.
Gabrielle was a great fighter, but she knew she was no match for this one. Even though she had the blood of

Dracula surging through her veins she made no attempt to defy her companion. Minutes later the waiter returned with two middle aged men and introduced them to their meals.

"This is Armand and Louis, I hope you will enjoy," he sneered as he walked away.

The men sat down next to the ladies at each end of the semi circular booth and immediately embraced their patrons for the night. Gabrielle reluctantly accepted the embrace and after giving Katrina a defiant smirk sunk her fangs into the man's shoulder and began to feed. The Louis writhed in ecstasy as the sensation of the blood draining from his body filled him with endorphins and drove his body to near collapse from the sensual high. Katrina was about to take her meal when they were both interrupted by Vincent, the club owner.

"By the saints, who has offered these distinguished ladies such slop? George, where is the V Sangus?" Vincent barked irritated with his underlings for having embarrassed him.

He pulled Armand away before Katrina could feed and pushed him aside. George appeared before his master much more humble than he had been a few moments ago.

"Sir, it is what they ordered. I showed them the list of available Sangus, but..." Vincent slapped George before he could finish his phrase.

Weakened from thirst and unable to focus her attention, Katrina had trouble reading their minds, but could sense something was wrong. Gabrielle drank her fill and let Louis drop to the floor worn out from the experience and stood.

"How dare you interrupt my evening you insignificant peacock? What business is it of yours what type of meal we prefer for the evening? You've interrupted my companion's supper. I believe she should be compensated and put on your tab for having caused the disturbance," she said with all the rage she could muster, grabbed Vincent by the throat, and held a blade to his jugular she had produced from thin air.

The two behemoths intently watching from the door were shocked to see what had happened. They rushed to Gabrielle but were stopped in their tracks as Vincent waved them away.

"Haven't you embarrassed me enough?" he said as the men approached. "It will be my pleasure Madame to make amends in whatever fashion you see fit. I'm here for nothing else but to serve."

"You," Gabrielle pointed at one of the door men. "Didn't I say we did not wish to be disturbed?"

The man stood motionless not knowing how to reply or what to expect next.

"It's the policy of the Protectorate that all distinguished officials and agents are to be reported to the Mayordomo upon granting entrance to a Legion establishment," the man finally said trembling.

Gabrielle released Vincent slowly and lowered her blade, but did not put it away.

"Had I been on a mission you would have blown my cover and I would have drained both of you. Make sure the next time I give you the courtesy of announcing my presence in your club, that you extend me the courtesy of discretion. Do we understand each other?" she said as the tone of the situation began to change.

Katrina's thirst was starting to overtake her. She stumbled back into her seat.

"Let's get my guest her meal before something horrid happens. She's getting hungry. You wouldn't like her when she's hungry," Gabrielle interjected sarcastically.

"Nice move. I'll have to remember that one if I'm ever in this predicament again," commented Katrina under her breath.

George cautiously approached the table with a wonderfully bronzed young looking man. An extremely well built individual with perfect hair and model looks. He had exotic features and a nonchalant demeanor that completely exposed his Vintage as V.S.X.O. House of Dracula. He sat next to Katrina. Her eyes fixed on her prey as she sensed his heart pulsating the blood through his veins. She took a deep breath as if inhaling his essence and savored the aroma.

"Kemosiri Jibade, V Sangus extraordinaire, compliments of the house," said Vincent and hastily walked away.

Katrina pulled her victim down to her and he lay on top of her at the seat of the circular booth. She was too weak to subdue her meal as usual. Her skin ached as he caressed her body then at the moment she could not stand anymore she sank her fangs deep into his chest almost as if digging for his heart. The blood that ran down her throat and through her body filled her with euphoria. She had never tasted or experienced anything like this. It was as if he had been created just for her. He embraced her and within a few seconds he was the one collapsing at her touch and Katrina became the aggressor. He writhed and squirmed under her touch, lost in the ecstasy of the moment. Her body fully restored and juices flowing once again, she felt the urge to indulge in his sexual favors, but she took control of herself and left Kemosiri in euphoric despair.

"You are definitely a stronger person than I," joked Gabrielle. "I would have been all over that."

"No one has ever accused me of being a person," replied Katrina and then she smiled to let Gabrielle in on the joke. "Had we more time, I'd rip him apart and thrown you the pieces."

They laughed as they walked away from the table. Katrina grabbed an innocent clubber dancing in the wings and pushed her onto Kemosiri.

"You won't mind if she finishes my meal," she told Vincent with a glare.

Vincent wanted nothing to do with the whole thing. He waved an affirmative and gleamed at her with the best smile he could. After experiencing the wrath of Gabrielle, he wanted no part of her obviously more vicious counterpart. He rushed to the back room and watched them leave on his surveillance monitor. He sighed as they walked out the door and collapsed into his chair.

"Marcos!" Vincent yelled for one of the doormen. "If those two ever come near this place again, you keep them out no matter what the fuck happens, and sound the alarm or I swear to you by the Dark I'll rip your soul from your flesh and feed it to the Jengals."

Vincent sat in his overstuffed nail-head leather chair, tipped a decanter of blood wine into a glass, and tried to relax. He wasn't used to being treated like a punk in his own club.

The Shack at the Road's end
Chapter Eighteen

Gabrielle led Katrina through the streets of Veracruz. They walked for miles keeping a low profile and staying to the shadows. As they walked, the smell of the sea breeze mingling with the aromas of spices and meats simmering over open stoves streamed through the air and tempted the senses like the ebb and flow of the sea at the city's shores.

They soon reached the end of Mario Molina Avenue. The road narrowed and the buildings got closer together. The area was so densely populated that the thought waves were flooded with activity from every direction. There was also such a strong pungent odor of spices, meats and cooking oil that it was extremely difficult to pinpoint anything else. Katrina's powers were nearly useless in this environment.

All except her night vision, which at certain moments was blurred by the sudden blast of light from a random oversized porch light that would have served better as a search light. Even vampire eyes need a few moments to adjust to drastic changes in illumination. Katrina had long learned a very helpful trick for such situations; the wink. In areas of complete darkness, one keeps an eye open and closes the other. Some might keep their shooting eye closed so that if needed there would be no need for adjusting. It sometimes interfered with depth perception, but it was better than being blinded for a few seconds while being pummeled by an attacker.

Gabrielle arrived at the entrance to an alleyway, stepped in, and curled her index finger at Katrina for her to follow. They walked through the one-person-wide corridor between two small apartment buildings. Gabrielle led Katrina to a small house at the end of the alleyway. It wasn't much to look at and if not led there, Katrina would have missed it completely. There is no way the Professor would have been discovered here. Gabrielle did an excellent job of locating the perfect hideout for a human avoiding any Legion pursuers. This shack at the end of the road seemed like a good refuge and rally point should things get hairy in Veracruz.

Gabrielle stood at the door and knocked. Katrina stood a few paces away and observed the surroundings. There was no answer.

"Ronald, it's Gabby," she called with a smirk of embarrassment on her face as she noticed Katrina's expressive reaction.

"I should have known," Katrina muttered, still more interested in her surroundings.

Gabrielle knocked one more time and after not getting an answer or hearing any sign of life, Katrina kicked the door open. They both stormed in, found the room in disarray, but no one was there. It appeared that no one had been there for a long time. There were papers and notes tossed all over the place. The professor had definitely been busy. Some artifacts, strewn about the place littered the small abode. They seemed to follow some strange form of order, probably only decipherable by the professor. There were vampire skulls stacked in one place, and then some bones that looked like tibias in another. A box full of canine teeth and fangs, which under the circumstances probably belonged to Canis, sat on a stool in the farthest corner of the room. There were a few rubbings on the wall that resembled hieroglyphics from the Pyramids in Egypt next to some that looked like they were taken from a Mayan ruin. Gabrielle nor Katrina could make any sense of them.

"Where's the professor and why did he leave all this lying around?" Katrina asked the question that was already lurking in both their minds.

Katrina handed Gabrielle a plastic bag and they started collecting anything of interest as they rummaged the place for clues to those questions. Gabrielle poked around the pile of wadded up and crumpled paper beneath the makeshift crate-and-plank desk and found one that drew her attention.

www.chroniclesofthedamned.com/theparchment.aspx

"What the hell is this?" Gabrielle asked as she showed the paper to Katrina.

"I guess our professor isn't giving up on this scroll business," replied Katrina.

"What do you mean? I thought we found them," Gabrielle asked confused and upset that he kept this from her.

"You found one of the scrolls, but it is believed by those who know the legends that there are six scrolls, each one detailing aspects of creation, mysticism, spirituality and the all mighty. Its origin and writer have been a mystery, but as we both now know, they do exist," replied Katrina as she folded the paper and tossed it in her bag.

They continued to filter through the mess. Gabrielle found a human skull with some interesting markings on it and picked it up to look at it. It had a string attached to it that pulled a lever by the lamp on the table that lit the place up like a blast from the sun. Temporarily blinded they both ducked their heads into their arms to shield their eyes from the light. Katrina pulled out her Gurkha and held it in her hand pressing the blade outward across her forearm as she covered her face. She sensed the impending danger, grabbed her bag with the other hand, pushed Gabrielle out the front door with a perfectly thrown cross-body block and they landed outside just as the room exploded in a fiery ball of bluish-green flame. The concussion from the blast shook them up and knocked them to the ground temporarily disorienting them. Dogs started barking in the night and the sounds of people rushing from their sleep echoed through the corridor.

In the confusion, Gabrielle caught the silhouette of a man watching from a nearby rooftop. When she pointed him out to Katrina the dark figure ran into the night through the rooftops. Gabrielle and Katrina sprang up and gave chase. Gabrielle climbed to the roof and ran after the dark figure. Katrina followed through the alleyways. A crowd was starting to form through the passages as the chase continued. Katrina fought her way through the growing mass of people keeping pace with their quarry. Before the fool could get beyond two more roof tops, Gabrielle was on him and knocked him to the alley below. Katrina arrived as Gabrielle, with fangs out, held the man by the neck as she was about to rip his head from his shoulders. The crowd, seeing the horror before them scattered in panic.

"Wait!" she yelled "You can't learn from a dead man," she continued.

Luckily for the man, Gabrielle came to her senses and only dropped him on his head once more. Katrina reached down, pulled the man up by the scruff of his shirt, checked his vital signs, and said "He's still alive. The sun will be up soon. We better take him back to the ship and find out what the hell he was doing watching us. I'm sure Captain Olivar will have him spilling all he knows by the time we rise for our evening meal."

"I'm sure he'll be spilling more than that by the time Olivar is done with him. Shame, he looks like he might be some fun given the proper form of dominance," Gabrielle replied knowing Katrina would not be amused.

Gabrielle grabbed the two bags, saw her lucky-skull, picked it up, and started walking. Katrina looked down at the man, looked at Gabrielle, and said, "Oh, well thanks for all the help!"

"Don't mention it! I know the stuff in these bags is real important," she replied sarcastically as always.

The alley had cleared by now, but they could sense the eyes peering from the windows and cracked doorways. The faint sound of distant sirens began to snake their way through the air. Katrina swung the man over her shoulder and they quickly ran back to the ship. They arrived just as the sun was starting to crest over the horizon. The captain was waiting for them at the gangway.

"Ah, just in time and bearing gifts! How thoughtful of you Madam," he joked.

"Not funny Olivar; this bastard is heavy," Katrina voiced her anger and glanced at Gabrielle.

Olivar grabbed the man by the back of the neck and lifted

him up in the air. He was still unconscious from the blow to the head.

"Food, work, or fun?" asked Olivar.

Katrina looked at him and smiled at the remark and said, "Information." She looked at Gabrielle and said, "Might be fun for her." Then pointing at the sharks in the water said, "Food for them if I don't like what he has to say."

The sun's rays hit the top of the sails by the time Gabrielle and Katrina disappeared below deck for their daily required slumber. It was a welcomed break after that night's events. Shortly after they had gone below, three stragglers from the night's shore pass stumbled onboard still drunk and dragging themselves along. Captain Olivar looked at the more sober one of the trio, handed him the man and said, "Here; secure this piece of shit below, release the wolves and make sure he doesn't get eaten in the process."

The sailor mockingly stood at attention, saluted, and dragged the man below along with his comrades.

"Holy shit this guy is heavy!" he said as they reached the bottom of the stairs.

A few minutes later, three Plebian Sucanis groggily walked on deck and sat next to Olivar.

"Stay alert. I don't know what the ladies got into, but it can't be good when they drag an unconscious man onto the ship," he said, as the gangway was brought up to secure the Invidia.

Odd Discovery
Chapter Nineteen

Gabrielle rose from her chamber and crawled out to the floor. She lay on the satin sheets and pillows she insisted were brought onboard for her and thought about the artifacts and notes she saw in the professor's shack. She wondered where he might be. Then it hit her; that thirst that slowly creeps at first rise, at the moment when the beast within begins to awaken. The hypos were great for sustenance, regeneration, and relaxation but at the end of such a long trip the blood got a bit stale. She threw on the first thing she found, which happened to be a leather trench coat, and walked out to see what was on the menu this morning. As she stepped out of her chambers and into the corridor one of the crew members was bringing a Plebian in for the night.

The Sucanis looked exhausted. Sweat poured from his body like water off a swimmer and his eyes were completely bloodshot. The sailor helped his shipmate to his bunk then stood at the doorway to make sure he was going to be okay.

"Those transformations can really take it out of them can't they?" Gabrielle whispered in the sailor's ears startling the man.

"Oh my God! You nearly scared me out of my shorts!" exclaimed the sailor.

"Is that all it would have taken," she coyly replied.

She pressed herself close against the sailor pushing him up against the wall. He took a deep breath as she grabbed him by the collar and slowly ran her tongue up the left side of his neck, up his face, and stopping at his lips to land a big wet kiss. She paused, looked straight into his eyes, and then dragged him into her quarters. The man gave little resistance.

She closed the door behind them and pulled him down to the sheets on the floor. He kissed her face and traveled down to her neck leaving kisses in his wake. She quickly spun her cheek and buried her fangs in his neck. She suckled on the wound long enough to gain her blood glow.

At that moment, she released him and slowly pushed his head down guiding his kisses to her breasts. Her skin erupted in goose bumps as his lips sucked at her flesh. Her excitement grew with his as she continued to drive his head passed her navel, down her belly, and finally between her legs. She wrapped a leg behind his neck as she took all the pleasure his mouth could give. As her arousal grew the air was filled with the aroma of her flowing juices. She turned him over, sat on his chest, and released his member from his pants. She then slowly slid down and took him in as she dropped and bit him on the shoulder to feed once again. Joined at both ends they writhed and bucked in rhythm until the excitement, or loss of blood was too much and he collapsed in her grasp. She continued to take his favors climbing in euphoria until she hit her climax and fell to the floor exhausted from the encounter.

She lay among the sheets basking in the sensation of the blood glow for a few moments then rose to her feet, energized by the crimson elixir. The sailor still did not move. She lifted him up off the sheets to his feet and walked him out the door. As they turned into the hallway Katrina appeared behind them.

"I see you've had your first meal," she commented as she helped her with his weight.

"And then some," said Gabrielle with a big fang-filled smile, eyes wide, looking like a Cheshire Cat.

"Must have been good, you just walked out into the main hallway on a ship full of men bare assed naked grinning like a fool," Katrina said, barely holding back the laughter. "Go ahead, I got this. Go get dressed."

Gabrielle released the sailor, stretched her arms out to her sides, turned her hands up, curled her fingers, and wiggled her ass with ever step all the way down the hall until reaching her doorway. She then looked back and gave one last wiggle before stepping through the door. When Katrina turned away to continue dragging the exhausted sailor, she was surprised by a mob of men cramped between the walls of the corridor, jockeying for position, and trying to get a better look at the spectacle. She handed the sailor over to the closest of them and slapped one of them, whose elicit thoughts just jumped out at her, clean across the face knocking him to the floor.

"Anyone else want my undivided attention?" she asked with a glare on her face.

The men all came to their senses very quickly, realizing who they were messing with and scurried off to carry on with their normal nighttime activities. Katrina walked to the cargo hold, passed the Sucanis holding cells, and entered the hold. Olivar was quietly talking to the man from the previous night. He was sitting in the center of the room, shaking like a leaf in the wind, and sipping a cup of tea he held in his hand.

"Ah, Mademoiselle Katrina Le Giroux, so good to see you this evening, let me introduce Señor Jesus Guadalupe Santa Maria de Concepcion. I think he's ready to talk," he said with a smile.

"What a name, quite a mouthful. I bet you were real popular in grade school. I guess your parent's wanted to cover all the bases when buying your salvation for the after-life. May I just call you Lupe, like one of your friends? I mean we are all friends here now, No?" Katrina said as she cast a look of pure death at the man.

Lupe was puzzled. How did this woman know what his friends called him? It could just as easy have been Jesse, or Chuey. He was scared.

"I'm sorry I missed the proceedings, how did it go Captain?" she said as she turned to Olivar.

"Oh it was quick. As soon as he saw me transform the bullshit ended and the stories just started flowing," replied the captain with a proud smirk on his face.

"That's just wonderful," Katrina replied and then something caught her attention and ruined her mood. "Lupe, you obviously are a dense person. How could you have those thoughts in my presence when I just gave you such a good hint as to what I can do? Since that's the approach you want to take in dealing with us, then so be it. I was so looking forward to a wonderful conversation with you, but I can't allow you to escape with your buddies that are watching the ship at this very moment, and tell them all about us," she said before reaching down and ripping into Lupe's neck, violently sucking the blood from his wound, and draining him till his extremities twitched as his body gave up the ghost.

Gabrielle walked in just as Lupe's body hit the floor.

"Damn it, I miss all the fun!" she exclaimed.

"Actually, you're just in time. We have a voyeur problem. I'm not sure how many, but they should be lurking around the warehouse at the dock. Can you take care of them for me?" Katrina asked Gabrielle.

"Oh, it shouldn't be a problem. Hey there Captain, feel up to a game of search and destroy? The one with the most hearts wins!" Gabrielle jostled Olivar.

"Let's do it!" he replied and flared his fangs to Gabrielle's complete delight.

"Okay, now let's not turn this into an 'innocent' killing frenzy. Make sure what you kill is an adversary," Katrina interjected. "I don't want any more attention drawn to our presence, and make it snappy. We need to get back to our mission here. I know where the professor is and getting him is going to be much harder than I anticipated."

Katrina walked back to her quarters as Gabrielle and the captain went to fetch their gear. They met at the main deck and scanned for any movement in order to get a general idea of where to begin.

"These guys must be experts. Even I can't detect their hides," said Captain Olivar.

"Yeah, I can't see them, but I can smell them," replied Gabrielle. "This just makes it more fun! How do we get off the ship without them knowing?" asked Gabrielle.

"I have an idea," Katrina popped up behind them and ushered them back down below deck.

A few minutes later a group of sailors appeared on deck carrying a large shipping crate between them. Katrina walked out and was barking orders guiding them to take the crate off the ship. They lowered the gangway and walked the crate to the side of one of the warehouses farthest from the dock. There was a loading dock there that happened to be completely in the dark. The crates disappeared from view. The men then walked back to the ship and carried on with their business as every other night. Some left the ship on pass, others walked guard duty, and the rest went to their quarters.

A few minutes later, the sound of the first bone cracking split the silence of the night. A few more followed in rapid succession. Gabrielle was the first to act. She fell upon an unsuspecting agent stooping behind an air handler on the roof of the nearest warehouse. He was holding a video device and was in no way prepared for the onslaught that befell him. The shocked expression of surprise was still on his face after Gabrielle twisted his neck snapping it like a twig. From there she could see the other locations and silently, yet swiftly, dispatched them. She only delayed a few seconds to drive her fist through their chest and harvest her kill-token. To her surprise, they were all human. The captain initially met with the same success, although not as fast, until following the scent of his last quarry and turning a corner in a dark section of a warehouse, he came face to face with another Canis. He immediately transformed, but it was almost too late. The Canis drew first blood, slashing at Olivar's chest. The pain was intense, but it drove the transformation to a quicker end. He bounced back and managed to get a bite grip on his opponent's shoulder. The still of the night was broken by the howl of pain uttered by the Canis. He struggled to pull Olivar off of him and attempted to return with a bite to the neck, but his efforts were foiled by the custom made Kevlar collar the captain wore. They fought for a few more seconds, rolled on the ground, knocked over equipment raising such a racket, and then finally the Canis managed to get a grip on Olivar, and ripped him away. To Olivar's surprise the Canis did not try to fight back instead he ran.

"Big mistake," said Gabrielle as she appeared from around a corner and sliced clean through the Canis' neck with her razor sharp Ghurka knife.

The Canis head dropped to the floor; the expression of conviction forever imprinted on his face. The body dropped, twitching for a few seconds before it just collapsed and lay like a bear skin rug in the middle of the floor. Blood was spilling everywhere. She reached in to the monster's chest and pulled out its heart. It was still pumping even though all the blood had already spilled out of it.

"Isn't it amazing how that happens? We are so dead that once we bite it, we are stiff as a board; not a sign of animation left in any part of us. You decapitate one of these sons of bitches and every part of their remains continues to fight for life," she said holding the heart for the captain to see as it continued to pump.

"I would guess you won this round my Lady," answered Olivar. "I'm a little fucked up here. We better drag him to the ship. I'll have a few of the guys come out and clean up the mess we made."

"Olivar, did you happen to see any surveillance cameras?" Gabrielle asked, remembering in shock the fact that their actions might have all been captured by some device."

"You mean these," Olivar said with a smile as he held up the mangled remains of what can only be assumed were video devices. "Why do you think it took me so long to get started?"

Gabrielle chuckled and said, "You sly devil, you; I see

R.N. Matos

why the Madame keeps you around."

Gabrielle helped Olivar up. He was holding his shoulder and was bleeding profusely from his chest.

"Hey, what the hell is that thing around your neck? I've never seen anything like that; and you, I thought you guys had a serious set of recuperative and regenerative powers? What happened?" Gabrielle asked excitedly as she points to his wound.

"We do, but the game changes when we fight each other. It will heal. It might take longer, but it will heal. As far as the thing around my neck, it's a collar I had made a few years back. I wear it whenever I'm going to see any action that could involve Canis or Legion. It had a telescopic design so that I can wear it under normal circumstances. Should I transform the loose fitting collar adjusts and becomes a tight seal around my neck protecting me from any edge weapon blows," replied Olivar.

He walks over to the mound of fur lying on the ground and scoops it up. Despite his injuries, he was still able to perform feats of incredible strength and agility. Gabrielle was impressed.

"I'd watch out for her, Captain, I think she's getting turned on," exclaimed Katrina, appearing out of the darkness. "Nice job, you guys. I guess Gabrielle won. What prize should we award her?"

"I think there are a few sailors on board that wouldn't mind being tasked with that mission," Olivar commented jokingly.

"Does that include you? You old Tomcat," Gabrielle returned the banter placing her hands on her hips, turning, and teasingly shaking her butt.

"Oh, stop it before I throw a bucket of cold water on the both of you!" exclaimed Katrina with a smile.

They all turned away and walked to the ship taking the body of the Canis below deck to the Grand Chamber. Gabrielle went to her quarters, throwing the Canis's head on a desk by her bunk. She walked to the galley holding the sack of hearts she collected and placed them on the counter. As she reached for the blender in the top cabinet, the captain peeks in.

"Katrina wants to talk to us. I guess it's some sort of debriefing. She's still stuck in her marshal ways," he said. "By the way, you want my hearts? I prefer sirloin to guts," he continued as he waves a blood stained, dripping sack.

"Bring it, I'll use it," she replied.

He tossed the sack to her and without turning around she snatched it out of the air and laid it next to hers. He walked away and headed towards the Grand Chamber.
"I'll be there in a minute," she called after him.

Gabrielle plugged in the blender, dropped a heart in, and started the blades. The noise attracted one of the sailors, who was walking past the door way. He looked in just in time to see her drop in another heart. His eyes opened wide, his skin turned a shade of green and began to sweat, just before he coughed and spewed vomit all over the floor.

"Hmm, squeamish are we?" Gabrielle asked sarcastically and smiled as she licked some blood off her finger.

The man doubled over holding his hands to his mouth and ran off.

"Better get someone to clean that mess up, 'cause I'm not going to do it, and I never forget a face," she yelled after him.

By the time she dropped the last heart into the blender the mixture was thick and frothy like a milkshake one might get at an upscale restaurant. She pulled the container off the base and starts to drink from it when another sailor shows up with a mop and bucket to clean up his comrade's mess. He arrived just in time to see her tipping the container up to her lips and notices some floaty things within the mixture, he watches as some of the blend spills down her cheek from the corner of her mouth. The man passes out and fall flat on his face.

"Oh, by the Dark, I don't get it! You can mop up a deck full of blood and gore, but you can't watch a girl have a meal? Can we get someone in here with some intestinal fortitude to clean this mess up!" she yelled as she walked down the corridor to meet with Katrina and Olivar.

Gabrielle arrived at the Grand Chamber to find the body of the Canis they had killed lying on the conference table. Katrina and Olivar were inspecting this specimen as if searching for something.

"Eeeck- Oh, don't tell me he has fleas!" she said with a look of total disgust; shaking her free hand as if trying to repel something.

"Show some intestinal fortitude, will ya!" Katrina said sarcastically with a smile.

Gabrielle smirked and joined them at the table. Katrina held up the Canis's left shoulder so Gabrielle could see the tattoo on its deltoid.

"What the hell is that? I've never seen that before," said Gabrielle.

"I'm not sure; I've never seen anything like it either. Except for this symbol here: it's a Swiss Guard symbol," replied Katrina. "I thought getting to the professor was going to be hard before. If he is being guarded by these guys, we have some serious problems. I already knew the professor was held up in the Cathedral of Our lady of the Ascension, I was unaware these guys were involved. I guess Lupe managed to hide something from me after all," Katrina commented.

"So, does this mean there are Canis in the Vatican Guard?" asked Olivar.

"Great, it's not enough we have the freaking Nachtshutz hunting us, now we have to worry about religious fanatic knuckle-draggers, no offense intended to you- Oli," Katrina exclaimed, apologetically catching herself at the end of her outburst.

"Don't worry my Lady, I consider myself a more advance species of knuckle-dragger, too refined for this riff-raff," he said laughing.

"I'm not sure. Do you think in the wake of the new discoveries and the New World order, the Church has found new allies?" Katrina pondered out loud.

"If that's the case, then what else are we up against?" Olivar asked the obvious question.

They all just looked at each other with great concern.

"Okay, the end game here is to find Vlad. The professor is just a means to an end. How do we snatch this guy long enough to get what we need from him?" Katrina said.

"Wait, this part never came up in our conversations. What do you mean find Vlad? Are we going to go dig him up from the bottom of the Pyramids? You can count me out. If we find him, if he's alive, and if we pull him out he's going to be one pissed off, extremely thirsty blood raging vampire! I saw him pissed just once before and I don't think I ever want to go there again!" she exclaimed with real concern.

"I don't know where he is, or if he's even alive. But then, if he weren't alive why would the Potentate hand me an assassination order for Vlad?" replied Katrina. "How many times can one kill or phase the same vampire?"

"I've always heard the legends, but never believed them. They all seemed so fantastic. Do you think they are real?" Olivar mentioned.

"I heard the same. We both have. I always thought they were stories he drummed up to bolster his reputation, but then again, here we are," Katrina said, anger evident all over her face.

"I watched him get ripped to shreds, I saw that whole area collapse, and I pulled Professor Rosell out alone barely escaping with our lives. How can it be possible that Vlad is once again among the living?" Gabrielle's usual sarcasm was giving way to the fear seeping into her cold dead heart.

"You're standing on a three hundred year old ship, talking to a vampire and a werewolf, over the corpse of a werewolf with a tattoo containing a Vatican symbol, and you wonder how it's possible? I might not have the answers, but I no longer question the possibility of anything," Katrina quietly said, as she sank in to her seat.

"Well, we know what we are up against. We better do some serious planning, and I would seriously consider using the Sucanis on this one," Captain Olivar interjected, in an attempt to curtail the escalation of the tone of the current conversation.

Katrina looked at him, sighed away her desperation, and said, "You're right. No matter what, we have to analyze the current situation, and plan for everything or this might turn into the most terrible mistake we ever make."

Gabrielle knocked the corpse off the table and said, "Let's do it."

They all sat down and discussed the events of the past days. They searched through the junk gathered at the shack, they watched the video captured from the spies, and formulated a plan to take the professor the next night.

Nuestra Señora de la Asuncion
Chapter Twenty

It was a still night. The sky was speckled with the pinhole lights flickering from the stars. The full moon was slowly rising, a welcomed sign for the captain as he readied the pack for the night's actions. Sucanis are vicious, uncontrollable beasts if left to their own devices, but in the hands of a skilled Canis using their natural instinctive powers of communication, they are formidable adversaries.

Legion who possess telepathic abilities are able to control Sucanis to a degree, but in battle it's the Canis that are unmatched at this task. The natural ability of a pack to operate in unison towards a common goal is not lost on the cursed Canis or Sucanis. It is this ability that Katrina trusted would work in their favor on that night. She gave them space as Olivar went down into the hold and sat among the Sucanis to await that night's transformation, which had to be triggered by the moon to gain its full effect and power. The horrific sounds that managed to seep through the boards from below deck sent chills through the nerves of the sailors no matter how many times they'd heard those sounds before. A few minutes later, Olivar rose from the dark stairwell, a team of Sucanis following close behind, loaded down with all manner of weapons. They cheered as he transformed.

Katrina joined them on the gangway. Gabrielle had gone ahead to scout the church. Katrina handed Olivar a headset and radio. Even though she could read his mind, he couldn't read hers. Communication was paramount in executing the intricate plan they had devised. There was no allowable margin of failure. Any mistake would cost them their lives. Katrina lowered the gangway herself in respect for her comrade, turned to her team, and said, "to the last breathe."

The full moon gave them a distinct advantage. The Sucanis squad moved out quietly and unseen. There were plenty of shadows created by the buildings and trees of the city contrasted by the bright open areas that allowed for better visibility when looking out for innocents and foes.

They gathered at the tree line of the park between Marina Mercante and Ignacio Zaragoza across the street from the dock. The streets were busy, but there were just enough lulls in the traffic to allow for intermittent travel across the roads. The support teams set up at their perspective battle points along the way. Finally the assault team gathered at the base of the Plaza de Armas and assembled for the ensuing action. They waited silently for Katrina's signal.

Then the moment came. The guards around the church were on a shift rotation. At that time every night, a man identified as a member of the Swiss Guard walked the perimeter, inspecting the grounds; that night was no different. As soon as the man appeared, Katrina called over the radio, "Green."

Olivar and the first element of the assault team, designated Alpha, sprang into action, and quickly took down the sentries. He drove his silver blade through the center of the Guard's heart. Olivar and the Alpha team dragged the sentries away and stashed their bodies under the bushes. The team quickly entered the main vestibule. Keeping to the shadows they set up for the second stage of the assault.

Olivar only had to think- we are ready- and Bravo team executed stage two. The Sucanis teams, hidden near intersections between the Cathedral and the dock, blasted down power lines and knocked over poles causing widespread blackouts and stopping traffic. As soon as the lights went out in the church, Alpha team ran through the church searching for the professor. The priests, nuns, and friars were unprepared for the onslaught that ensued. In the dimly lit vestibule and cavernous passageways of the Cathedral, the candlelight offered by the shrines and candelabras was not enough to see the terrors coming. They only elevated the fear in the Sucanis' victims, as flashing shadows flew around them leaving a trail of crimson splattered stucco walls. In their panic the priests and friars tripped on the bodies and slipped on the blood pooling on the terracotta floors. Only the ones who huddled together in a circle of prayer were spared. Lucky for them, the leader of Alpha team respected their Lord, even if he no longer followed him.

Olivar, driven by Katrina's telepathic visions, locked on his target like a cruise missile. He ran through the passageways, up the stairs leading to the old bell tower, directly to a hidden chamber, knocked the heavy wooden door off its metal hinges, and stared down into the surprised eyes of Professor Ronald Rosell.

The professor knew there was no escape and rushed to grab his satchel of important papers. Before he could make a move, Olivar snatched him up and threw him over his shoulder. Part of the team led the way through the Cathedral corridors, out the back exits, and to the courtyard in the rear. The others collected as much of the Professor's things as possible and followed.

It was in the courtyard that things went sour. As they

moved through the meticulously landscaped garden enclosed by a fifteen-foot wall, they quickly realized they had run into an ambush. At the end of the garden, standing between them and the gate, were four Canis bearing silver plated spears. Olivar commanded four Sucanis from Alpha team to attack the Canis. The rest followed him as they back-tracked in an attempt to flee the way they came. It was a futile attempt. Waiting for them at the entrance were creatures stranger than they; gargoyles. Olivar was momentarily stunned and lost control of his pack. The pack went berserk and attacked the gargoyles viciously. The gargoyles turned their claws to stone, buried them in their attacker's hearts, and dropped their victims to the ground.

The Canis at the gate had managed to take advantage of Olivar's temporary loss of composure and claimed control of the four Sucanis he had sent against them. The situation was looking grim for the operation, until suddenly the courtyard was filled with howls and growls coming from the top of the wall that surrounded it.

It was Bravo Team poised to attack from the top of the wall. A menacing site even for the stone hearted gargoyles. Being out-numbered by a pack of Sucanis is never a good thing. Olivar, though, had fought too many battles to allow the bloodshed that would inevitably ensue should he charge. He had grown to appreciate his ship mates too much to allow them to be slaughtered needlessly. He opted for evasion. Olivar launched the professor to the top of the wall and then leapt to the waiting arms of his fellow Canis. The remainder of Alpha Team followed. The gargoyles reached for the stragglers who barely escaped their grasp. The gargoyles could not proceed beyond the walls and stood angrily watching the intruders escape.

The Sucanis assault team ran through the streets of Veracruz completely hidden in the darkness caused by the blackout. A few pedestrians who had been caught in the streets at the moment the lights went out were startled by the sensations that something had just brushed past them very quickly. It was one of those moments that cause one's skin to erupt in goose bumps and the hairs in the back of your neck rise on end from a chill in the spine. The next day the radio station would surely be flooded with tales of ghosts in the night, and possibly some Chupacabra sightings.

The Canis from the Cathedral followed, determined to retrieve their charge. They chased the Sucanis, following the professor's scent. They diligently followed the signs left behind, delayed only by random and swift attacks by the Sucanis that showed extraordinary skill in their retrograde actions, while trying to avoid contact with the human population of Veracruz. The trail led them to the park at the corner of Marina Mercante and Ignacio Zaragoza. The leader sniffed the air, but could find no sign of their quarry. It was as if they had vanished, but something told him they were still around. He just couldn't see where.

The trees!

It was too late; Olivar's Canis fell upon them knocking them all to the ground. Then, like a flash, Katrina and Gabrielle appeared severing their heads with those ominous silver plated Gurkhas before they could rise up off the ground. When it comes to the Legion, speed definitely kills.

"Hi there lover," Gabrielle said with a smirk. "Did you really think you could hide from me forever?"

The professor said nothing. He was in too much shock from the experience to utter a word. Olivar pulled him off the tree, where he had been placed by one of the Sucanis, and handed him over to Gabrielle. They all quickly moved out of the tree line and crossed the street. In the commotion caused by the blackout and traffic jam the entire party was able to get to the dock and slip onto the ship without being detected. Once on the ship the Sucanis were locked away to rest and recuperate from that night's action. The sailors had already prepared the ship to set sail. Provisions had been brought aboard and the sails were inspected, tested and adjusted. Gabrielle took the professor to the conference room and sat him down. One of the sailors brought in his stuff, at least what survived. Professor Rosell sprang to life.

"Is my laptop here?" he asked.

"What does it look like?" asked the sailor.

"What does it look like? Are you kidding me? Have I just got on the Neanderthal Boat? Gabrielle, please, tell me someone grabbed my baby?" he pleaded.

Gabrielle coyly walked over and slowly pulled the laptop out from behind her back. She moved so fast that he never noticed when she took it from the top of the pile the sailor brought in.

"Here you go, lover!" she said as she toyed with him.
Katrina walked in to find the professor feverishly inspecting his laptop computer while Gabrielle licked his neck with her arms wrapped around him from behind.

"Do I need to lock him up for the day while we rest or do you think he will behave?" Katrina asked Gabrielle.

"Once we set sail, what choice does he have?" replied Gabrielle. "It's either us or the sharks and he can't swim with that laptop. I think we're good."

Olivar walked into the conference room. He looked uncharacteristically distraught.

"How many?" asked Katrina. Already knowing what he would say. She just thought if he talked about it there would be a chance for release.

"We lost three. Melchor was among them. I was really getting to like that guy. He loved to get under my skin, but he was a good trooper. One of the gargoyles got him. Speaking of, what the hell was that all about? I had heard legends of the stone men, but what the fuck?" he said, his sadness quickly turning to anger. "How did we not know about them?"

"I think these are all questions the professor can answer, but the sun will be coming up soon. We'll have to interrogate him tomorrow night. It shouldn't be difficult," Katrina said as she started to walk away.

"We should be shoving off shortly. I've already given the order. I won't be resting today. I want to make sure we aren't pursued and I want to avoid any Federal entanglements. Once in International waters, I might catch a few winks, unless the pirates decide to take another crack at us," he said to her as she walked away.

"I wouldn't worry about the pirates. Trust me they won't soon forget this ship," Gabrielle reassured Olivar.

Katrina turned back and gave everyone a nod then disappeared.

Gabrielle took the professor by the hand and walked him to her quarters. Olivar watched them walk down the corridor, and then called one of the sailors. He told him to guard that door and make sure that egghead doesn't leave that room until nightfall. The sailor understood.

Olivar walked to the main deck and threw his blades down at his feet, sticking them into the wood floor, and stood watch over his ship as it pulled away from the dock. In the distance he could see the commotion their night time activities had caused. As they were clearing the bay, a line of police vehicles drove onto the port and parked where the Invidia had docked. Some officers got out of their cars and waved their arms gesturing for the Invidia to return to port. Olivar just smiled and waved good bye.

The radio came alive with Spanish chatter, as the Harbor Master was ordering them to return. It seemed the authorities wished to discuss something. Olivar ignored them, too. By the time the Coast Guard arrived, the Invidia had crossed into International waters and Olivar just waved at them, too. Olivar knew that getting into port in Tampa was going to be a little bit more tricky than usual.

We'll have to cross that bridge when we get to it.

R.N. Matos

Under New Management
Chapter Twenty-one

It was a very hectic week for Barabas. All the administrative preparations had been taken care of, the new staff was hired, and all the proper notices were sent out announcing the fact that the Castle was under new management. The impending visit from the Protectorate and its inspection would soon come. Lady Celeste made all her necessary adjustments and announcements declaring herself the new manager. In order for their charade to work, Celeste would have to appear to break all ties and allegiances with Madame Katrina. The most dangerous part of the scheme was the interview with the Protectorate agent. He would undoubtedly possess some sort of power that enabled him to detect falsehoods, maybe even read minds.

"I think it's best if you take an extended vacation, so that I can meet with them alone. If you are here and the Protectorate's agent happens to be another mind reader it could mean the end of it all," she said.

"Thank you, my Lady, but I wouldn't know what to do with myself on a vacation. I might drive myself crazy from boredom," he replied.

"You might find yourself dead from sudden loss of blood syndrome if you give the right answer to the wrong question when the Protectorate interviews you," she replied with a hint of sarcasm for effect.

"Oh, that is true. I see your point. Not to mention putting you and the Madame at great peril. I think I believe a trip to see my aunt in Miami is in order. I'm sure she will be just thrilled to see me," he said with a touch of humor.
Celeste gave him the screw face look of – that's not good enough.

"Ah, not far enough eh, maybe my brother in the Bahamas?" he asked.

"That sounds more like it. The Protectorate won't go through all that trouble, and it won't matter later. Especially, when the money starts rolling in, and the blood keeps everyone in the glow," she said.

Sergei walked into the office.

"Excuse me, just 'cause I fuck you doesn't mean you walk into my office without knocking," Celeste reprimanded him.

"Uh, sorry," he said as he turned back and knocked on the door.

Celeste shook her head and said, "Who is it?"

Sergei stood at the door with a puzzled look on his face and softly replied, "Uh, it's me, Sergei."

"Fuck off, I'm in a meeting," she replied.

"Oh okay, but the painters are done. They want you to look at the place, and they want to get paid," he said even more puzzled than a second ago.

"Fuck 'em," she said laughing from the other side of the door.

She didn't get a response, she just heard his footsteps recede and go down the stairs.

"Go after him, before we end up with paint splattered all over the place. These guys don't know who they are messing with, but they seem to have very little sense of humor. I wouldn't want to have to paint the walls with their blood," she told Barabas.

He was out the door by mid phrase. Celeste just laughed and followed. She walked down the stairs and looked at the walls, the stairs, the rails, and the ceiling.

These guys do good work. I'm glad Barabas recommended them.

She walked out onto the dance floor and looked around. It all looked very good. She was impressed. The black and red motif was carried out expertly. The different tones of red accented by black on the walls were a striking touch. The mahogany floor accented with red lines between the boards was an unusual touch that tied the floor in with the rest of the room.

"Thank you, gentlemen; I am very pleased. I expect you will be our guests at the grand re-opening," she said as she extended her hand in greeting and their check in the other.

"We are usually very busy, but I've always been curious about this place and the women that frequent it, so I'll have to come by. Not sure about my partner though, he's squeamish. The sight of blood makes him faint," the man said with a chuckle.

Celeste smiled.

The men had already packed their equipment and walked out the door as soon as they received the compliments and the check from Celeste.

"Barabas, call the staff. I want to have a final meeting before the opening this weekend. Make sure everyone is here tomorrow night," Celeste ordered.

"You do realize that they are all human, we don't have a Legion among them yet," said Barabas.

"I don't care. Some of them want to be Legion, they might as well start acting like one," she replied. "In fact, anyone who does not make it in time to the meeting will be demoted to Sangus. If they don't like it they can forget about working here. I have a stack of resumes from hopefuls begging to work here, so not my problem."

Celeste then turned to Sergei and said," Hungry yet?"
"I could do with a late night snack, before hitting the chamber," he said nonchalantly.

"I feel like a hunt. Let's see what's out and about in Ybor tonight," Celeste replied. "I'm going to put something a little less appropriate and more revealing on."

"You go ahead and do that I'll lock up and put the car in the garage. I suppose we won't need it tonight," Sergei said and walked away.

Barabas walked back to the office, picked up his briefcase, and walked out to the parking lot. Sergei was returning from the garage and met Barabas at the side of the building as he drove by in his Mercedes.

"I don't know how you do it B; stay up all night with us and then take care of your stuff during the day. I really don't know. Sometimes I think you're a closet vamp," Sergei joked with Barabas as he drove by.

"You two be careful, this thing with the Protectorate scares me. I wouldn't be surprised if he already has someone watching our every move," replied Barabas and then drove away.

Being a newbie to the Legion, Sergei had no idea what the implications of what Barabas was saying were. He opened the door just in time to catch Celeste walking down the stairs from the office. Her bright red curly hair pulled up in a geisha-style bun, held together with chop sticks, and strands of curls hanging down the sides perfectly framed her alabaster face. Her green eyes accented by the black eyeliner and eye shadow in stark contrast to her ultra pale complexion complimented her voluptuous black painted lips. She wore a long brocade black highwayman's coat with dragons and roses embroidered into the fabric, accented with thorns and skull shaped buttons. Under the coat she wore a long sleeved mid-drift-bearing black fishnet top that exposed everything except her black tape covered nipples. Her long legs stretched down for each step on the staircase, teasing the eyes with the rise of the black and red plaid mini skirt decorated by the same thorn accents on her coat, and right at the moment of pubic reveal it dipped down again leaving Sergei to question; panties - no panties? A tightly cinched spiked buccaneer style belt held it all together. Her legs adorned by sheer black knee high stockings and a pair of Doc Martens Marnie style shoes. She looked stunning; in a Gothy kind of way. Sergei was dumbstruck.

"So, are you just going to stand there and gawk or are you going to say the words I want to hear?" She snapped.

"Dude, you look awesome!" Sergei, struggled, but finally got the words out.

"Not exactly what I wanted to hear, but I'll take it," she said with an air of disappointment. "Pick your tongue up off the floor and let's get on with it. I need to kill something."

They walked out of the club, passed the parking lot, and crossed the street to Centro Ybor. Not a bad place to survey the crowd and get a pulse of the action for the night.

"Not much of a crowd tonight. That damn hockey game must have driven away some of the usual patrons," Celeste observed with some disappointment.

"The college is always a promising alternative," said Sergei.

They walked back out into the street and turned up 9th heading towards Centennial Park.

"How about Crow Bar or Prana?" asked Celeste.

"I'd rather go to the Bone Yard. They seem a little more tolerant of us," replied Sergei.

"Yeah, but that's cause they get free drinks at our place. I don't know how accommodating they would be if that policy changed. Doesn't matter, we get what we want out of them. I think I'm just going to stroll over to the park and just ambush some lonely unsuspecting derelict, get the hunt bug out of my system and then you and I can go home and enjoy each other. What do you think?" said Celeste.

"I think that would be a good idea, but," Sergei said before he was interrupted by a voice from behind them on the corner of 17th.

"Oh my God, you guys look awesome! That is such a cool outfit. Where did you get those shoes," a pair of college girls wearing their Greek Gamma Delta allegiance shirts marveled and praised Celeste's wardrobe.

Celeste could not believe her luck. She was ready to give up, go slay a hobo when fate stepped in and turned the course of the night. That was too bad for the Gamma sisters. The night also had greater promise for Sergei. Celeste wasn't known for her generosity and she really didn't like to share, but when blood was the currency all is acceptable. The evening started with, "And how may we make you lovely ladies' evening an unforgettable one?" Sergei practiced using his newly acquired silver tongue. It would have sounded like a total come on and lame pick up line coming from any mortal, but it rolled off the lips of this Legion like honey into the Gamma sisters' ears. They strolled down 17th and wandered into the Green Iguana. The usual stares from the crowd emphasized how out of place they were in this crowd. Then again, it would be hard for this group to find somewhere they didn't look out of place, of course, barring the Castle. Still, Celeste rejected the Gamma's offer to find another place.

"Don't worry about it. I'm not uncomfortable to be here, you girls look fine," she joked and they laughed.

They patiently stood waiting to be seated, and then Celeste got upset when someone was seated before them and used her usual charm to get a booth. She leaned over to the hostess and said, "You don't get us a booth in the next ten seconds I'm bleeding you dry by morning." She flashed some fang for effect. In no time at all, a booth was made available in the back by the bar.

"Amazing what people can do when properly motivated," Celeste said staring at the hostess with a smirk.

They sat at the booth, and a few seconds later a waitress stopped by to take their order. She leaned over and flashed a little cleavage for Sergei's benefit. Celeste was not amused, but Sergei seemed to be enjoying himself so she put up with the flirtation for a moment. The Gamma girls were a little put off.

"Excuse me, bar wench, there are ladies at the table and anyone of us could be his date.

Celeste was impressed by their companions. She stepped in before things got a little out of hand.

"Ladies, ladies, let's just take it down a notch. I don't think you want to upset a Legion even if she is - serving. I wonder how a Legion becomes a bar maid in a human bar? Have we done something naughty or are we just that good?" Celeste said and then grabbed the bar maid's wrist and twisted it to expose the small blood brand on the inside of her forearm.

"I would be more careful of what you do next," said the bar maid.

Celeste stared at the brand and said, "I'll keep that in mind. Get me a bottle of that new Vampire brand blood wine. I haven't tasted it; we may bring it in to - The Castle.

The bar maids tone changed and said, "What will everyone else have?"

R.N. Matos

"I would like a classic Mojito made with Matusalem® rum please," said one of the Gamma's.

"I'll take a Whiskey Sour on the rocks," said the other.
"What is Matusalem®?" asked Sergei.

"A rum made by Cuban Americans in the old-style Cuban tradition from an old family recipe," replied the Gamma.

The night moved on just fabulously. Celeste even forgot her objective for the night. The girls from Gamma ingratiated themselves to one of the toughest members of the most murderous, calculating predators on the planet. At this point they felt very safe. Then, all the levity just dissipated when two meat heads were guided to the table next to them. These were no ordinary meatheads: these were major league assholes. As soon as they sat down, it started.

"Yo, Joey, what's up wit' da odd bunch ovah theah'," said Mike the biggest of the two.

"I don' know Mike, but that pale one in the Goth outfit looks like she needs some swellin' lovin'," replied Joey.

They spoke loud enough for everyone within three tables to hear. They were of the obnoxious type with an unascertainable Italian, Georgian, maybe Bostonian accent.

"How about I give you some swellin' right around your eye," Sergei rose up from the table ready to pounce.

Celeste put her arm up and pulled her jengal down.

"Umm, I love it when a man comes to my rescue, but the Goth girl doesn't need any kind of swellin', and even less protection. I'd be more careful who you address in such a loathsome fashion around this neighborhood," Celeste growled as she leaned over the top of the booth reaching over to the jerks.

"Someone's on da' rag," Joey said laughing right in her face.

That was all Sergei could stand. He got up, pushed Celeste out of the way, reached over, grabbed Joey by the neck, and pulled him out of his booth and into the air.

"Say another word and I'll rip your heart out of your chest and show it to you," Sergei said, ready to launch Joey across the table.

Celeste moved just in time, preventing Sergei from killing this moron in front of their guests and the world. Just as quickly the waitress and the manager showed up at their booth.

"Is there a problem here?" barked the manager.

"These jerks have been harassing her ever since they sat down!" yelled one of the Gammas.

"Hey, dis fuckin' mook put his paws on my boy heah. What ya gonna do 'bout that?" protested Mike. Weez jus' sittin' heah waitin' fo' our drinks, and this punchy fuck grabs my boy like a rag doll and dangles him ovah ma head."

The waitress looked at the manager. He shook his head and said, "Sorry gentlemen, but you're going to have to leave."

Just as he finished that sentence, a group of extremely large individuals stepped up and curtailed any more protests from Mike or Joey.

"Dis is fah from ovah," Joey leaned over and told Sergei

as they were escorted out by the manager and his henchmen.

"Good riddance," said the Gamma girl.

"Waitress, we are ready to order," said Celeste.

The Gamma girls ordered their food and Celeste ordered another bottle of blood wine. Sergei just sat, still seething from the commotion. He finally took another glass of blood wine and sipped from it. He hadn't been drinking blood long, but this bottled stuff still took some getting used to. It just wasn't enough to satisfy his blood lust especially after the incident with the two meat heads. He was starting to look at the Gammas with an added interest. Celeste just smiled and did her best to help keep Sergei under control until the right moment. The tension grew within the group. The Gammas mistook the attentions from Sergei as nothing more than sexual flirtation and coyly reveled in the moment. They enjoyed every minute of the cat and mouse fondling under the table. Celeste enjoyed every minute plotting their demise. After the meal and a few drinks they all walked outside.

"Hey, thanks for letting us hang out with you. We had never really been brave enough to approach one of you and get to know them. It was fun," said one of the Gammas.

"Yeah, we have to get back to the house, we have a busy day tomorrow," said the other.

Sergei wrapped his arm around one and said, "It doesn't have to be over. The night is young; there are so many places to explore, and so much to experience."

He pulled her up and planted a wet kiss. She was captivated by his touch. She closed her eyes as she accepted his lips. She sighed and nearly collapsed in his arm as he held her weight.

"Oh, but really we need to get back," said the other one.

Sergei paid no attention and walked the girl further down the sidewalk.

"I think your sister has other ideas. If you prefer, you can go on home, we'll take care of her and get her home safely," Celeste said with deep concern on her face.

The Gamma looked at her friend, then at Celeste and said, "I have a lot to do tomorrow, but I can't leave her out here. I'll come along for her sake. She seems to be having fun. I don't want to ruin the night for her."

Celeste kept the Gamma entertained with an in-depth discussion of the nuances of Goth fashion. They spoke of brand name versus thrift store purchases, and the interesting emergence of Goth sub-culture into certain areas of the mainstream. All this served as a distraction to get the Gamma sisters to Centennial Park. At the park they made their way to the center of the park and sat on the concrete ledges under the trees.

Sergei and his Gamma were engaged in a vicious bout of tonsil hockey. Celeste continued to distract the other Gamma and initiated some physical contact by demonstrating how some creative use of black could enhance her look. Celeste put both her hands on the Gamma's face and was about to go in for the jugular kill, when a familiar voice called to her from behind.

"I told ya it wasn't ovah!" Joey called out to them standing in the shadow of the trees.

At this point the anticipation of a fresh kill and meal had gotten the best of Sergei and he was in full fang attack mode with blood red eyes. Instantly Sergei dropped his Gamma and jumped to Celeste's side. Celeste was irritated; she hadn't tasted a virgin in years. She turned to her Gamma, fangs brightly shining in the night, and said, "Run!"

The two girls quickly sobered up and tore down the street like the devil was chasing them with a pitchfork and their asses were on fire.

"Oh you two meat heads have obviously mistaken us for chumps," Sergei said glaring at his next meal.

"Nah, no mistake heah," said Mike as he pulled out a pair of stakes.

"Wanna be vamp hunters," Celeste smiled.

"Wanna be nothin' we're full fledge members of the Nachtschutz," said Joey.

In a split second and before anyone else could say another word, Celeste pulled an iron spike off the garden fence surrounding the bottom of the trees, jumped over to Joey, blocked his feeble attempt at striking her, and drove her fangs deep into his neck instantly dropping him to the ground. She ripped a deep gash into his flesh and stood up. She let the blood pour down her chin and onto her chest. It panicked Mike and he attacked with a violent thrust of a stake. He wasn't quick enough. Before the point of Mike's weapon could find its mark, Sergei broke the stake with one swipe of his hand, and landed on top of him dumping him to the ground. Sergei gorged on his victim ripping the flesh from his chest and sucking up every drop of blood in the man's body.

"I don't want to be like you," gurgled Joey through his crushed larynx as blood seeped through the wound.

"You don't have to worry about that, Joey. You're just my most recent meal," she said as she pulled him up, bit into his neck, slammed him to the ground, and helped Sergei drain him dry. "Nachschutz my ass," she said as the last twitch of life trembled through Joey's body.

This was not what Celeste had in mind when she set out on a midnight hunt. This was too big of a mess to just leave it in such a public place.

"Sergei, call Barabas. Tell him we need a clean up job.
Barabas showed up an hour later. Two men got out of the Mercedes and Celeste and Sergei got in.

"What the fuck?" was Barabas first words.

"It was an accident. They attacked us; said they were Nachschutz," defended Sergei.

"And you believed them?" replied Barabas looking at Celeste.

"Watch your tone old man; I've already done one thing I regret tonight. Don't make me increase my regret," said Celeste with a sneer.

"Okay, okay, don't get excited. I'm only concerned that this might have drawn some attention. Attention we don't need at the moment. I would much rather be the object of your regret, than the focus of Lady Katrina's rage if we mess this up for her," Barabas said remembering who he was talking to.

"I agree, so make this go away," she replied.

"I don't get it. Isn't this what we do?" asked Sergei.

"It's what we used to do," said Celeste. "With the rise of the New Minority and the treaty of Global Acceptance, we were supposed to adhere to certain rules. We just broke one of them."

"But, they attacked us," replied Sergei.

"Yeah, try to tell that to a jury of humans after they hear of our little encounter at the Green Iguana," replied Celeste, getting angrier by the minute at how the whole night had progressed.

"What about the Gamma girls?" Sergei reminded Celeste.

"We may have to kill them too," Celeste said further regretting the decision to go on a simple hunt.

"Gamma girls, there were witnesses?" asked Barabas with frustration.

Celeste just looked at him with complete defiance.

The two men knocked on the trunk lid, Barabas hit a button, the trunk lid opened, and the men tossed in two black vinyl bags. They walked to Barabas's window; he slid the window open with the press of another button, and said, "Hay unas muchachas tambien. Traiganlas al club."

He turned to Celeste and asked, "How can they identify the girls?"

"They were wearing Gamma Delta sweat shirts," replied Celeste. "But they left over an hour ago, how the hell are they going to find them?"

"Did any of you touch them?" asked Barabas.

"That dope made out with one," said Celeste pointing at her boyfriend.

Barabas opened the window nearest Sergei and one of the men leaned in. Barabas gestured to Sergei to open his mouth. The man closed his eyes smelled Sergei's breath, inhaled as much as he could, and then walked away.

"How about the other one?" asked Barabas.

"Well, I touched her with my hands," said Celeste.

Barabas lowered the other window and the man walked over, reached in, pulled Celeste's hands up to his face, and licked both of them quickly before Celeste could pull away. He then looked into the darkness and walked away.

"Who the hell are those guys and why do you want them to bring the girls back to the club?" asked Celeste. "You expect me to kill them there?"

"The two gentlemen in question are what we call Kirkos. They are mystics from the old world," he answered.

"Legion?" asked Celeste.

"No, just hired hands, they'll find those girls, and what you do with them is your problem, but we have to get to those girls before they say anything to anyone about what they saw. This isn't just about the human related consequences; it's about the Legion's eagerness to take the club away from us. We can't give them any excuse," Barabas explained.

They drove off and headed towards the Castle. It was a short ride, but a necessary one. The two vampires were in no condition to be seen by anyone. Barabas parked on the side of the building where the staircase outside the club led to the back door and the office on the second floor. Celeste and Sergei climbed the stairs in the dark and walked into the club. Barabas drove around and parked the car behind the building. As he neared the front door of the club he was met by the Kirkos holding the Gamma girls who appeared to have fainted. He opened the door to the club, let the two Wraiths in, and followed them. He then closed the door and led them across the dance floor and to the stairs at the back of the club. They climbed to the second floor and opened the door to the office. Two blades zipped past Barabas on each side of his head, split the Kirkos' heads wide open, and dropped them to the ground. The two girls they were holding tumbled to the floor.

"I'm gone for a few days and look at the mess you guys get me into," said Katrina eerily staring at Barabas as Gabrielle walked over and picked up her blades.

"Um, sweet meat. Where did these two come from? Planning a feast in our absence?" Gabrielle added as she stroked one of the girls hair, while the Gamma girls were slowly recovering.

Barabas stood in complete shock without saying a word.

"Oh, don't worry about those two goons. They were going to betray us the first chance they got anyway. Now the girls are a different matter, they were so scared they ran all the way to the dorm, and shut themselves in the room, but they will eventually blab," said Katrina as she turned to her understudy, "What do we do Celeste?"

"I guess we have to kill them too," she replied.

"That would be the obvious thing, and I'm sure Gabrielle would be just ecstatic to rid us of them, but we need to think beyond that. If we just kill them, people will be looking for them and everyone saw you with them I suppose," stated Katrina.

"Um-um, didn't anyone teach you not to play with your food," Gabrielle found it amusing to torment Celeste and did so any chance she got.

"Did anyone ever teach you to respect your elders?" Katrina shot back, in an attempt to put Gabrielle in her place.

Gabrielle smirked and walked out. "I'll make sure the professor is comfortable," she said as she left the office.

The Gamma girls came to, just as Gabrielle was walking out.

"What's happening here? How did we get here? Oh my God, don't kill us please," said one of the Gamma girls as she looked around the room and recognized Sergei and Celeste.

The other panicked and started screaming. Celeste sprang to her and cupped her hand over her mouth and shushed her quiet. The other one was too stunned to say anything.

"Barabas, you may leave now. Close the door behind you. Wait in the lobby. I'll take care of everything from here on, and Barabas, yes: I'm very disappointed," Katrina directed the threat to Barabas as a reminder that he is only worth the weight of his last accomplishment.

Barabas left quietly with his eyes looking down at the ground in order to avoid any eye contact with anyone else in the room.

Celeste grabbed both the Gamma sisters by the arms, walked them to Katrina's desk, and sat them in chairs in front of it. Katrina walked around the desk and started to speak.

"So, what attracted you to them?" she asked.

"Well, they looked so innocent and their blood was just calling to me," Celeste began to explain but was interrupted by Katrina.

"I wasn't talking to you," said Katrina. "I was asking the Gammas."

The two girls glanced around in panic as tears streamed from their eyes.

"Oh come now, you must have known they were Legion. You are college girls, not maidens locked away in a convent. Let's go, I already know the answer, I just want to hear it from your own lips," said Katrina surprising the Gammas.

"We just thought they looked cool," gasped one of the sisters.

"Yeah, we didn't mean any harm. We just wanted to say we had hung out with vampires, I mean, Legion," said the other.

"We won't tell anyone, we promise. We'll act like nothing ever happened," said the first.

Katrina startled the girls with her abrupt laughter. Celeste and Sergei were also startled. Everyone watched her laugh not knowing what was so funny and afraid to ask what the joke was.

"How appropriate, Lindsey and Brittany, this is just too much. So your names are Lindsey and Brittany," Katrina managed to say through the laughter.

The girls still had no clue what was so funny and stared at

each other with looks of complete astonishment. Suddenly, before anyone could realize it, Katrina leapt on Lindsey knocking her back to the floor, burying her fangs deep into her neck, and sucked violently till her body began to loose all signs of life. Celeste dove towards Brittany, but Katrina reached up, grabbed her, and pulled her off course making her fall to the ground.

"Let her be! I'll take care of this! Get out!" Katrina growled.

Sergei picked Celeste off the floor and they walked out of the office.

"Don't stray too far, I'm not done with you yet," Katrina called out behind them. Brittany was screaming in the background.

A long while later, during which everyone was wondering what was going on and contemplating the different avenues their fate might take them, Katrina called them to the office. As they all walked in, looks of horror and surprise crept into their soulless faces at the sight of Katrina sitting at her desk with Lindsey, Brittany, and Olivar standing right behind her.

"This place is now under new management," Katrina said with a stern look on her face.

The Castle Charter
Chapter Twenty-two

From that night on, the college girls from Gamma Delta were in charge of the Castle, Celeste and Sergei were in charge of security, and Barabas kept doing his job making it all look good for the Protectorate and legal for the government. Lindsey and Brittany had special talents. They were able to attract humans like ants to sugar water. They charmed everyone they met. Their unique charms even worked on some Legion, which would make them instrumental in the plans Katrina had for the Castle and for building a new House within Legion society. By the end of the following night, the girls had brought in enough applicants for Katrina to fill all the staff positions. Every one of them were morphed by and answered to Katrina. Celeste was not happy about being demoted, but she was relieved to no longer have the responsibility. Security was closer to what she wanted to do anyway. The chance to kill something every now and then was tough to beat. Sergei became the head bouncer and with his brute strength, even unwelcome visits from the other families were easily discouraged. Invitations to the Grand Re-Opening went out to all the dignitaries and industry executives of both the Legion and human society. This promised to be a great event, but everyone had to be cautious.

The night before the grand re-opening was also an

important special event.

"Madame Katrina, the gentleman you asked me to invite is here for your meeting. He's not alone," said Barabas.

"Show them up. I know who it is that's with him," replied Katrina.

Barabas stepped outside, then returned with the one known as Slinky and his body guards the Hammer from the House of Kharsag.

"Gentlemen, be seated. I have a fresh bottle of Blood Wine from the vineyard of Paso Robles. Would you like a taste?" Katrina greeted her guests.

"Look here lady, I didn't come here for some sort of morbid tea party. I've got better things to do than sit here and waste my time with some fugitive traitor bitch and sip some fucking bullshit wine," Slinky replied with hostility.

"Now, now Mr. Slinky, I may be a traitorous, fugitive bitch, but I'm sure you know what else I am and how good I am at it. So, let's dispense with the bullshit male posturing and keep things civilized," Katrina answered with an eerie tranquility.

"Let's get to the point, I don't want to risk being seen with you," replied Slinky.

"Oh, so, we arrive at the issue, Fear! Fear is why your house has been faltering ever since your mentor fell at the hands of some of my associates, fear is also the reason you all scurry about like rats through the streets, even though the Potentate granted papers of charter for House of Kharsag,," Katrina stated with the serenity of an evening breeze.

Gabrielle entered the office and stood next to Katrina.

"What the fuck? What is this bitch doing here? That's it," Slinky said, as he stood up and walked towards the door.

"I offer this only once. I suggest you listen to my proposal before leaving a mutually profitable offer on the table," Katrina continued, forcing all of her being to express amiability, her voice dripping with conciliation. "I don't feel the obligation to explain myself to you but, in the spirit of the negotiations . . . Gabrielle is here as my guest and as a key component to my vision. An irritation you will either have to forget or live with; or not. Either way I wish you would sit and listen before making a decision ."

Slinky stood at the door, looked back at Gabrielle, looked at Katrina, and then asked, "How do I know she won't hold a grudge?"

"You'll have my word in assurance that she will behave like a complete lady during these proceedings," replied Katrina.

Slinky walked back and sat in the nail-head leather chair, threw his hands up in surrender, and said," Let's hear it."

"Allow me to introduce my new associates who will take over this part of the proposal; Brittany and Lindsey Gamma. We affectionately call them the Twins," Katrina said as she summoned the Gammas to the room.

"Oh… hey, now that's more like it. What family are they from?" Slinky's demeanor instantly changed.

Even the Hammer, who had been standing by the door completely emotionless, eyes shifting back and forth like a robot, perked up and took interest.

"Never mind that, just listen," Katrina replied.

Slinky sat back in the chair and listened to the twins present their proposal as best he could between the distractions while he ogled over their physical attributes.

"The purpose of this proposal is to establish a business relationship between House Kharsag and the proprietors of the Castle. Both attempting to avoid scrutiny by the Potentate and the Protectorate, we feel it best to join forces under a secret pact for mutual benefit. This pact would benefit both in the financial arena and in collaborations to advance each other's agendas within Legion society. The Castle will fall under ownership of House Kharsag and silent partners represented by Mr. Barabas, and overseen by Madame Gabrielle Vazques. All decisions regarding policies of operation shall fall to the board in which the House of Kharsag shall share equal vote with the silent partners, and Madame Gabrielle shall hold a tie breaker vote as Sergeant at Arms. Board members shall be selected by the principles. The principals shall have the greatest portion of the vote in their respective alliances and each board member shall have one vote. This commission will also consider all House issues brought before it as an entity of arbitration to resolve disputes without involving the Potentate. Each board member shall have a financial share of the Castle equal to their vote on the commission. Barabas will continue to preserve the appearance of legal and loyal operation for the benefit of the Potentate and the government, but what we do is our business and our business only. Any board member has the authority to call a meeting for whatever reason, but the principles must be present for a vote and acceptable outcome. Anyone signing this charter is bound to its regulations and policies and subject to its penalties. Signatures shall be required in blood from all parties involved. Do we have an agreement, Mr. Slinky?" said the twins as they presented the Charter in a manner reminiscent of Tweedle-Dee and Tweedle-Dum.

The Gamma Twins had the exact effect on Slinky Katrina had hoped for. He fell on their every word despite the momentary lapses of attention caused by the twins charming physical attributes. By the time they were done Slinky would have stripped down to his bare essentials, gotten down on all fours, and barked like a Chihuahua if they asked. Gabrielle shook her head in disgust and disbelief.

"I guess we have a deal," Gabrielle said with her usual sarcastic smirk.

"I still don't understand what your part is in all of this, but I'll agree to the Charter and its terms as long as the money flows," Slinky said holding some suspicion.

"Very well then, Barabas, draw up the paperwork. Mr. Slinky, please meet us back here tomorrow night with your board members, and we can all sign over a bottle of Blood Champagne. I will arrange some entertainment for you and your associates. I would definitely make plans to stay for that," said Katrina.

"What the hell is Blood Champagne?" replied Slinky.

"One of the many benefits of owning a Legion night club is being ahead of all the latest trends by virtue of our distributors and patrons. We will be the first to sample the fruits of the first barrel of Champagne produced from the vineyards of Paso Robles," Katrina explained.

"Well then, count me and my boys in for the night," Slinky said with a smile.

Slinky and the Hammer left the night club, Sergei flexed up as the Hammer walked past him through the double doors at the entrance. The Hammer glared back into his eyes and smiled. The Hammer was a giant in stature and a bull in girth. Still, Sergei refused to show any intimidation. The Mercedes Benz limousine pulled up and the Hammer opened the door. Slinky slid into the back seat, followed by the Hammer, who squeezed himself in.

"Catch you later," the Hammer said pointing his fingers at Sergei like a gun. It was the only thing he said all night.

"Fucking blood-sucking gangsters," Sergei said bitterly under his breath.

Grand Opening
Chapter Twenty-three

The Castle never looked better. Through the participation of Mr. Slinky and his associates, there was a variety of resources added to the club that was not available before. At this point, the secret partnership looked promising. When one arrived at the club by vehicle, there was the option of self-parking at the public location down the street or Valet parking. For an added fee, and if the vehicle was flashy enough, one could park in the limited spaces in front of the door; this service of course at the doorman's discretion. The array of ultra luxurious sports cars and sedans announced that the club had attracted a new level of clientele. It still catered to all walks of life and society, but a new upscale crowd was stepping through its doors. After the vehicle was taken care of, one could stand in line, or walk right in. The latter is a benefit of valet parking. Once through the imported mahogany doors, one was teleported back to an earlier time in American history where lavish decorations adorned the theaters and dance halls of the age. Red drapes with black frill trim covered the walls of the foyer, plush red carpet adorned with black dragon silhouettes over black marble floors led to the old style ticket counter where one selected special bands which identified the patron as Legion or human for the benefit of the waitress, servers, and staff. Surrounding the old style ticket counter were various styles of red and black sofas and love chairs for lounging and conversation, something nearly impossible in the midst of the music and dancing in the main chambers of the club. Long red and black brocade drapes hung from the passageways to the chambers; one led to the main chamber on the first floor, another to the stairs leading to the main chamber and dance floor on the second floor, and yet another to the balcony. On the first floor the Goth / EMO crowd could mingle, dance and frolic. The DJ stand blasted heart-shaking rapid bass tunes by VNV Nation, Apoptygma Berzerk, Combi Christ, Lords of Acid, and many more whenever the stage didn't have the likes of Phoenix Nebulin, the Cruxshadows, Sunday Munich, or the Last Dance performing their euphoric musical trances. The second floor chamber was where the hip hop aficionados would strut their wares, impress and socialize. The bass pumping through the speakers courtesy of DJ Calaco's spin table sometimes launched barrages of phone calls to the local police station for miles around whenever lyrical crooners like Young Gator, AJ Lundy, Kollosus, and Uptown Hawk weren't orchestrating the ebb and flow of the human wave on the dance floor. From the balcony, VIP's could watch the action on both floors from the privacy and luxury afforded by sound proof glass. The wait staff and upscale furniture, including a twenty foot "orgy bed," provided the comforts even some VIP's weren't accustomed to. Dignitaries from every industry and walk of life would enjoy the best music, liquor, wine, cigars, blood slaves, and attention their money, influence or status could buy. On any given night one might catch Curtis "fifty-cent" Jackson sharing a blunt with Billie Joe Armstrong, or Marilyn Manson and Eve comparing tattoos over snifters of Courvoisier. In all of Tampa and possibly the nation there was no better place for those seeking discreet alternative entertainment.

The Castle was a great place for those seeking a change of pace from the mainstream night club experience, but it held a more secret and sinister purpose. The House of

Kharsag used it as a venue from which to recruit soldiers and "concubines" for the cause. Katrina, mostly used it to keep tabs on the pulse of the Legion and to finance her now covert operations. Both would enjoy a virtually never ending stream of volunteer Sangus and plebes. The allure of near immortality and eternal youth drew many to their doors. Others hoped to escape the consequences of the ill conceived decisions in their life. A slight few were willing to trade whatever it took to escape whichever disease had ravaged their body. Those with no moral value put none on their soul and unwittingly trade it for fleeting strands of vanity. Under the new ownership arrangement, the Castle would vastly surpass either party's expectations. This was a welcomed surprise to both, but they knew it would eventually attract the interest of the Protectorate, and raise suspicions in the Potentate.

The night the agents arrived, Gabrielle and Slinky were ready. It was the second night of the Castle's grand re-opening. The place was full of the glitzy, glamorous, beautiful, and trendy clubbers, that had heard about the debauchery of the night before, wanted to experience it, and who would soon disappear leaving the club to its rightful patrons. The atmosphere was festive and awe-inspiring in its grandeur; fire jugglers, contortionists, acrobats, and street magicians complimented the usual array of entertainers. Three agents of the Protectorate and a business representative of the Potentate visited the Castle to inspect the establishment and reinforce their involvement in the venture. The Hammer was at the door along with Sergei. The Hammer escorted the dignitaries up the red velvet staircase to the VIP room and seated them at the large leather sectional in the center of the room. Sergei closed the doors to the club, only VIPs were permitted from this moment on. Everyone in the VIP room stared like star struck teenagers at the magnificent appearance of the agents. Their clothes of tailor-made custom-fitted brocade silk and cashmere exuded class and elegance. Their skin as smooth as alabaster and just as white gave them an eerie yet sensual appeal like one might experience when admiring Bernini's statues. A few minutes later Slinky appeared with his best "Blood Ho's and Blood Studs," as he referred to them, in trail.

"Greetings and salutations to thee, my distinguished guests," Slinky said as he approached the agents.

He then pointed to his stable of Sangus behind him and said, "Please enjoy the hospitality of my Castle."

"You've kept us waiting," said the Elder, who in this case looked like she was fifteen. "I don't appreciate being made to wait on anyone. Especially, Neomorph upstarts such as you."

Slinky knew at that moment that it was going to be a long night. Still, he motioned for the Sangus to walk past the Elder and her companions to exhibit their talents. Blood gifts usually heal all wounds between the Legion. The Elder touched, sniffed, and tasted their skin with her tongue. She then waved for the next one. She did the same for each, looked at Slinky, and said, "I am Elder Alexandra Epsilonia, you have great stock here. In all my years I've come across very few that aroused such lust."

She walked over to the Sangus who were standing with their backs to the glass partition, did a visual inspection of them all, they smiled, trying to be polite, and then she pounced on one with such force that she nearly ripped the Sangus' head off at the neck. The blood sprayed into the air as the Elder gorged on his crimson elixir. The other Sangus cowered away from the scene and hid behind Slinky. The man collapsed in the Elder's arms. She did not drain him. She pulled away just at the brink of killing him.

"This one is mine," said the Elder as she carried him away to a more private corner of the VIP room. A couple was already sitting on the love seat when she walked over to it. They quickly got up and let her claim the spot.

"You go ahead now, Mama," said the man with his hands in the air in surrender, and then he dragged his girl away by the arm and settled in another part of the room.

Slinky noticed the shocked look on everyone's faces and asked, "What the hell did you expect?!"

Everyone looked away and carried on with whatever activity they were engaged in before.

"We shall inspect the rest of the establishment now," said one of the agents. "And, we shall like to look at your books."

"Whatever you say, brother. Hammer, keep an eye on our special guest. Make sure she doesn't eat any of the VIPs, we're trying to run a business here," Slinky said as they walked down the stairs.

After hearing this, several of the people in the room made their way to the stairwell attempting to make a discreet exit, but the Hammer moved into their path, offered them a bottle of Dom, and motioned with his head for them to go back to what they were doing. No one was leaving the club until the Protectorate's agents and the Elder had left.

Slinky led the agents on a tour of the Club, first showing them the dance floors, they moved on to the bar, followed by the kitchen, and then finally the conference room and office. On the dance floors, the agents walked through the crowd looking at all the clubbers, pulled some aside, stared into their eyes, and moved on. This annoyed a few people, but they all took it in stride and continued with their dancing and drinking. One human male took offense to the treatment his date received at the hands of one of the agents, but one look into the piercing stare of the blood red eyes diminished any courage or insanity the boyfriend might have had. At the bar they ordered some drinks, which surprisingly they paid for, made their comments on the bar maid's attire, and then moved on. In the kitchen they were very nonchalant and uninterested. They only took interest when shown the amount of meat in the walk in deep freeze locker.

"Is this all up to government standards?" asked one of the agents.

"Just recently inspected; most of it exceeds their standard. Some is, shall we say, awaiting proper disposal; Collateral evidence of Legion Final Solution operations. They were left here by the former proprietor," Slinky replied.

They did not probe the matter further. Not only did they not want to hear the rest of the explanation, they didn't want to be reminded of the one they had severed relationships with. They made their way to the conference room where Barabas was waiting with the books. The agents perused the ledgers, asked for the disc version.

"I only see this human, where are your partners, we must meet them too," said the other agent.

"I represent them," said a voice from behind them startling everyone in the room.

It was Gabrielle arriving just on cue. She had a pair of Olivar's goons with her.

"What are they doing here? Do you allow such filth into our establishment?" said an outraged agent.

"This is our establishment, and by law we can't refuse entry to anyone based on color, creed or species," replied Gabrielle. "Besides, they're my personal watch dogs and are useful when Legion patrons get out of hand."

"Aren't you afraid of the consequences if one gets a hold of a human?" the agent responded.

"I'm in complete control of my dogs, which is more than I can say about the Protectorate," replied Gabrielle.

"Watch your tongue, you degenerate whore!" blasted the other agent.

Slinky knew what might come next and stepped back to avoid getting caught in the cross fire, but it was not necessary. Lady Celeste appeared with the twins and the climate of the moment took a different turn.

"Excuse us; let us keep the focus of the proceedings in proper perspective. She represents certain partners who wish to remain anonymous due to the current climate of the human Legion society. They selected Lady Gabrielle as a representative in order to use her clout to keep the other partners in their place. Humans can be so, how do you say, petulant," The twins charms were hard to resist especially as they handed them the suitcase with the full amount owed the Potentate. The agent laid the briefcase on the table and looked inside. He looked up at Gabrielle and Slinky, then moved the briefcase over to the other agent and presented the money with a motion of his hand. The agent pulled out a couple of stacks and peeled the money back; he continued through the briefcase and inspected each stack in the same way.

"Can we expect this kind of tribute every month?" asked the agent.

"Guaranteed," replied Slinky.

"Keep your partners in line," the agent told Gabrielle.

Everyone made their way to the VIP room. When they arrived the Elder had gone through her second Sangus and was starting on her third. The first two lay on the floor unconscious, but still alive.

"This one's got quite the appetite," Slinky whispered in the Hammer's ear.

The Hammer nodded in agreement. The agents handed the briefcase to the Hammer, selected their Sangus, and fed in anticipation of the nights coming activities.

"Lady Gabrielle, will you be joining us?" asked the Elder.

"Not at this time, but the twins will gladly keep you company," she replied as she introduced Brittany and Lindsey.

"Ah, of course, the Neomorphs everyone is talking about. Come here, let me examine you," she motioned to the girls.

The twins walked over and she peered into their eyes, then quickly pricked their necks with her nail, ran her fingers across her tongue, and tasted their blood. She walked them to the orgy bed leading them by the hand, tore off their clothes, kissed them, then turned to the VIPs, and said, "Now you gaze upon the marvel of the Legion. Join us if you wish, but beware; for you might fall victim to its charm and lose yourself in ecstasy."

With that, the remaining Legion in the room picked a Sangus or VIP and fed. What followed was an indescribable display of debauchery not seen by human eyes since the days of Caligula. The VIPs that did not accept the Elder's invitation watched the orgy of blood and sex in complete astonishment and shock. Some could not bear the sight and wretched, others were so aroused by the scene that they engaged in their own sexual debauchery with which ever human partner stood next to them. Gabrielle walked out knowing their agenda was completely secure and endorsed by the Potentate and Protectorate.

A few hours later the Hammer escorted the Elder and her agents down the stairs. Gabrielle waited by the front door. She looked out, did a visual check of the perimeter, waited for the driver to pull around in the black Mercedes, and then opened the door for the dignitaries. She glared at the agents as they walked past, and then changed her expression as the Elder approached. She had a Sangus in tow. Gabrielle looked at her and motioned with her hand inquisitively.

"As I said, this one is mine. Next time you see Katrina tell her if she brings us Vlad's head all shall be forgiven," said the Elder leaving Gabrielle with a cold feeling.

The Elder let the Sangus in the car first, then climbed in, and closed the door behind her. Once the car drove away, Katrina appeared from behind the building.

"I know what you're going to say. Forget it. I want to know why these Methuselah want Vlad so badly before I risk my immortality trying to destroy one of the oldest among us. You think the professor has had enough time to look over his notes, research, and give us an answer?" she asked Gabrielle.

"Let's go ask him. I'm sure after a few days in a cell surrounded by Olivar's men he's ready to say just about anything to anyone," replied Gabrielle and they started walking around the back to the staff parking lot.

"Good point, let's make sure he says it to us first," Katrina said as she climbed into the GTR.

"Wait a minute, isn't this Celeste's car? I thought it was all about the Muscle Cars or nothing with you?" queried Gabrielle a strong air of sarcasm in her voice.

"Oh shut the fuck up and get in the car. One cannot live by muscle alone, and after the stunt those assholes pulled with their so-called bail out I'm considering other options," Katrina said completely dejected. "Of course, that baby fart exhaust note is going to be hard to get used to."

They drove off the Castle's parking lot and headed towards the Invidia at the docks.

Clarity
Chapter Twent-four

Professor Rosell looked emaciated, dehydrated, but completely captivated. His work had engulfed his every being. The more he researched, the more he found, and the more he found the more he thirst for answers. At times it infuriated him. It was also amazing to him that locked up in this cell in the bottom of a 16th century Spanish Galleon he had better access to equipment and information than he ever thought possible. He was so enthralled in his work that he didn't notice Katrina and Gabrielle standing in the cell.

"Let's go Ronald; wake the fuck up, play time is over. Time to put the toys down and talk," Katrina yelled somewhat annoyed.

"I think he prefers to be called Professor Rosell," Gabrielle whispered.

"Yes indeed; I worked hard enough for that title," he said with attitude.

"Oh, it's alive!" said Katrina sarcastically referencing the classic movie.

"Did you know Angels walked among us?" he said with the enthusiasm of a boy who had just discovered sex.

"Get him washed up, fed, and to the conference room please," Katrina told Gabrielle.

"With pleasure," replied Gabrielle.

"Let's not, we don't have time for pleasure," answered Katrina, and then she smiled. "Don't take too long."
They all walked up the stairs, reached the next level, and separated. Katrina went to her quarters. Gabrielle took the professor to hers.

"I'll meet you in the conference chamber in an hour," Katrina said as she disappeared into her cabin.

Katrina wasn't surprised when she walked into the conference room and found no one else there. She knew they were coming, so she just sat at one end and thumbed through all the crap the professor had accumulated while doing his research. A few things caught her attention, especially the fax photo of a page from an old French manuscript with the name Arias in the title. Her French was a little rusty, but she could still read what it said. It was part of a dossier the Vatican was keeping on the family.
How in the hell did Ronald get his hands on this?

Among some of the other interesting things were a lot of notes referencing Kharsag and a word that kept popping up in various notes; Metatron. That word rang a bell of familiarity loud and clear within her head, but she could not place it no matter how hard she tried. Finally, Gabrielle and Professor Rosell stepped in. He looked considerably better than an hour ago. He stood across the table from Katrina. Gabrielle stood by, looking at all the pictures and papers.

"Well Professor, let's have it. Where's Vlad and how is it he's not at the bottom of that mess in Egypt?" Katrina said with a stern look on her face.

"Aren't you interested at all in this stuff I got from the Vatican?!" the Professor replied, as excited as a boy with a secret he couldn't contain.

"Later Professor, right now Vlad is all I'm interested in," she responded harshly.

"Fine, fine, what if I told you that Vlad, at one point took refuge somewhere deep within the catacombs below the Vatican City in Rome? What if I told you that Bruno Castañeda is also looking for him? Also, what if I told you that there might be more who survived that battle besides your friend Bruno, Lady Gabrielle, and I?" he said with a serious look on his face staring right into Katrina's eyes.

"I'd say you're suffering from delusions and need to check your sources. Legion cannot step on consecrated soil; which includes churches. Last I heard the Vatican is one big consecrated piece of land. Bruno is too busy living his life as the great artist to want anything to do with Vlad, and there is no way anyone survived that catastrophe in the desert. So, stop answering my questions with questions and give me some answers or I'll toss you in a steel chamber with Celeste for a month and see how long you last," replied Katrina.

"No need for dramatics. I'm going to let you know everything you want to know and more, I just wanted to know how much I needed to explain. It seems it's everything," sighed the professor, and then he continued.

"The phenomenon of how Vlad Tepes III survived the Catastrophe in the Desert, as you so eloquently put it, is of yet a mystery to me, but I can attest that survive he did.

You see, when I was taken from that place to the Potentate's headquarters by Lady Gabrielle, or Drone Six-One as I knew her, they feared something, and put me in a so-called safe house. I say so-called, because that's where I was kidnapped by the men of the Nachtschutz. They took me to the Jesuits and the Jesuits stashed me in some secret part of the Vatican. It was an area I had never seen or heard of before. I spent a lot of time there, but I don't think I could ever find my way back there again. I never saw it from the outside. I only know it was the Vatican because I could hear the sounds coming from St. Peter's Square. The prayers were so beautiful.

"Anyhow, while I was there, I was instructed to help them look through some extremely old manuscripts. Their point of interest was one manuscript in particular which was written in an ancient language that I didn't understand, but they had a sort of code book that I was using to try and decipher the text. I was extremely puzzled to find that the book made references to cloning. It was actually a step-by-step guide on cloning, but the things it talked about were impossible. I wondered, what interest the Vatican had in cloning? There were times I would become bored with what I was doing. Ever spend extended periods of time among men who had taken a vow of silence? It's completely frustrating. Even my insults did nothing to make them utter a sound. I began to wander the area and ended up deep within the catacombs. I found so many interesting manuscripts, scrolls and tablets. I would sometimes lose myself in the books I found, forgetting to eat, or sleep. I spent entire days looking through the pages of these ancient books. There were ancient Greek translations of different scrolls, letters between the apostles, and edicts from the early days of Christianity under the Romans. One day I strayed and became lost in the labyrinthine catacombs. I reached a place that was sealed by a large stone. Over the stone door was a brass plate with the inscription 'Alexandria' in old Roman text. As I analyzed the stone looking for a way into the chamber, I heard a noise coming from behind me. It was too late. By the time I turned around I was knocked to the floor and I passed out. When I came to, after who knows how long, I was face to face with Vlad. He had his whole weight on top of me and some blood was pouring from the corners of his mouth. I then heard some voices calling out to me in the distance; Vlad was startled and he struck me across the face, knocked me out, and the next thing I know I'm waking up to some nun giving me a sponge bath.

"Do you know how creepy that is, a nun touching my privates? She must have taken a vow of silence too because she said nothing after I threw her out of my room with a few choice words.

"So, you see, Vlad is alive. Well, maybe not alive, but he still walks among us," Professor Rosell explained.

The professor settled into a chair, crossed his arms, and had a screw face of dejection like some five-year-old that is denied his candy. Olivar happened to walk in a few minutes before and caught the tail-end of the story.

"Did he tell you about the gargoyles yet?" he asked with a grimace.

"What about the gargoyles?" said Gabrielle.

The professor didn't feel like saying much more. He was feeling unappreciated, so he just tossed his head up in defiance and turned away.

"Well, it turns out the professor discovered documents that say something about them being evil spirits looking for restitution and so their penance is to serve at the walls of the church as guardians. He found all this on some scroll he said is part of the ones found in Egypt. What was it he called them? Oh, yeah the Chronicles. Chronicles of the Damned or something like that," Olivar continued.

"So, there's more to those scrolls, Professor?" asked Katrina.

The professor did not answer.

"Olivar, ask Lady Celeste to come in here please," Katrina said threatening the professor.

He still ignored Katrina. Moments later the twins stepped into the room.

"Have you fed yet my dears," Katrina asked.

"Actually, I had a bite at the club, but used up all my energy in the strenuous encounters on the orgy bed. I could tear into some walking blood sack right now," Brittany assured.

"Why does it have to be her?" protested Gabrielle.

"Because you'll show some compassion," replied Katrina.

"Aren't they supposed to be watching things at the Castle?" Gabrielle resented having the twins around when Professor Rosell was concerned.

"Things in the Castle are just fine. The place is in good hands. So mind your own business," Brittany snapped at Gabrielle.

"Why don't you just do your thing and get it out of him? Can't you read his mind?" asked Lindsay.

Gabrielle had a look on her face like the only thing keeping her from thrashing the two little upstarts was Katrina's retribution.

"I can't, that's the problem. Most people have one train of thought at a time. Some might jump from one to the other. Some even play entire events like a movie in their heads. Not this guy. He thinks of a bunch of things at once, keeps no real track of anything, and jumps between completely unrelated subjects so often I can't make any sense of what he's thinking. He's going to have to tell me what I want. I'll be able to tell if he's telling the truth, but I won't be able to get anything out of him that he doesn't want to tell me," answered Katrina.

"Maybe if you rewarded him instead of threatening him he might respond favorably," Gabrielle interjected.

"Yeah, a little pleasure for the pain," Lindsay threw in her two cents.

Just then a coherent thought escaped the Professor's mind.

"By the Nyx, Ronald! You tell me what I want to hear right now or I'll tell Gabrielle what little naughty things are kicking around in that melon. Tell me what I want to hear and I'll make sure they happen," Katrina offered.

"Are you serious? You could make that happen in exchange for telling you where Vlad is now? How do you propose to protect me once I tell you what I know?" asked the professor with a heightened level of enthusiasm mixed in with caution.

"I am sure I can arrange both very easily," Katrina said with a smirk on her face as she looked right at Gabrielle.

"What the hell is going on?" Gabrielle said, feeling a little threatened.

"Fine," conceded the professor. "But, I'll only talk to you."

Katrina ordered everyone out of the room and shut the door. A few minutes later she opened the door, called Olivar inside and told him to take the professor down below. When Olivar reached down to take the professor by the arm Katrina whispered into his ear. Olivar nodded and continued out the door with the professor. Lindsay and Brittany turned around and started walking down the corridor.

"Not so fast. I have a treat for you two," Katrina yelled out to them.

"What the fuck is this Katrina?" asked Gabrielle.

They followed Katrina below deck. They walked through the dark corridors and arrived at one of the Sucanis holding cells. Two of Olivar's men were waiting inside the cell.

"For me?" said Lindsay, "You shouldn't have."

"Are we supposed to share?" Brittany protested at the indignity.

"I think you two need some together time," replied Katrina.

They sashayed into the cell like cats playing with their prey. Lindsay had a big smile on her face as she approached her chosen partner for what was left of the night. Brittany's mouth was starting to water and then she got a very unfamiliar sense of danger. The men morphed. Before either one could react they were in the grasp of Sucanis.

"What the hell is this?" Lindsay yelled out in protest.

"So, this is how you betray us? I knew you were devious, but turning us over to them; now that is low," said Brittany looking at the Sucanis.

The Legions' one big advantage over Canis and Sucanis is speed. That advantage is nullified once in the grasp of these vicious monsters. Oddly, they didn't decapitate the ladies and rip their hearts from their chests. Instead one pulled Brittany to the center of the cell and shackled her hands to chains hanging from the ceiling. He reached down and locked leg irons around her ankles. Her arms and legs were spread far apart as she hung from the cell ceiling. The Sucanis hung Brittany from the ceiling as well, facing Lindsay, but just out of reach from each other. Once both the Legion bad girls were securely strapped in Katrina brought the professor to the door.

"Here you are Ronald, they're all yours. Don't do anything stupid. You know I'm going to cut them loose eventually," Katrina said as she smirked at the vamps.

The professor stepped into the cell without saying a word. He looked back at Katrina and smiled as she shut the door.

"What the fuck," Gabrielle protested again.

She stared at Ronald through the opening in the cell door looked at Katrina then walked away.

"Is he going to be okay locked up with them? You know they can break out of those shackles just about anytime they want," Olivar asked with some concern.

"I don't think they will. They're both open to new experiences and those shackles can restrain Sucanis, they should be adequate for the Neomorphs. My only concern is the condition of the professor when Lindsay and Brittany start competing for his affectionate attentions as one might say," Katrina replied.

"What about Gabrielle, she looks really upset?" Olivar asked.

"She'll get over it; and besides, if she has an issue with it she needs to take it up with the professor," Katrina replied.

"I'd hate to be in his shoes," said Olivar.

"What about tonight?" Katrina teased.

"Well Madam, I prefer human company for the urges that surge through my flesh," replied Olivar.

"Bigot!" Katrina answered with a glare, then smiled letting him in on the joke.

"Make sure the cook delivers a medium-rare seared porter house steak with all the fixings in the morning; the professor is going to need it, and get ready to set sail. We have an appointment with my master," she said sarcastically.

"Do I have a course, heading, or destination yet, Madam," asked Olivar.

"You could say we're heading home," she said cryptically and continued, "How long?"

"Madame Giroux, I think about three days to prep and stock. Most of our provisions were depleted on the last trip," replied Captain Olivar.

"Not good enough, I want the ship to sail in no more than two," Katrina insisted.

"I'll get it done," answered Olivar.

Katrina walked out and headed down the corridor.

"Is the Madam stepping out?" asked Olivar.

"I need to take care of some last minute issues at the Castle. I'm taking two plebe Sucanis with me," Katrina answered.

"Must be serious," said Olivar.

Katrina gave no answer; she just walked up the stairs, and disappeared into the darkness.

A Night Best Forgotten...
Chapter Twenty-five

Professor Rosell was on the verge of fulfilling one of his greatest fantasies. He was locked in a cell with two bound women at the mercy of his impulses. Having devoted all his energy into studies he never took the opportunities afforded him by campus living to explore his sexuality. A decision which left him branded a nerd and made him a social pariah late into his adult life. Just because he did not take the opportunities didn't mean he did not think about them. It is this same kind of self-imposed oppression and abstinence that drives men to commit inappropriate acts, at inappropriate moments, on inappropriate victims, and become monsters enslaved by their desires.

This night he was free to act upon the urges that haunted him for so long with eager participants in his explorations of the flesh. He once gave in to the moment, felt a Legion's lustful touch, and pitied them for it. Now, he let his inhibitions fly, fearing no consequence or retribution. He would lose his humanity with them in order to bathe in all the ecstasy the Legions pleasures offered.

The first barrier when engaged with a Legion in fancies of the flesh is the taboo of blood lust. Without the blood that brings life to the flesh allowing the juices to flow there can be no gratification. This can also be part of the whole experience. One can call it Legion foreplay.

The professor approached one, then the other offering his neck and at the point of contact he teasingly pulled away. The desire within the two women increased as they heard his heart beat and sensed the blood pulsing through his veins. He was well aware of how consuming jealousy could be in these settings. He approached Brittany and pulled his shirt off. In the glow of the limited light offered by the single warm light bulb of the cell, his emaciated body gave off a gleam from the sweat that beaded on his body, projecting the illusion of a tight ripped physique. He reached for her face with his hands and caressed her cheeks then slid his hands slowly down to her neck and kissed her forehead. Her lips got close enough to his neck to feel the warmth of his skin. When she opened her mouth, bringing her teeth closer to his flesh, he pulled away coyly, and left her yearning for blood. He backed away slowly, walked around and behind Lindsay, pulled her blouse open, and exposed her breasts. He reached down near her navel, pulled his hands up slowly squeezing her skin until he reached her breasts, and kneaded them hard. Lindsay gasped and Brittany growled in protest. She shrieked as the professor leaned over Lindsay's shoulder, offered his neck, and allowed Lindsay to feed first. The jealousy builds to a rage and the shackles barely contained Brittany's fury.

The next part of the interlude is the arousal. One needs to focus the Legion's attention towards the physical pleasures their revived flesh could sense and divert their attention from feeding. Lindsay sucked at the wound swallowing the stream of blood that poured into her mouth. When she reached blood glow the professor felt the heat coming from her skin and quickly pulled away leaving her straining at the chains that bound her, leaving her gasping for more.

He moved in front of Brittany and once again cupped her

face in his hands. She squirmed around attempting to bite him, but he reached away, pulled her blouse open, grabbed her collar, pulled her close and kissed her hard on the lips. He moved around and left a trail of kisses down her neck and offered his neck to her. She bit and sank her fangs deep into his flesh. He felt a sense of euphoria caused by the Legion saliva mixing with his blood and the loss of blood itself.

Both Legion women were now in full blood glow and deep in desire. Their skin erupted in goose bumps and their bodies shuddered as the yearning sent shock waves racing up their spines. The professor knelt between the two bound girls; they were just out of reach. He then pleasured each one in turn in every way his imagination devised.

The twins were in a heightened state of blood glow and the surge of sensation was causing a deep irritation and lust for flesh. The professor produced a scalpel from a leather medical bag that was sitting in a corner of the cell. A prop no doubt left there by Katrina for their enjoyment. He held the scalpel in the air and showed them the gleam of light bouncing off the edge. He reached out to Brittany, dragged the blade across her skin, traced her curves, and sliced a cut across her chest just above her breasts. Brittany screamed then gasped as the pain triggered her overactive Legion endorphins. The wound bled and then began to heal. Lindsay watched, frightened by the whole scenario; anxious about what he would do to her, but eerily aroused by the whole scene playing out before her.

He reached for her with the scalpel and dragged the blade down from her neck to her navel ever so slowly. She let out a shriek that lasted the entire length of the wound. The blood streamed from the cut painting her body in red. The sight and smell of the blood running down Lindsay's body increased Brittany's arousal. She fiercely struggled against her restrains, but could not break away. The wounds mended, but the blood was still there, and it drove them insane with need. They struggled against their shackles, hissed, gasped, and moaned, but the professor wasn't done tormenting his subjects.

The professor reached into the leather case and pulled out a vial containing some clear liquid. The girls' hearts pounded and their breathing became rapid as they hyperventilated in desperation. Their anxiety swelled as the professor uncapped the glass container and the bitter smell of garlic crept into their noses. They whimpered and squealed like little girls when they saw him dip the blade of the scalpel into the vial. He walked over to Brittany, held the blade to her nose as she desperately shook her head to avoid the stench. He walked around and stood behind her. He reached around her with his left hand and cupped her breast and squeezed. Brittany sighed both from pleasure and relief. He caressed her mounds then slowly slid his hand down across her ribs, over her tight stomach, finally stopping between her legs and began to stroke.

It agitated Lindsay to watch as Brittany writhed in pleasure, and then she screamed with Brittany as the professor dug the scalpel deeper into her flesh. He sliced a trail of small dashes from her neck leading down between her breasts, traveling over her belly, and stopping at her mound. He sliced another trail of dashes running up her body to the other side of her neck. This time the wounds did not close right away and blood flowed freely. He cut her pants off with the scalpel, threw his down to the ground and explored her erogenous zones with his member.

Brittany gasped, moaned and finally screamed as the pleasure and pain sensations surged through her body. Lindsay watched and struggled against the chains trying to get some release from her yearning. At the moment when Brittany was reaching her climax, the professor pulled away, and left her yearning for release.

The professor then walked over to Lindsay, he picked up the vial and dipped the blade in the solution again. He came up behind her. Lindsay panicked as she knew what was coming. Brittany watched as he plunged the scalpel into

Lindsay's chest with his right hand, reached around with his left hand, cupped her breast, and then simultaneously cut, sliced and stroked her skin leaving the same pattern of bloody dashes to her mound then up again. Brittany's wounds were starting to close, but they left behind small white scars tattooing her skin forever.

Brittany became so aroused when the professor sliced off Lindsay's pants that the shackles crashed to the ground from the force of her thrusts for release. She walked over to Lindsay and released her from her chains. The professor was stroking her from behind. Lindsay and Brittany pushed him to the ground, Lindsay straddled his lower torso, and Brittany pressed down on the other end and faced Lindsay. It was a literal lover's triangle as they licked the blood off each other's body and he pleasured them to screams of climactic ecstasy. They finally fell spent to the floor and held each other for the rest of the night.

The next morning the ship's cook opened the door and found them wrapped around each other in the farthest corner of the cell. He gently woke the professor and laid down a plate in front of him. The professor groggily rose up, grabbed the flatware, and cut into his meal. The juices flowed from the porter house steak as he cut away the first piece and put it into his mouth.

"My compliments to the Chef," he said with a look of complete satisfaction on his face.

"I'm glad you like it Sir. Enjoy it, it could be the last meal of a condemned man," joked the cook.

"Gabrielle?" asked the professor.

"She wasn't happy, Sir. The last time I saw her she was tearing one of the Sucanis up in a sparring match. I hope you can heal as fast as they do or you're done," replied the cook.

"I guess I'm done, because I have no special powers other than my intellect, and that only gets you so far in a fight against a Vampire," said the Professor.

"Oh now, Sir, I wouldn't be adding insult to injury. You know they hate that word," said the cook.

"Yeah I know, I know, it's just hard to get used to," replied the professor.

"I'll leave you to your meal, Sir. Those two look like they'll be looking for a hardy meal themselves when they wake," said the cook pointing at the twins.

"I'd hate to be their next victims," answered the professor. "Poor souls won't know what hit them," he continued.

"Yes Sir, the hunt is going to be heated tonight. You must have worn them out good, my man. Takes a special kind of man to wear out a Legion, even more so two. So, how'd you do it?" asked the cook.

"Not that I would talk about those things, but I think I would rather forget last night. I felt like I wasn't myself. It was like some strange force was compelling me. Don't get me wrong I wanted to do both of them, but what happened last night was just beyond what I was after," the professor replied.

"Well, they say these two have some kind of psychic powers; almost like mind control," divulged the cook.

"I don't believe in that, and besides my intellect is above any sort of hypnosis. I think I just let my urges run away with me," the professor scoffed at the notion.

"Many strong and intelligent men have been brought

to their knees by a woman's cunning wiles," the cook answered as he walked to the door.

"Regardless, I hope to soon forget my actions of last night," the professor submitted.

The cook stood at the door looked back and said, "I don't think that is going to be very likely!"

He pointed to a bloody mess of a man outside the door being dragged to his quarters by his shipmates.

"He was Lady Gabrielle's sparring partner," said the cook.

"I guess she won't likely forget it, and so neither will I," the professor said defeated by the thought.

"Well, good day and good luck, Sir," the cook said as he made his way down the corridor.

Last Minute Errands
Chapter Twenty-six

Katrina stepped on deck and called out to one of the sailors, "Make sure Lady Gabrielle is awake and ask her to come see me."

The man was not happy with his task, especially after having witnessed the events of the previous night. Lady Gabrielle had become well versed in the destruction of Canis and other creatures. She held an unmatched disdain for the Sucanis. Something he's glad he's not. The man walked down the corridor and ran into Professor Rosell standing just outside Gabrielle's door. He knocked.

"Lady Gabrielle! Lady Gabrielle, Madame Katrina awaits you on main deck," he called to her through the door.

Gabrielle opened the door; she was wearing a lacy negligee, she looked at the sailor, and then noticed Professor Rosell standing behind him. She grabbed the sailor by the collar, pulled him in, bit him on the neck, wrapped her legs around him, closed the door and said, "Did you have a good night, Ronnie?"

The door shuts on the professor's face just as he was going to answer.

I guess I deserve that.

He walks away and heads towards the main deck. He saw Katrina and avoided her eyes as he walked past her. Katrina smiles and starts to say something to him, but is interrupted by the professor.

"She's going to be a while," he said.

"I gathered that from the look on your face," she said.

The professor goes to the rail of the ship and stares out into the bay.

"Do you want me to describe what's going on in there?" she teased.

He didn't answer, just looked away into the night.

"I can assure you it's nothing like the adventure you had the night before," she said as she laughed.

He angrily walked to the other side of the ship. Katrina chuckled and paid no further attention to him. The twins walked up the stairwell from below and greeted Katrina.

"A glorious night to you, Madame, when do we eat? Brittany and I are starving," Lindsay said excitedly.

Katrina noticed the scar patterns on their chests.

"My, my, those are really interesting. I'll have to consider that style for my own tattoo. Did it hurt?" said Katrina, taunting the girls.

"It was fun," said Brittany looking towards the professor.

He ignored them and continued to stare out into the horizon. Just then Gabrielle walked up. The twins slid over to Katrina's side as soon as they saw her appear. Gabrielle gave them a look of death, then rolled her eyes, and asked, "So what's on the agenda for tonight?"

"I'm glad you are all feeling feisty, we need to take care of some errands at the Castle and I believe it's going to get bloody," Katrina told them.

"Oh, that's just great. I'm not dressed for this type of activity," Lindsay complained.

"Yeah, we thought we might just catch something tonight," Brittany added.

"You're going to catch something alright," Gabrielle said under her breath.

"Don't worry about that, you look fine. In fact, you look exactly how you need to look, for this particular errand. We need your disarming demeanor for this job," Katrina assured the girls.

"Let's get on with it already," Gabrielle said as she made her way to the gangway.

"That's all good, but I don't want to get my boots all stained with blood and scuffed up," Lindsay complained.

"I guess we'll have an excuse to go shopping then," Brittany called out.

The girls hollered and giggled, giddy over the thought of treating themselves to a night of shopping. Gabrielle was not amused. She resented them before, after the incident of the previous night, that resentment was cemented, and quickly developing into hatred. As far as Gabrielle was concerned the only thing keeping them in one piece was Katrina.

"You ladies hurry up and get a head start. Gabrielle and I are taking the GTR back to the Castle," Katrina told the girls.

"Oh my god, I love that car! Maybe Celeste will give me a ride in it tonight," Lindsay exclaimed.

"Maybe she'll let me drive it, since I'm the one that can drive stick," Brittany taunted.

"Oh shut up, she's not going to let anyone else drive that car. Especially not you, and for your information, that car is automatic!" exclaimed Lindsay repelling the taunt.

"Whatever, bitch," replied Brittany.

"Aaahh, what the hell was that? You're the bitch, in fact you're a ho-bitch so there," answered Lindsay.

They ran off and were heard giggling some more way down the street. Gabrielle plopped down in the seat of the GTR. She turned to Katrina, who was getting her stuff together in the seat next to her, and said, "Let me kill them, please. I'll make it quick and painless. Let me just end it."

"Now, now, they serve a purpose and their special abilities have come in handy, are paying dividends, and will continue to pay dividends even for you. We just have to put up with their quirks and nonsense. Don't forget, not only are they young, but they're Neomorphs. They've had their blood, but they haven't had their first kill. Tonight all that will change," Katrina said as she drove off.

It was a busy night in the old town. Ybor City was alive with party people, window gawkers, and middle class socialites. The Prana was jumping, the Green Iguana was packed, and the Castle looked like a Star Wars premiere; the line of patrons waiting to get in stretched out around the corner and down the block. The new policy of separate doors for VIP patrons was paying off greatly. The only thing keeping people out now was the Fire Marshall enforced capacity of occupancy. Separate exits also helped with crowd control. It was going to be a tough night for what Katrina had planned. They arrived at the Castle and pulled into the Valet drive up. The valet took the keys from Katrina.

"Park that in Lady Celeste's space. She'll be happy to see it back and in one piece," Katrina told the boy.

The ladies entered through the VIP entrance and went up the stairs. Just as they reached the top landing Gabrielle noticed that the twins arrived just behind them. She told Katrina of their arrival, and she went back down to meet them. Katrina whispered something in their ear; they nodded, and walked past the curtains into the main chamber. Katrina and Gabrielle continued up the stairs to the VIP room and rushed some people off a sofa by the window that looked out on to the dance floor. Gabrielle watched as the twins mingled and quickly hooked up with a pair of muscle-bound college jocks. Sergei walked up and said hello, had a short conversation, and then walked towards the VIP room.

"Where's Celeste?" Katrina asked Sergei as he approached.

"She's upstairs with Barabas, they're discussing table cloths or something or another. I'm not sure exactly," Sergei answered.

"How are things with our new partners?" Gabrielle asked.

"They're a bunch of assholes! They keep calling me Neomorph and treating me like shit," Sergei replied.

"Don't let it get to you. The next time they call you a Neomorph just say 'for the House of Dracula', that should bring them down a notch," Katrina told Sergei.

Sergei laughed and then asked, "What can I do for you tonight; the twins mentioned you had something for me to do?"

"Assemble the staff. Tell Lady Celeste to give you a list of all the humans who wish to be morphed. Then, tell her to bring Barabas to me. Take Lady Celeste's list and go through the crowd, and if anyone on the list is here tell them they have been invited to the VIP room. Once you've done that announce that the club is closing and that everyone except for the humans in the party room with the twins must leave. If Slinky gives you any resistance tell him to come see me. Make sure those Kharsag pricks leave. Then you stand by the door and don't let anyone in or out. I don't care who it is, and Sergei, if anyone does get in or out - it's your ass," Katrina ordered with a stern warning.

Moments later, Celeste and Barabas walked up the stairs to the VIP room and stood next to Katrina looking down at the club floor. Katrina could see a few people that Sergei selected were walking towards the stairs. It wasn't as many as Katrina had hoped, but it was an adequate amount for the purpose they would serve. The moment Sergei announced that the Castle was closed, to Katrina's surprise, people starting filing out without complaint. No complaints of course except from Slinky, who, judging from his demeanor, was hot. He pushed through the crowd that was trying to make it out the door, and stomped up the stairs.

"What the hell is going on?" Slinky stormed into the VIP room looking like he was going to eat the world until he noticed Gabrielle and Katrina standing across the room from him.

"Lay-deez, Lay-deez, no one told meh you was here. So, is dis a private Par-tay? Is there an invitation for me somewhere, cuzz I didn't get it," he quickly changed his tone.

"You could call it that, and no; you're not invited," Katrina replied.

"Oh come on now, not long ago I partied up here with the Elder. How is it I can't partake of the soirée with the Dragon Queens?" he remarked with a sneer referring to their unit affiliation.

"This is an intimate affair with my staff congratulating them on their performance so far," Katrina replied.

Slinky stared at Katrina like a poker player trying to read his opponent. Katrina just stared back with a fire that only her red eyes could summon in situations such as this. Slinky approached and stood right in front of Katrina. He leaned over and whispered in her ear.

"Don't mad dog me bitch. I'll turn this whole place into the fucking St. Valentines Day Massacre; you dis' me like that again," he said doing his best to keep his composure. He paused, looked at Gabrielle then slid his eyes to his right to look at Katrina.

"Are these sanctioned morphs?" he continued to whisper in her ear.

"You know the answer to that and since you are the only one in this room that knows that, I would hold it as a great personal insult should the Protectorate find out. You do know how well I take insults," Katrina responded with equal composure.

Slinky realizing his mind was being read quickly stood back and walked away without another word.

"You're letting him go?" asked Gabrielle.

"He's no longer a threat to this operation. I made it crystal clear in his mind exactly what would happen to him if anyone ever found out about what we are about to do here. Trust me, he's going to do all he can to keep this a secret," replied Katrina.

Once Sergei closed the door he went to the party room where the twins were waiting. There was already a mini-orgy going on. The twins had every one in there completely mesmerized and playing to their every whim like puppets on a string. He nodded and they understood the message.

In the VIP room, the staff and the seven morph candidates were finally gathered in the suite. Katrina called them to attention and they gathered around their master.

"This is the moment you've all been waiting for. On this night you will all be granted immortality through the blood which races through my veins. You will all become members of the Great House of Dracula. Barabas, come here. Barabas has been a loyal employee, a true follower, and a trusted friend for many years. He has been the guardian of my business endeavors and my personal security for most of his life. He has wished to become one of us for almost as long," Katrina proclaimed to them all as she held him by the arms and faced him towards the group.

"It wasn't possible then, and it isn't possible now," She continued as a hulking figure slowly emerged from the darkness beyond the curtains that surround the room. There was a panic in the room as the figure drew closer to the light and everyone realized it was a Canis. He walked towards Barabas stood in front of him just a few feet away and stared at his victim.

"No Madam please, how have I wronged you? Oh please don't do this to me," Barabas pleaded.

"Barabas, you are dying. The cancer that is eating away at your lungs will soon get into your nervous system and kill you but not before rendering you useless not just to me, but to anyone else. This curse I allow is your only salvation," She said with a cold stare.

Before Barabas could let out another word the beast attacked him ripping at his flesh until Katrina called him off with just a thought. The crowd was in shock. His body fell to the floor and Barabas cried from the terrible pain and the betrayal he felt. The Canis picked him up and carried him away. The Staff was bewildered from what they had just witnesses and wondered about their own fate. Katrina then walked to the first staff member and gently cupped his face then bit him on the neck. The man went into convulsions and Katrina let him fall to the ground. She moved on to the next and she fainted just as Katrina was reaching Blood Glow. She then walked back to the man, who was starting to fade, and asked the question that had sealed the fate of so many others, "Do you want to live?" The man responded, she slit her neck, he fed.

The rest of the staff who were watching this spectacle for the first time became uneasy. A few even tried to escape, but Gabrielle blocked their path. Soon everyone took notice as Katrina and her Neomorph lost themselves in the heat of passion that the Blood-Glow offers and their curiosity was aroused. For some of them the scene aroused more than their curiosity.

When Katrina was satisfied, she approached the girl, who by this time was very near death. She offered her the dark gift of immortality and the girl accepted. After feeding this girl, Katrina's body craved more blood; she moved on to another staff member and bled him dry. The cycle continued until all the staff members and loyal Legion hopefuls had been morphed and the VIP room had transformed into a den of debauchery that rivaled any orgy Nero could have imagined. The activity left the group of Neomorphs and Legion thirsty with blood lust. The twins' party on the dance floor below took a bad turn for the participants. The Neomorphs and Legion swarmed upon them and ravenously fed upon their victims. Katrina demonstrated the full power of her telepathic ability and with one thought pulled them all out of bloodlust. Gabrielle was shocked out of her bloodlust by the sudden stop of her peers. Still in full influence of the Glow, she stopped, looked around, and marveled at what had just happened. Gabrielle, with blood pouring from her mouth dripping down to her chest, got up, wiped her lips clean with her forearm, walked past Katrina, and said, "Fang blocker!"

Gabrielle walked towards the back staircase, passed Celeste and Sergei who were still going at it hot and heavy, and said," It's over assholes! How about you go get a room or something, you exhibitionist fuck bunnies? No one here wants to see what you do to that bitch!"

"Who you calling a bitch?" challenged Celeste.

"Hey honey if the shoe fits wear it, but I was referring to your Bitch," countered Gabrielle as she slipped into the shower room upstairs.

Once that whole drama settled down, the staff and other Neomorphs were allowed to leave. Katrina pulled the twins aside and spoke to them.

"I'm going to need you to take care of things for a short while. Help Celeste get rid of these bodies. Barabas is going to be indisposed for a while. There is a Plebian Canis watching over him, so you won't need to worry. Celeste is going to have to handle Slinky and his crew so, Sergei, will be away also. It will all fall on you girls to keep this place functioning under the radar until I get back. If I don't make it back, there is a box in the lower drawer of my desk with a document that gives you, Celeste, and Sergei equal share in the Club. Make sure you present that to Barabas so he can make the arrangements or else the Potentate will take it all. Do you understand," she said calmly and clearly making sure they understood by reading the thoughts in their mind.

The twins were excited, then as if by some magical power between them turned around at the same time and said, "Does that mean we can throw a party?"

Katrina smiled, shook her head, and walked away.

"Stupid, see that's the kind of thing that makes her want to kill us!" Brittany snapped at Lindsay.

"What? You fucking said it first," Lindsay replied.

"How did I say it first, you practically knocked me over as you blew past me to open your big fat mouth," Brittany countered.

"You are obviously delusional from all the blood you sucked… among other things!" Lindsay growled.

"Oh, you're just fucking jealous 'cause my guy had hair,"

Brittany hissed.

"Yeah, he had hair all right. He had hair coming out of his eye balls. You sure he wasn't a Canis or maybe a Carebear?" Lindsay replied.

"Hose Muncher!"

"Carebear fucker!"

They both turned away and stomped up the stairs from opposing sides of the hall. By the time they met at the top they were laughing and talking about going shopping for boots. Katrina watched the whole spectacle and chuckled.

They might be a ditzy pair of vampires, but at least they're my ditzy pair.

Katrina walked up stairs to check on Barabas and heard the twins quarreling with Gabrielle as she passed the shower room.

"You girls go ahead and get that shit out of your system I want to take a soothing warm shower when I'm done here, and I do mean soothing?" Katrina yelled to them.

There was no reply. Katrina continued towards the back of the hall and entered Barabas' office. He was laying on his side with his back to the door. She called, but there was no answer. She realized that even if he was awake he was probably in no mood to talk. She couldn't tell. She couldn't sense anything from him at the moment. The Canis walked up behind her, peeked in, and then just shrugged.

"He should be okay in a couple of days. It is really bad timing that this shit had to go down on a full moon night, it's going to wreak complete havoc on his system, but he should be okay. I'll keep an eye on him. How long will you be gone?" The Canis said trying to show some compassion for the old man.

"I know I leave him in good hands. Olivar vouched for you and had great things to say about your abilities. I hope you live up to the expectations. This old man is dear to me and essential to our operations. I would not be kind to anyone responsible for allowing any harm to come to him. Am I clear?" Katrina whispered as calm and cold hearted as only she could be.

The Canis nodded and walked away.

Katrina closed the door and locked it behind her.

"Furball,... here - catch this," she yelled as she tossed him the key to the door.

She turned around and walked towards the shower room, once she was sure he had the key. She stepped into the shower room, took her clothes off, and slipped into the shower. The girls were still enjoying the water rushing over their skin. Katrina had emerged at just the right moment; the quarrelling had just ended and now there was a serenity that accompanies this rare ritual. Katrina still had some lingering effect from the Blood-Glow and her skin erupted in goose bumps as the first dew-like drops of warm water speckled her skin. The stream that followed relieved all her tension and melted her anxiety about what she felt fate had in store for her. They all stood motionless under the shower that fell like rain upon their bodies. It's these little things that vampires crave the most; a small taste of living that only blood can offer.

Once the showers were done, Katrina and Gabrielle disappeared into the night and walked towards the Invidia.

Celeste and Sergei took over the showers and explored their pseudo-humanity further under full Blood-Glow. The twins went outside, relocated the cars to the garage, locked the doors, and sealed the building in preparation for the coming day. Slinky and the Hammer had a routine habit of passing by the Castle just before daybreak to make sure the place was sealed up before heading to the safety of one of their many lairs in the city for their daily rest. They parked their car, checked the garage, and then walked towards the building.

Meanwhile, the Canis, being part human after all, slipped out to indulge in one of the few habits he picked up in his many years of living among the culture of Tampa; an occasional stogie. His senses were somewhat muted by the ecstasy of the swirling smoke from this Cuban Cigar, the fabled effect of being rolled on the thighs of a latte-skinned Cuban girl, his favorite were these Cazadores. The presence of the two Legion rounding the corner to the alleyway where he was smoking on the landing of the fire-escape surprised him into transformation.

Slinky and the Hammer wasted no time eliminating the Canis. A silver bullet through the heart from the silenced Sig Sauers they carried would have put any Canis down; the four that hit him sealed his fate.

"So much for Katrina's impenetrable security; she's gonna owe me big for this one. Bitch don't know how much I do for her," Slinky complained to the Hammer.

"I don't know boss, this doesn't seem right. That bitch is way too careful to leave with some Canis hanging around. Especially with all this attention from the Protectorate," the Hammer said with an uneasy tone to his voice.

"Well, that bitch isn't as smart as she lets off as you can see. Check that door up there make sure it's all sealed tight before we split," replied Slinky.

R.N. Matos

The Hammer walked up the staircase on the fire escape and checked the door at the top. He opened it.

"See What I mean; stupid bitch. Close that mother fucker and let's get the hell out of here. She and I are gonna have words," Slinky told the Hammer angrily.

The Hammer locked the door from the inside, closed it, and walked back down the staircase. The two men walk back to the car and drive away.

Oblivious to what had just happened, the twins sat at the bar and indulged in a bottle of blood wine from a sample case the good people at Vampire Wine provided the Castle in hopes of gaining a foothold in the rising local market.
"Damn, this shit is good," Lindsay exclaimed.

"Hell yeah, and unlike the real thing, it gives you a buzz instead of the blood-munchies," said Brittany.

"Yeah... WTF- is that all about? Drink blood, then crave blood, use it all up doing the Nasty, and need more blood! By the Dark?!" commented Lindsay.

"That's another thing, so like we can't say OMG anymore? Like what happens, is our skin going to erupt in flames, turn to ash, and blow away like in those creepy old movies?" Brittany remarked.

"I guess we have to say 'by the Dark',... BTD... or maybe we can say 'Oh My Dark'... OMD, get it?" said Lindsay.

"Nah, I don't get it. WTF?" said Brittany with a blank look on her face.

"OMD... you stupid blonde bimbo! Don't you get it?" Lindsay snapped at Brittany in complete astonishment.

"NO, I don't get it Blondzilla!" Brittany snapped back making faces at Lindsay.

"Fucking Orchestral Maneuvers in the Dark… OMD you retard," Lindsay squealed through her laughter.

"Oh … I am a retard, what the fuck? How did I not get that?" laughed Brittany.

"It's the bubbles baby, blame it on the bubbles. All that air just went to your head," Lindsay said laughing hysterically.

A thunderous noise interrupted their laughter and jarred them into a panic.

"Dang, those two are still going at it," said Brittany breaking the tension.

Lindsay started laughing again and they both broke down doubled over with laughter until the next explosive sound reverberated through the empty hall.

"Holy shit, that came from the other side," Lindsay shouted.

The twins ran up the stairwell on the right and into the shower room. They found Celeste and Sergei on a bench basking in the afterglow of an intense intimate encounter. They were suffering from the lethargic effect of a prolonged Blood-Glow induced session of copulation.

"I don't know what you girls are doing, but you need to tone it down, the neighbors are gonna complain," Celeste stammered in a droopy state.

"Oh shit, what the hell was that noise then," Brittany hollered to Lindsay, and then realized she had taken off searching for the source of the noise.

Brittany ran in another direction to search. The noise led Lindsay to Barabas' office. She tried to open it but the door was locked tight. From the noise coming from the room it sounded like a tornado had swept inside and was ripping the place apart. The next sound they heard brought chills to their bones and made their skin erupt in fear bumps; a howl like they had never heard before echoed through the Castle and surrounding streets. Brittany ran up the left stairwell to meet with Lindsay. As she reached the hallway, the door to Barabas' office erupted into chards that dug deep into Lindsay's chest; blood spraying from the open wounds. A furry claw-filled paw grabbed Lindsay by the neck and lifted her up in the air. Brittany looked on in shock as Lindsay struggled and punched the beast. A hairy head appeared from the darkness through the doorway and bit Lindsay's face almost completely engulfing her head. Brittany rushed to help, but the beast shook his head viciously from side to side violently ripping Lindsay's head clean off. Blood splattered everywhere and speckled Brittany's face with big red splotches of blood.

"Oh shit, crazy werewolf, run!" screamed Brittany as she came out of her shock and realized she couldn't take on this beast by herself.

"Fucking run, there's a werewolf loose in here!" she yelled trying to get Celeste and Sergei's attention.

The werewolf formerly known as Barabas was hot on her tail when Celeste and Sergei drowsily stepped out of the shower room and into the beast's path. Brittany kept running, heading for the stairs. The monster opened up his right paw, the claws glistened in the dark as he ripped Celeste open from her crotch to her neck nearly taking her head off with the blow. Sergei jumped on the werewolf, but in his blood-depleted state of exhaustion, a result of the romp in the shower, he was no match for the powerful striking force of the beast in lunar rage. Barabas caught Celeste with his left paw as she stumbled toward the floor; he swung and struck Sergei with the other paw knocking him over the railing down to the dance floor below. The monster flung Celeste off the balcony pathway tossing her right on top of Sergei. As he tried to get up, the beast landed on both of them and ripped into their flesh. This gave Brittany a chance to make it to the front door. She wasn't sure where she was going, but she knew staying was not an option. She struggled with the locks for a few seconds spurred by the occasional sounds of bones crackling and flesh ripping. Just as she made her way to the last one she heard footsteps and the sound of nails scratching on the floor the way a dog tries to get traction on a slippery floor. She managed to get the door open just in time to find a man standing in front of her whose eyes told the quick tale of what was happening behind her. The man jumped over her, did a back flip, pulled out a blade, and buried it deep into Barabas's chest. The beast let out a heart wrenching squeal and dropped to the floor spilling blood everywhere.

"I heard Tampa was a party town, but this is a little more excitement than I expected," said the man as he pulled the knife from his victim's chest and wiped the blood off the silver blade.

"Oh shit, you don't know what you have just done. Lady Katrina is going to destroy both of us," said Brittany, completely as she turned and watched Barabas's blood sluggishly spread onto the dance floor; he slowly transformed back to the sweet old man she knew.

"Oh don't worry about that Doll, me and Katrina are tight; real tight. Where is that uptight bitch any way? Hey-hey sweet cheeks, Marcus is here, time to tear it up!" he yelled out searching for Katrina.

"Mister, I don't know who you are, but things are going to get real ugly for you when Lady Katrina...," Brittany was barely able to get another syllable out when her head was severed from her shoulders from behind and landed next to her body as it hit the floor.

"Oh look - what a surprise, it's Mister Nottingham. We're going to have to stop meeting like this or people are going to talk," said Deni as she stood in the doorway looking at Marcus with those piercing yellow eyes that sent quakes of fear down a lesser man's spine.

"Why'd you have to do that to that nice girl? It was such a pretty head, too. Ah, look here, those fetish tendencies you like to explore are going to need another partner cause I'm still trying to recover from the last session, and honestly I don't have the time so I'll just be on my way," said Marcus trying to find a good escape route that didn't involve going past the one legged terror standing in the doorway.

"As much as I would love to revive our passionate bondage interlude of past, you know for old times sake, I'm under orders, and can't mix business with pleasure. I was supposed to intercept Katrina but I see I've arrived a little late. I guess you're coming with me instead," Deni told Marcus.

"Well, I'd like nothing better, but I had plans on doing the town, literally, and must be on my way," Marcus replied with sarcastic disdain.

"I don't think so and if I must I will drag you with me," Deni threatened.

"Oh yeah, and what army is..." Marcus didn't get

another word in before Canis flowed into the Castle like a river and surrounded him.

"Hmm, I should have known, you fuckers travel in packs. I guess I'm your guest. Any funny business and I start splitting fur. You might take me down, but I'll drag as many of you with me as I can..." again Marcus was interrupted; this time by a blow behind the head that knocked him unconscious.

"Looks like we're going to have to tell the Nachschutz that their experimental club works very well; They'll have to tell me what it's made of, or make one for me," Deni smirked as the Canis put Marcus in a black burlap sack and carried him away.

They all jumped into the waiting black SUV with blackened windows and drove away.

The next night Slinky and the Hammer arrived at the Castle to find the mess left behind from the previous evening's event. Slinky rushed up to his office, opened up a panel and rewound the video on the surveillance equipment he had secretly installed a few weeks back.

"Now ain't this some shit. I spend one night away from this place and look all the fun I missed. If I knew this is what it was going to take to eliminate the competition I would have done it a long time ago. Hell, I have some furry friends of my own that owe me some favors" said Slinky.

"Yeah, that's great boss, but, what the fuck are we going to do now? Katrina is going to be back soon and she's going to be pissed as hell," said the Hammer.

"Don't worry about that. Leave all that shit to me. Get some assholes in here and let's clean this joint up. We need to open this bitch up for business, and do me a favor; kill that fucking DJ. What's his name? Frankenstein's Daughter, Voltaire's Wife, Dracula's Daughter - whatever his fucking name is... kill the bastard. Fuckin' DJ buzz kill is what they should call that son of a bitch," Slinky told the Hammer as he walked to the bar and opened up a bottle of Vampire Blood Wine.

A Return Home
Chapter Twenty-seven

As the Invidia neared the coast of North Carolina's Outer Banks, the hairs on the back of Olivar's neck stood up and his heart started to race. There are things that even hundreds of years don't erase. The horrors of everyday life are magnified by that which lurks in the mist and darkness on the blurry edge of reality.

"This might be home to you, but it definitely doesn't feel much like home to me," Olivar told Katrina with a sneer.

"Come now, you know killing things is part of your nature; at least you're not killing friends, family, and neighbors," Katrina said.

"Not mine anyway," he replied.

"We need to find our old cove, so we can drop anchor and get to shore without notice," Katrina commented.

"I suspected that was the case. I'm heading towards the cove now, but all this looks so different. The level of development around here is impressive. I wonder what one of these seaside homes costs," Olivar rambled.

He tried to match what he saw with the memory of what the shore looked like before. He followed the ships navigational instruments and arrived at the spot that was once their favorite shore landing. To their astonishment it looked much as it did years ago.

"Olivar, leave the sailors to watch the ship. Everyone else comes with us. Make sure the Sucanis are ready. This will probably get ugly," Katrina ordered.

"I thought we might stay here for a while since the sun will be rising soon," Olivar inquired.

"I need to get everyone off the ship in case it is discovered. I have an idea where I want to spend the day. It shouldn't be too far away from here," replied Katrina.

A few minutes later, Gabrielle, five of the Sucanis, and the professor walked to the main deck. The crew hauled up two rolled up Zodiac rafts. One of them pulled the inflation device and they tossed the boats over the side. As the boat inflated, the outboard motor rolled out from the center of the boat.

"Good. I wasn't looking forward to rowing ashore. That shit sucks," said Gabrielle, grouchy at the fact that they'd have to get in the water at all.

A Sucanis snickered at Gabrielle, jumped overboard, and landed in the water just as one of the Zodiacs finished inflating. He reached a Zodiac, climbed in, and attached the motor.

"Show off," Gabrielle yelled as she jumped and landed

in the other Zodiac.

Everyone else roped down to the Zodiacs and they sped away into the darkness.

"Everything around here might be over-developed, but this cove looks like it is still the most secluded area for miles around," said Olivar as they reached the shore.

Katrina quickly gathered her team and formed them up. They all took their positions in the tree-line and waited patiently making sure they were not discovered and no one lurked in the shadows.

"Excuse me, I get the whole 'we need to make sure we maintain security', but if we don't get to cover soon it ain't going to matter from all the screaming I'm gonna do as the flesh burns off my bones," said Gabrielle annoyed at how long the process was taking.

Katrina gave the order and they moved out. Once she got her bearings the team moved a lot faster. She found the old tree with the opening to the Shinobi cavern and the last of the group made it in the cave just as the sun was peaking over the horizon.

"A few seconds more and there would have been a strong barbecue odor filling the morning air. Probably would have called every Billy Bob, Billy Joe, and Mary Lou in this place," Gabrielle was still her cheery self.

They walked deeper and deeper into the cave and with every step; Katrina feared there might be an ambush waiting for them. She could sense that the rest of the team wasn't crazy about this whole situation either.

"Don't worry people, there is more than enough of us

to take on anything that might pop up in these parts," she tried to reassure them and herself.

Finally they made it to the inner sanctum where she once learned her trade. It was bare. The statues were gone, the weapons no longer hung on the walls, and the bundles of raw materials were missing.

"Nice place, we couldn't book a rock quarry or maybe a nice mausoleum," Gabrielle continued to nag.

"Oh, shut the fuck up and get some rest," snapped Katrina having reached her limit.

Gabrielle sneered, grabbed a dirty sack and curled up on a far corner of the chamber. The professor did the same and settled on the other side of the chamber. Everyone picked a spot and then Katrina opened the hidden compartment that folded out into a makeshift bed.

"Oh, well that figures," said Gabrielle as she turned away.

A few minutes later, Gabrielle dragged her rags over to the professor's side and cuddled with him in the corner.

As per Katrina's orders, Olivar took three Sucanis and they went out to scent out Vlad's trail. He left one of them at the opening of the cave to secure his master as she slept, then darted off into the forest. It wasn't hard to pick up the trail. There were plenty of hidden carcasses lying around to find the fiend. Olivar concluded that he must still be in hiding otherwise he would have just fed in the open and would not have had to kill his victims. There likely wasn't anyone with him who could secure him during daylight; therefore leaving a Sangus walking around was not a good idea. Olivar followed his senses to a roadside rest stop. There were plenty of hidden cadavers there too and even more that led off into the woods. They came to a meadow at the edge of the forest. In the center of the meadow was a power substation. It had one road in and several power cables leading out of the station. The place was surrounded by a ten foot high fence and a security guard at the gate. Olivar's Sucanis was going to rush over to get a closer look, but Olivar stopped him.

"If he's in there, he's probably found a way to monitor the security video. This area isn't really known for Timber Wolves so wolves our size will definitely set off some alarms in his head. Not to mention we're talking about Vlad Tepes III, I'm sure he's seen more than his share of Canis. He'll sniff us out quicker than we could say 'aye'," he said and showed him the security camera that pivoted back and forth.

They ran back to the cave to get some rest. Once night fell, Olivar grabbed a coal from the furnace and drew a layout of the substation. They worked out a plan to take down the place and search for Vlad. Olivar led everyone to the meadow at the edge of the forest.

Once there, Katrina ordered them to form up along the edge of the forest and wait for her signal. Katrina and Olivar ran off in the direction of the road. Shortly after reaching the road, they saw the substation vehicle was driving up towards the gate. Olivar transformed and lay across the road. Katrina jumped across the road and waited in the ditch. When the vehicle stopped and the man got out to investigate the pile of fur lying across his path, she jumped out grabbed the guy by the collar and slammed him against a tree. Olivar got up and ran over to the passenger side, but there was no one there. On her signal, a few of the Sucanis ran up from their positions and jumped in the back of the truck and lay down within the bed. Katrina sat low in the passenger's seat, while Olivar pulled the man's shirt, jacket, and hat off and put them on. They moved out and pulled up to the gate. The buff young man that had relieved the elderly man from earlier jumped up from his seat and ran over to the window.

"So, what's up Harry," Said the man as he approached.

"Oh hey boss, Harry is sick, I'm his replacement for the night," said Olivar trying to act like it was the most natural thing in the world.

"Well, sir, wait here a minute. No one notified me. Let me confirm that and I'll gladly let you in," said the guard.
As the guard walked back to the security shed he was knocked flat on his ass and rendered unconscious by Katrina who had slipped past him, while he challenged Olivar. Katrina let Olivar in through the gate, and then gave the signal. Gabrielle led the remaining team in the woods to the gate. Everyone jumped out of the truck and the search was on.

"Kill everything, leave no one alive!" Katrina yelled.

The Sucanis transformed and rushed through the doors. They ripped through several workers and tore their heads off ensuring there would be no unintended morphs in this raid. Olivar and Katrina found the map of the facility hanging on a wall and quickly took separate routes that would complete the search and bring them right back to that location. Gabrielle stood guard with three Sucanis at the doors. Olivar turned the lights out in the facility, and bolted away. Katrina had already disappeared. Many innocents died that night, but as far as Katrina and her crew were concerned, if they were guarding Vlad, they were combatants. A half-hour later both Katrina and Olivar appeared at the rendezvous.

"No sign of him," said Olivar.

"I know he's here. I can feel him, but I can't sense where he is," answered Katrina.

"I have a strange feeling too," said Gabrielle.

Katrina and Olivar searched the complex. Olivar heard sounds coming from the floor as if something was below them. The other Sucanis did too. Katrina looked for an elevator or stairwell, but found nothing. They met back where they started. They sat quietly in the dark waiting to hear something that would guide them to their prey. One of the Sucanis noticed a door slowly closing.

"Over there!" he yelled as he transformed and darted out into the darkness.

Olivar and a few of the Sucanis gave chase. Katrina waited, something didn't feel right. When they finally arrived at the door they found the Sucanis lying dead in front of it. His head had been severed.

"That's just great, we're being stalked by the deadliest predator of all time," said Olivar nervously with his senses scanning the darkness for their assailant.

"Why are we still breathing? I know how he is. We should all be a withered pile of dust right now," said Gabrielle.

"You sure know how to put one at ease," said the professor nervously.

Katrina then picked up what she was waiting for, just a moment of thought to escape Vlad's mind in his attempts at emptiness. She rushed to a wall and pulled a section away that revealed a stairwell leading down into the unknown. They rushed in when they heard footsteps leading away. Once they reached the bottom they were all struck by a blinding light that lit up the whole area momentarily blinding them.   As their eyes cleared and their vision returned they saw the strangest thing any of them had ever witnessed.

They looked around the grand hall built into the remains of a railroad tunnel.   Cautiously they searched and stared in awe at the sight of giant copper framed glass tanks filled with some strange green liquid.   Each tank was connected with a series of copper pipes spiraling and spider-webbing throughout the ceiling.   In each glass tank was a human body coiled within thin copper pipes.   The bodies floated in the tanks with no breathing devices, no feeding tubes, and no monitoring system. There was row after row and column after column of these vats filling the whole vicinity of the space disappearing into the darkness.   Katrina approached one of the vats trying to pick up any signs of life.   As she got closer she recognized the man that was coiled up inside.

"Vlad?" she asked incredulously staring into deep red eyes that held no sign of life.

"Holy shit, how many of them are there," exclaimed a Sucanis echoing the thoughts of everyone else in the room.

"I have 700 of them," a voice called out.

"Why?!" yelled Katrina.

"Once one tastes immortality as I have, one doesn't want it to end," replied the voice.

"You are one of the oldest, most powerful vampires known, none but the Elders can count your days, what more do you want?" asked Katrina as she searched the cavernous chamber.

"You speak as if there was anything left of my once

298

human self. I haven't been that human since the second time I came face to face with the Nazarene," said the voice.

"You are Vlad Tepes III, your followers call you a hero, your enemies called you the Impaler, and your comrades call you Master; your immortality is secure!" said Olivar trying to throw his voice in the mix to distract their stalker.

A pack of wolves sprang from beyond the light and ran straight at them fangs and claws exposed. A Sucanis was taken down to the ground by a wolf and was being shaken in the grasp of the giant wolf's jaws. Another Sucanis was downed in the ensuing skirmish until Olivar and Katrina snapped out of their momentary shock and attacked. Katrina quickly threw silver spikes that found their mark deep into their targets chest. Olivar charged another of their attackers; the collision bouncing into one of the vats with enough impact to bring it crashing down to the floor. The body inside fell out and seemed to melt into the liquid as the skin hit the air. Olivar ripped his attackers head off its shoulders with one swipe. Together they laid waste to all their attackers. Each one met their fate at the end of a silver plated blade, spikes, or claw and fang. Then the last one hit the ground a victim of a Sucanis' claws to the throat. One by one they began to transform back into their natural born states. Katrina recognized the tattoos and markings.

"Wanchese, what happened to you my old friend?" asked Katrina.

"That is the problem with the Wendigo, they are immortal, but they age quickly. Soon there won't be any of them left," said Olivar.

"Vlad, where are you? How could you allow this? They were your servants," Katrina yelled.

"I am called Legion; for I am many. My story begins long before I took possession of the vessel you know as Dracula, and long before Lucius Valerian Teppe was tricked into hosting my essence; that which you call the spirit. The world has only known my power for a short part of my existence. For most of that time I have struggled to free myself of the one you call Satan. The beloved one of the El who once called us his children, called him his son, and now we call enemy," said the entity in a voice that crackled as it reverberated through the cavernous walls of the lab.

Katrina and the Sucanis could find nothing. They searched the whole area and it was as if he wasn't there at all, but yet he was. The professor took advantage of the lull in activity and looked over all the scientific data around the lab. He picked up clipboards and examined the information, then found a reference he recognized. He was off searching through drawers and cabinets frantically searching for something.

"Who the hell is Lucius and what exactly are you talking about. Don't you speak English?" Katrina tried to toy with the entity in order to get a fix on his position.

"Don't bother. I will reveal myself when I am ready. That is a story for another time and place. Just know that what is in you, is a part of me. We are all made one by the darkness that we share, and if I can free myself of his grip you can too," said the voice.

"He's talking in riddles. Do you understand him?" asked Olivar.

A loud crash coming from the stairwell broke the tension of the moment and the bodies of the three Sucanis that were guarding the doors came crashing down. The lights went out and guardians of the Potentate came rushing down the stairs. It did not seem like they were going to ask any questions, now or later, it was all going to be shooting and slicing. Katrina and her crew were ready for a fight, but hopelessly outnumbered.

"Ah, Katrina, you have done very well for us. I have to thank you so much for your assistance," said Alexandra as she walked down the stairs.

"We did not..." Katrina tried to explain.

"I know, this is what I was waiting for," said the entity as he suddenly appeared looking every bit like the Vlad everyone knew.

Katrina looked over at Vlad, they stared at each other for a moment, then drew their katanas. Vlad, Katrina, Gabrielle, Olivar, and his Sucanis crew drew together and attacked the Elder and her minions. The fighting was vicious. It was easy to see why Katrina was widely considered one of the most dangerous Legion in the world. Even among her own kind the name Katrina Le Giroux struck terror in their lifeless hearts. She launched herself, ducked into a cartwheel passed a barrage of bullets, and delivered duel deadly blade strikes to the hearts of two over confident attackers. This was followed by swift decapitation by blade strike.

"It's the only way to be sure," she said as the heads dropped to the floor beside her.

Olivar morphed and charged the horde of vampires that fell upon them in waves. He ripped open so many of his attackers that his arms began to fail him. Gabrielle and her lightening fast blades cut their heads off right before the already damaged corpses hit the ground. Vlad demonstrated the skills earned in blood through a millennia of battles. As everyone raged around him in furious flurries of blade and bullets, he downed all opponents with minimal, almost sublime movements delivering deadly accurate strikes. No wasted motions, no flashy acrobatics, just graceful, deliberate assaults to essential points of life. They managed to break through the first attacking force and pushed the fight to the confines of the stairwell. The professor continued his frantic search while the battle raged on around him; narrowly escaping with his life on several occasions.

"We stand more of a chance here; this is the only way in. They must face us in smaller numbers— numbers we can manage," said Vlad.

Katrina stabbed the first of the next wave of Legion through the chest, turned the blade, and split him in half all the way through his head. The Sucanis behind her took care of the one that followed; bit him on the head, shook violently, and ripped it from his shoulders. Olivar started to fatigue. His constant ripping and slashing took its toll and made his arms near useless. Two Legion soldiers managed to pin him down. One split a gash across Olivar's chest with a silver sword, raised his head by the fur on his nape, pulled out a Gurhka, and held it in the air ready to strike through Olivar's neck. Gabrielle left the professor, leapt into the air, landed between them in a crouching position, then rose up and sliced the two Legion from groin to gullet. She then spun and took both their heads off with her Gurkhas. She stayed by Olivar's side, fending off any assailants, while he recovered. He regained some strength and resumed the fight at Vlad's side. His agility and strength, matched only by his ferocity, made it difficult for any Legion to stand against him. Vlad stabbed and sliced his way through the deluge of fiends he once called his comrades, raining down destruction without mercy. They fought hard but their opponent's numbers did not seem to diminish. As the last of the Sucanis succumbed to the relentless attacks from the vampire horde the valiant team started to lose ground. Many still fell to their blade or claw, but every kill pushed them further back into the lab until they had precious little space to maneuver. They were overwhelmed by the sheer numbers and held in place as they looked down the barrels of MP-5s pointed at their heads by the Legion soldiers that stood at the ready in a semi-circle in front of them.

"Don't throw your existence away. You have fought a valiant battle, ended many of my soldiers, and now face destruction in vain. Look around you. Even if you die here, we take what you have so valiantly protected. Surrender and arrangements shall be made..." said the Elder Alexandra. Before she could finish her plea, however, a commotion from behind the ranks interrupted her.

There was gunfire, the clashing of blades, and then an eerie howl—a howl that those who ever hear it don't soon forget.

An Unexpected Turn of Events
Chapter Twenty-eight

"**B**runo!" Katrina and Gabrielle yelled in unison.

Vlad, Katrina, and Olivar attacked with renewed fervor. Alexandra made her way to the top of the stairs. What she saw filled her with fear. The substation was surrounded by Canis and they were on the attack. She ran back down the stairs.

"I got it!" yelled the professor, holding a small bag.

Gabrielle sliced a vampire's head off, spun and sliced

through another, and made her way to her absent-minded scientific boyfriend to protect him.

"I can handle one of those things," said the professor, "I'm not completely useless."

Gabrielle spun around and cut an attacker's hand off, took his blade, handed it to the professor, and then cut the victim's head off. The professor instantly jumped up, took a fencing stance reminiscent of the Olympics, and proceeded to stab his opponents as if in competition.

"No, you dimwit! Slice their heads off like this," Gabrielle yelled as she decapitated the professor's opponent.

"My God, how brutal! You're a beast!" exclaimed the professor, bothered by the blood that spattered on his face.

The battle raged on, though the opposition began to wane. Vlad and his cohorts battled their way up the stairs, and saw the waves of Canis closing in on the surrounded vampire horde. As they battled in the doorway to the substation, Alexandra appeared from around a corner, knocked Gabrielle to the ground, struck Vlad in the chest with a blade, and swung her sword aiming for Katrina's neck.

A Canis leapt over the fence and slapped Alexandra's blade away. He stood face to face with the Elder holding out his sword defiantly. The Elder lost all her composure and growled at the Canis violently. She slapped the blade to the side and pounced on the Canis sinking her fangs deep into his chest. The giant creature rolled over and pinned Alexandra to the ground, held her by the neck, and flared his claws ready to bring them down upon her chest. Vlad jumped, speared the Canis on the side of the ribs and knocked him off the Elder. The Canis stood and growled at them. A few of the Dragon Praetorian guard appeared and stood by the Elder's side pointing weapons at the

Canis. They then turned their weapons on Vlad. Katrina, Gabrielle, and crew fought desperately to get to Vlad's side but were heavily engaged in combat with other opponents.

"Traitors," Vlad hissed.

"We are under orders," said one of the guards.
Right when everyone thought Vlad was done, a pack of Canis leapt over the fence and landed on the guards. The weapons discharged and bullets ricocheted in every direction, but none found their mark. Each of the pack members bit into their victims and shook them till the limbs ripped off. The first Canis finally brought down the Elder as she tried to run. He drove his claws through her back as she struggled and pinned her to the ground. He then bit her on the back of the neck and pulled. The skin stretched until it ripped, blood spilled out of the cracks, and strings of flesh strained against the force until the head snapped off. Vlad attacked the pack and sliced one of their heads off. He was brought down by a pair of Canis and at the very moment they were going to dispatch the Legion to the great unknown, Vlad rolled over pulled silver daggers from his jacket and buried them deep in their chest. As he growled at them in rage he was struck on the back of the head with what appeared to be a club or mace by the first Canis. Vlad's head wobbled as he tried to look at his assailant and then to everyone's surprise passed out. A pair of Canis quickly ran up and dragged the fallen Legion away. By now the Canis forces had completely overrun the substation. All around them Legion were being slaughtered by the vicious lupine attackers. The Canis holding the mace then turned to them and morphed to his human form. It was Bruno. Concerned they might be next, Gabrielle rushed out to attack Bruno, but was met half way by Marcus.

"Wait, they only want him. There is something going on, that you are not yet aware of," he said to all of them.

Bruno stood silently in front of them without saying a word. Some Canis rushed past Katrina and her crew and ran through the doors of the substation. A few minutes later they came back dragging the body of one of the many Vlad's from the glass enclosures in the lab. One of them yelled, "Fire in the hole."

Everyone around scrambled for cover, away from the substation. Katrina, Olivar, and the rest of the crew chased after them. Gabrielle and the professor headed off in a different direction.

"Fire in the hole!" yelled the Canis again.

By now, everyone was nearing the tree line.

"Fire in the hole," yelled the Canis once more and a large explosion ripped through the night, completely destroying the substation in a blaze of orange and yellow light that would be seen for miles around. Almost immediately, screaming sirens could be heard approaching in the distance.

Everyone scattered. Deni appeared in the black SUV and Bruno threw Vlad in the back. He looked back searching for Katrina, hoping to catch her gaze. Their eyes met in the distance and Katrina caught a message traveling through the darkness.

I think that's payback...

Katrina was not amused. Marcus came to her side with Olivar in tow.

"Where the hell is Gabrielle and the professor?" she asked.

"I assume their halfway to China right now," said Marcus sarcastically. "The last time I saw them they were hauling ass through the forest," he continued.

"I guess we'll catch up to them later," she replied.

"What do we do now? We lost Vlad, we got the Elder killed, and the lab was blown up. There's no going back now," said Olivar.

"There's always the Invidia," said Katrina.

"Now wait a minute. Everyone calm down. Let's take a minute, and analyze the situation. They don't know what happened here. Take that crispy critter lying over there back to the Protectorate. Say it's Vlad. They're gonna be pissed that he's dead, but as far as they know, you brought him back. The circumstances of the Elder's demise fall under the category of casualty of war, and anyone who knows otherwise is dead or has no stake in saying differently. I don't see how we can lose,"Marcus commented on the obvious points that seemed to escape everyone in the heat of the battle.

Katrina and Marcus arrived at the New Minority's corporate office gates with a giant box. The guards at the gate scrambled to action pointing weapons and sounding alarms. Three guards approached and spread to either side of the visitors. Katrina and Marcus held their hands up in the air. They were ordered to kneel on the floor and hold their hands behind their heads. They did so, confident in their ability in killing every one of the guards from this position, if the need should arise. Another guard opened the lid to the box and, with an expression of horror that never left his face, called for a supervisor. A sharp dressed man in an Armani suit stepped through the gate. Tentatively, he looked at the two that were kneeling and proceeded to the box. Only when he felt secure did he look inside then proceeded to rush everyone inside. The guards carried the box away. Katrina and Marcus were escorted to holding cells and waited. The next night an Elder came to Katrina's cell.

"I see you still play a brilliant game of chess," he said.

"I absolutely do not know what you mean. I have simply accomplished the mission you entrusted me with," she replied recognizing the old member of the Potentate.

"I know there is more than you are letting on, the effort you are making to cloud your thoughts from me are evidence enough," he said.

"What happens to us now?" she inquired.

"Every member of the Dragon Praetoria will be executed... Oh no, my dear, do not panic. We can't very well phase the newly appointed Protectorate of the New Minority," he said with a devious smile.

"You jest!" replied Katrina.

"Oh come now, my dear, when have you ever known me to do anything in jest? After I leave here the guards will release you and your companion. I wish to see you in my chambers. We have much to discuss," he answered.

The Elder walked out the door and disappeared into the darkness as usual. A guard walked up just as the Elder said would happen and released the pair. Katrina was taken to Vlad's old quarters and Marcus was escorted to one of the dignitary suites, where he was tended to by a sultry blond and a red head much to his delight. There was a knock on Katrina's door. She opened the door and a slouch pushed in a blood slave.

"Compliments of the Potentate," said the slouch with a

glob of drool drooping from his lips.

Katrina dismissed the slouch and fed on the slave. She wasn't completely convinced this was truly happening and wanted to make sure if her suspicions were justified, she could defend herself. A couple of hours later, a slouch opened the door. He walked into the room holding a red silk robe and placed it on Katrina. He then pulled her away and dragged her all the way to the Elder's quarters.

"Ah, there she is; the woman of the moment. What a vampire you have become. Vlad was right about you. There is no doubt he had a great eye for talent," the Elder said.

"I would prefer not to speak of him, Sir; I did a mission. I take no pleasure in its accomplishment," Katrina snapped at the Elder.

"Ah, such a good tactic; masking your thoughts with anger. Anger is a very good shield, but there is no need. I know it was insensitive of me to bring up your mentor, but it goes to the subject at hand. As Protectorate you are responsible for the security of the Legion Empire and there is a great threat looming in the horizon. A threat we once thought was extinguished. We expect you to execute your duties as diligently as you accomplished that most difficult of tasks. Here is the seal of the Protectorate, wear it with pride, it will open doors that you yet do not understand, and its authority is absolute. You now answer to the Potentate and no one else," he told Katrina.

"I'm honored by the confidence you are showing in my abilities. If I may ask, what is to happen to Gabrielle Vazquez? She was a member of the Praetoria and would make a good ally in completing my duties. She would make a great Final Solution agent, I assume there is a vacancy," Katrina inquired.

"We are currently looking for her. She has slipped under

the radar and seems to be extremely skilled at avoiding our detection," said the Elder.

"What is to become of her, once you find her?" Katrina pressed.

"I'll leave that up to you, but will you really feel safe with a sworn body guard, minion, and assassin for the man you just eradicated?" asked the Elder.

"I'll have to interrogate her and see where her loyalties lay," said Katrina.

"Very well, we shall elevate our efforts and notify you as soon as we find her. Now, go; I need to feed and then I have a long list of meetings to attend. You will find a dossier on your desk in your chambers when you return. The individual in that portfolio is to be placed on your highest priority for elimination. Do not fail us. The fate of the Legion depends on the capture and subsequent execution of this menace," the Elder said as he walked away and entered his inner sanctum to feed in the protection it offered.

Katrina returned to her quarters. She saw the sealed manila envelope on the desk and decided to ignore it while she settled in. She looked around and found a cache of weapons, some scrolls and a book of ancient art. She found the TV remote and turned it on to occupy her mind. The news was on and a report came on that caught her attention.

World renowned physics professor turned archeologist Dr. Ronald Rosell has produced another extraordinary relic that promises to further explain the creatures that we now know we share the world with. The message appeared on his now famous website the scroll is currently being translated. Its contents will be posted soon for all to read in the near future...

"That son of a bitch is looking to get his big brain

separated from the rest of his body," Katrina said out loud.

A gruesome thought slipped into her mind and she rushed to the desk to see who this all important dead man was. She hoped it was not the professor. That would definitely seal the casket on her relationship with Gabrielle and that was one vampire she did not need as an enemy. She ripped the flap on the package and pulled out the contents. There was an unusual amount of information on this target. It all fell out. Conspicuously absent from the packet was a photo of the individual. She fumbled around and finally found the piece of paper that crushed her soul.

I wish it was the professor. Either way this is a death sentence.

She grabbed a bottle of blood wine that was in one of the cabinets and sat on the floor. Taking a long swig from the bottle, she stared out into the city through her panoramic window as a painful tear of blood ran down her cheek. The name of the unfortunate soul, the target of all the force of the Potentate under her direction was Bruno Maximus Castañeda.

A voice from her past crept into her mind and said-
Be careful what you wish for, for some day, you might get it. Envy is the greatest of the seven deadly sins for it causes even the brightest of angels to fall.

Katrina's tears flowed from her eyes as her heart broke from the pain of her grandmother's words and the weight that they represented now. She closed the window, wrapped herself in a blanket and cried herself to sleep.

-Finito-

Glossary

Aeacian- a vampire hybrid resulting from the morphing of a human pregnant with a canis child.

Blood glow- near human state of vampires after a full feeding.

Blood slaves- humans willingly allowing vampires to feed on them hoping to be morphed.

Braves - term for the man in native american indian culture.

Canis- humanoid being capapble of transforming to any animal.

Cohorts- A group or band of people.

Croatoan- relating to the Croatan who were a Native American tribe living in the coastal areas of what is now North Carolina.

El- the name the ancients used for the one and only God.

Flanked- to be placed or situated at the flank or side of.

Gurkhas - a Nepalese soldier in the British or Indian army.

Holy Roman Empire - designation for the political entity that originated at the coronation as emperor (962) of the German king Otto I and endured until the renunciation (1806) of the imperial title by Francis II .

Jengal- A vicious dog hybrid animal Legion keep as pets.

Jibade- Egyptian name meaning "related to royalty."

Kemosiri- Egyptian name meaning "Black Osiris."

Kirkos- Decendants of the enchantress Circe, who lived on the island of Aeaea.

KUKRI- a formidable and effective weapon of the Gurkhas and an exquisite piece of local craftsmanship that symbolizes pride and valor which also represents the country and it's culture.

Legion- Preferred name of the vampire race.

Lycanthropes- a werewolf or alien spirit in the physical form of a bloodthirsty wolf.

Max-Sec- Maximum Security.

Mayordomo- Owner or boss – title for the regional Legion official answering to the Protectorate.

Methuselah- term for the vampire ancients.

Morph-the act of turning a human to a vampire.

MP-5 - a 9 mm submachine gun of German design.

Nachtshutz- ancient society of vampire hunters started by the Canis.

Neomorph- Newly turned werewolves or newly turned vampire before its first kill. Sometimes used as a derogatory term.

New Minority – the public name for the vampire society.

Newbie- a newcomer or novice.

Nyx - goddess of night, nightmares and darkness.

Nyxians- the remnant spirits of ancient gods who rule the darkness.

Palookas - Slang A stupid or clumsy person.

Phase- Term used to describe the destruction of a vampire.

Plebeian - a servant of the vampire nation.

Potentate - the governing body of the vampire nation.

Praetorians- a specially trained force of bodyguards used by Roman Emperors.

Protectorate- Security agency responsible for the protection of Legion affairs through the New Minority. Also, the title for the head of the Protectorate organization.

Sangus- Legion term for a human who sells their services as a blood slave allowing vampires to feed on them for a price.

Sucanis- (Soo-Kan-is) word meaning lower Canis; a person that has survived a Canis attack and becomes a werewolf or shapeshifter.

Slouches - creatures resulting from the failed attempts at vampire hybrids.

Strumpet- a prostitute; harlot.

Sunlighter- canis term for human.

V.S.O.P- (Very Superior Old Pale) cognac is made from the two finest crus the Grande and Petite Champagne and aged for eight to twelve years.

Wendigo- In native american folklore a malevolent cannibalistic spirit into which humans could transform, or which could possess humans.